F

FISHER & ASTER

FOLSOM
Fisher & Aster

Cover Design by Hang Le
Formatted by Jovana Shirley, Unforeseen Editing
Proofread by Erica Russikoff and Christine Estevez

ISBN-13: 978-1719341127
ISBN-10: 1719341125

ONE

FOLSOM

The clock in the lobby reads 7:20 a.m. I already have a hard-on, one that will last for most of my day. I'm surprisingly awake, considering my late night. I smell of aftershave and coffee, tangy like a hopeful morning. I grin at the people who stare at me and ride the elevator to the top floor. Apartment 922 is unlocked, as it's supposed to be. I open the door and I'm greeted by Silica: long-legged, thin as a rail, hair a deep amber. She's wearing nothing underneath an open robe. Typical.

"Hi." Her walk is catlike, rolling shoulders and nimble legs. She laces her hands behind my neck and stares up at me expectantly.

"Hi," I say. I'm waiting for my cue. Cues are important for accuracy.

"I missed you," she says. She burrows her nose into my neck, breathing me in. "I'm glad you're home."

Ah. There it is. Keyword: home. I wrap my arms around her waist and pull her against me. She feels that I'm hard and her head lolls back as she grinds her pelvis against me. A cat in heat. Biting onto her bottom lip, she makes eye contact.

"I made dinner," she says. She releases me reluctantly, her eyes on my dick. "I hate it when you work late."

I follow her into the kitchen where a table is set with a candle and two place settings. Nothing like a romantic dinner at 7:30 in the morning. I stretch before sliding into my seat and then I loosen my tie. That's always a nice touch—tired husband loosening his tie after a long day. She smiles and then moves to the kitchen where there's a mess of pots and pans scattered across the sticky counters. I look out the window as she bangs around, the silverware drawer sliding open and closed, a clatter of metal as she grabs a fork. The traffic on the street below thickens every ten minutes. I'm glad I left early to get here. She returns with only one plate, piled high with food.

"Aren't you eating?" I ask.

She makes a show of placing it on the table, reaching around me so that a breast brushes my arm. She wants to think she's seducing me, but my body is ready. It's always forced to be ready.

"I ate," she admits. "Don't be mad."

"How could I be with this spread?" I glance down at my fish, the shrimp, a loaded baked potato leaking butter and sour cream. This is not what she ate. If I lifted the lid to her trash can there would be a half-eaten container of yogurt—I'd bet my life on it. She slides into the chair next to me, leaning her head on a hand. Still full from my own breakfast, I cut into the potato eagerly. Silica watches, her leg jiggling under the table. I close my eyes for effect when I swallow the first bite.

She wriggles in her seat, pleased. I force down a few more bites, feeling sick, before setting my fork down and pushing my chair back.

"You're not hungry?" She pouts.

"I'd rather eat you," I say. That does the trick. She's in my lap, moaning, spreading her thighs and wrapping her legs around my waist.

"I've been thinking," she says coyly, "that we should start a family."

I jerk back, looking at her in surprise. She looks vulnerable, soft brown eyes blinking slowly.

"Really?"

She nods. I kiss her neck and she tilts her head up to give me better access.

"I want that too," I say. "Let's go put a baby in you." I carry her to what I hope is the bedroom and breathe a sigh of relief when it is. A husband should always know where his bedroom is. Then I fuck her senseless.

In my old life, I was a patriot. That was before, when there was a country to defend, and when there were men to defend it.

Now I'm this.

I kiss my "wife" goodbye for both the first and last time as she leans against the doorframe in her nightgown. My driver is waiting downstairs with the car door open.

"We have twenty minutes," she says.

Robin is in the car where I left her. My handler. We have a precarious friendship. She doesn't look up when I get in.

"How'd it go?"

"We decided that we want to start a family..."

She lifts her eyes to my face then promptly looks back at her Silverbook. "I love it when they want to play house. Only time I wish I was a fly on the wall."

"Where to?"

"The suburbs," she says. "Take your pill…"

I am Folsom Donohue. The other men call me Foley, the women…they call me many things. I was the first man in the Society of Regrowth. The first they recruited, the oldest of the twelve at thirty-four. The other men respect me and see me as a figure of leadership. I have impregnated two hundred and three women over the course of sixteen years. Five of those pregnancies have resulted in male children. I fuck my way through high society; the women who can afford to pay to have me come inside of them, their daughters, their sisters. Twelve men. We are the last hope; our dicks are worshipped.

My two o'clock is obsessed with cats. I'm led to her bed and told to undress. She rides me with her eyes closed and her tongue caught between her teeth. She looks feral as she hisses instead of moans. I've been instructed not to touch her, so I prop my arms behind my head and count her cats. Six total. One lounges on a pillow above my head, another watches from the dresser nearby. At one point I feel a furry body lay across one of my feet. When we're done, she tosses my clothes at me, picks up a cat, and retreats to the bathroom.

"You can leave!" she calls before shutting the door.

My life is fucking weird.

Women are not stupid. That's why they outlasted us. While men destroyed each other with hydrogen bombs and wars, Mother Nature took care of the rest, sterilizing what was left of the already dwindling male population. The women who had to bury husbands, and fathers, and sons were already rebuilding, looking for solutions. Already superior in their physical design, their bodies build life with two key ingredients. One they need from us, but give them time and I'm sure they'll find another way. I live in their world now: the age of women.

TWO

FOLSOM

I get ready to leave the End Men compound, a place they keep us before we're moved on to a new Region, new women, new pussy. The only other man here is Jackal, and he leaves tomorrow for the west side, an area known as the Green Region—what used to be the Pacific Northwest.

"You out?" he asks, eyeing the duffel at my feet. He's standing in front of the full-length mirror, holding his dick up while using a razor to shave his balls.

"Yeah," I say. "You're going to nick your shit one of these days and bleed to death."

"Always so negative," he says without looking at me. "I like to fuck, smooth."

Jackal is one of the guys who likes this job. Probably the best-looking of the twelve of us, he's known to hold orgies instead of the one-on-ones most of us prefer. He once got three women pregnant in one night—all female births—he's yet to father a boy, which despite his looks makes him less in demand than some of us. He suddenly puts down his razor and turns to look at me, an unusually serious expression on his face.

"You're going to the Red Region?" he asks.

"Yes."

He nods, still holding his dick, but he looks less cocky now. "Be careful there, man. That place is…" He shakes his head while he searches for the word. "The women are different there."

My curiosity piques. I haven't been to Red in seven years. As the oldest of the End Men I consider myself an expert on women, and so far I've yet to visit a Region where I'd call them "different." Most of the women are the same: grateful, horny, accommodating…

"In what way?" I ask.

"I don't know, man." He runs his hand through his hair, making it stand up. He won't look me in the eyes.

"It was my first Region. Maybe I was just too new to know better. They're cunning there. It's not just about…sex."

I zip up my bag and throw it over my shoulder. "What's it about?"

"Control."

Our eyes meet for a second before I put on my sunglasses. We are already controlled, it doesn't matter which Region we go to. "Thanks for the heads-up," I say. "Good luck."

He watches me go; I can feel his eyes on my back as I make my way to the elevator. Jackal is a drama queen. We consider it part of his charm.

"Lobby," I say once the doors are closed. The walls of the elevator are glass, and I watch the ground approach as I run my fingers across the stubble on my cheeks. They keep us high up, the thirty-sixth floor of a skyscraper; we have more security than the President—who is a woman.

"Morning." Robin meets me in the lobby, Silverbook in hand. We've worked together for the last year, though I know very little about her. I suppose she could say the same about me. She's allowed a government job now that she's post-menopause. She told me once that there could be a million men in the Regions and she'd still rather fuck a woman. I like that she's not trying to fuck me. I also like that she keeps her grey hair short when every other woman on the continent has it long. She touches the screen and we look over my schedule together as it hangs in the air in front of us.

"This is the time you should arrive," she says. "They have a parade to greet you. Do me a favor this time and try to look grateful for it."

I grunt.

"Tomorrow you have your first two appointments, then a party at the Region's capital building hosted by the governor, where you will have to select your first two lottery winners." She pauses to make sure I'm taking all of this in.

"Appointments," I say, glancing at her. "I wish you'd stop calling them that. I fuck women in their bedrooms."

She smiles briefly. "Right, well whatever you want to call them—your copulations start at 8 a.m. sharp. You have your pills?"

I pat my bag and my giant bottle of pills rattles.

"I have a supply of them too," she says. "If you run out, let me know, we can't have you going limp on the job." I grimace and she pats me sympathetically on the back. "Ready?"

A car takes us to the airstrip where I board my private jet. My crew is waiting on board: a doctor, a stylist, a massage therapist, a nutritionist, personal security, and Robin. We are given things like private jets and a full staff. The Statehouse is very accommodating for the last virile men on the planet. My jet is black—since I was the first, I got to choose. The other guys are bitter about it; two of them have said they're waiting for me to die so they can have my color.

"Your coffee." Robin hands me a cup as I buckle in. I click and sip at the same time. It's just the way I like it. I'm so bored with that. What does a man have to do to get a bad cup of coffee? Everything is perfect, my whole life orchestrated, spoiled, controlled. I am not this man they're forcing me to be. In my dreams, I own a cabin in the woods. I fish, and hunt, and everyone leaves me the fuck alone. I close my eyes so I don't have to look at their faces, expectant, waiting for their next instruction. I fall asleep before we take off.

The Red Region swallows up Virginia, West Virginia, North Carolina, and South Carolina—all shadows of their former selves, a quivering collection of reformed territory. We land among the solid red flags, which are whipping angrily in the wind. I remember what Jackal said before I left. He was paranoid. Probably overthinking everything since it was his first Region. There is a fleet of cars waiting when I walk down the gangplank and onto the tarmac—all black with dark windows. The Red Region representatives greet me, five women with long grey hair, their clothes the same deep crimson as the flags. They grasp my hands like they're truly grateful to have me here. Once a woman is past her childbearing age, she is forced to wear her hair grey, and those with white hair must dye it. It signifies a stage in life when their service to repopulate is over, and their service to the government begins. These women may have a career, and in general, seem much more relaxed than their younger counterparts, who are conditioned to want only one thing from the moment they first bleed. After the introductions, I'm led to an armored car, where my driver nods politely before she opens the door and I slide into silence.

My ride is a peaceful one, even Robin is taken to another car, and I am able to study the landscape without her monotone briefing. I relax, stretching my legs out in front of me. The houses all bear the same red tile roofs, and the colors of their doors vary depending on what branch of service they work in. This is the same for all of the Regions: yellow doors for anyone who works in medicine, blue for the politicians, green for the service workers, white for the elite. We drive down Governor

Street in the heart of the city where the people stand crammed on the sidewalk to welcome me and watch the parade. The parade floats—both in front of my car and behind—are phallic in nature, one so tall that five women are suspended from its shaft, wearing nude leotards and waving into the crowd. They throw something at the people, but I can't tell what. I hear a loud boom and red smoke erupts from the tip of the penis. The people go wild with applause while I flinch in the backseat, a disturbing piece of imagery for any man. The music starts up and I roll my window down so they can see me. Protocol is the same everywhere I go. Let them see you, let them celebrate. Dancers join the parade, flanking both sides of the car. They are naked except for the body paint. When the parade is over, we drive to the End Men compound, a smaller version of what I left this morning. The car pulls up to a security station and the driver shows the guard my papers. She motions for her to roll down the back window and eyes me accordingly, her cheeks turning a bright pink when I stare back. No doubt she wanted to catch a glimpse of me to tell her people later. We are waved through the gate, and the car stops outside of a building with marble arches. My home for the next year.

"Welcome to the Red Region, Folsom." The governor greets me as I step out of the car. Her name is Pandora Petite, though she is anything but. She is as tall as me, and her shoulders are broad, stretching out the suit she's wearing. Her grey hair is arranged in an impressive series of arches that rise above her head and look like a crown. I take her outstretched hand and shake, clutching her dry lizard skin against mine.

"Always dry," she apologizes. "I have a rare skin disorder. Don't worry, it's not contagious."

I hadn't assumed it was. Her excitement as she leads me into the compound is palatable, my staff trailing behind. I give male children; therefore, I am desired, good for a Region. I can see the hope in her eyes, possibly the greed as well. The Regions who produce the most male children are given priority by the Statehouse: more food, more resources, more money. The Red Region is rich in resources and low in luck in producing males from its pregnancies.

A line of women stand behind her smiling politely, clutching their Silverbooks like good worker bees. I ignore them, focusing my attention on Governor Petite.

"We're excited to have you, Folsom. Your reputation precedes you…" She pauses a moment to take me in, her eyes traveling the distance of my body. Most governors call on me after my sexual duty to the Region is done. It is a running joke among the men that you can't leave a Region without fucking the governor first: political pussy. Governor Petite will ask for it from behind; she'll want it hard and fast and will moan like a cow giving birth. I feel myself getting hard as I follow her into the building. Good, that's good. I need to be ready to fuck. This is a job, one that I'm good at. I touch myself through my pants, running a palm across my erection. My parlor tricks—part of the facade of Folsom is to be enamored with my own fucking dick. They love it. The women we pass look on in fascination. Most of them are of the working class; they'll never be with a man. Unless they win the lottery. For every week I spend in a Region, two lottery winners are randomly chosen. Two years ago in the Yellow Region, a lottery winner got pregnant from our night together and gave birth to a boy. She is a celebrity now, the face of hope among the common. Governor Petite leads me through a courtyard lined with brightly blooming cherry trees. An elaborate fountain sprays water in the center of the courtyard. When I peer through the spray, I see a man and woman entangled in an embrace, his hand in her hair and her face tilted up toward him. They're naked. Surprise, surprise. She sees me looking and smirks.

"We like to encourage a general attitude of…"

"Sex?" I offer.

"Productivity." She smiles.

I shake my head not bothering to conceal my smirk. It is the same everywhere I go.

"Your apartment," she says, stopping at the only door.

It's a massive wooden structure that hints at the size of what lies behind it. Too much space…empty, lonely space. I would prefer to be somewhere small, but I am their hope, and they shower me with luxury.

"I hope it's suitable. The rest of your team will take smaller, practical apartments in the building. You'll have two hours to rest from your journey before your arrival dinner," she says, looking at her watch. "The Red Region is very excited to meet their End Man."

I don't wait for her to dismiss me. I step into my mansion, flinging my sunglasses onto a table and kicking the door closed.

"Welcome home," I say to no one.

THREE

GWEN

The music is so loud in the streets I want to cover my ears. Though if I do, I'll get another scathing look from my mother and sister. I watch mutely from my tiny square of the sidewalk as the parade slowly moves by. I would rather be at work…or at home…or anywhere except here. It is day one of Phallus, the festival that celebrates the arrival of our new End Man: a tradition established by the Society when they stepped in to save humanity. By day, women paint their naked bodies and dance through the streets like they did in the ancient civilizations, crass and vulgar with gyrating hips and loose wild hair. They dance predominantly around penis statues, which could be made out of anything from grass to beaten metal. In the evenings, these same women slip on expensive silk dresses and sip gently on champagne at parties that play classical music and celebrate how refined we are.

What I have learned in my lifetime of observing Phallus is that you can get really damn creative when you want to make a giant penis to worship. My favorite statue ever: a giant penis made out of thousands of tiny penes. Since I was a child, the festival has made me giggle uncontrollably. I make such a fool of myself at these things that my mother and sister have left me at home the last few years.

But not today. Today, I am a modicum of maturity, a respectful penis worshipper with everyone else.

When his car drives past, I stand on my tiptoes to catch a glimpse of the famous Folsom. Naturally his window is rolled down. He waves rather limply to the crowd, his mouth set in an unemotional line. I look around to see if anyone else has noticed, but they're all waving back, screaming. My mother has a hand on each of her daughters' backs. I step away from her touch, closer to the road and to Folsom. For a moment I think our eyes meet as his car edges by. He's so close I can see the stubble on his cheeks, the dark sweep of eyelashes as he blinks. His features are hard, but his eyes are soft. I tilt my head trying to imagine what type of man lies underneath the skin. And then the car passes and I'm left staring after it.

"Let's go, Gwen." My sister's voice cuts through my thoughts.

I glance wistfully toward the car as I follow them. I'll know soon enough.

The first social event of Phallus is the Red Ball, where we're all required to wear the color of our Region. I choose something simple in a tomato red, with long sleeves and a Peter Pan collar; the hemline ends modestly right below my knees. There are no frills, or bows, or elaborate decoration. It's desperately out of fashion, but I like the way I feel when I wear it. My older sister, Sophia, has chosen a deep red dress with a waterfall skirt. Blond hair piled on top of her head, she looks like a goddess. For the first time she offers no cutting remarks on what I'm wearing, she's too focused on the night ahead of us.

"Will we be able to talk to him?" Sophia asks my mother as she climbs into the car. "We should have priority since we have appointments with him."

"I don't think that's how it works," my mother says. "And I'm sure everyone will be fighting for his attention." She sits in the middle and I scoot in after her.

Folsom Donahue is the most prominent of the twelve End Men. The first. The other men treat him with respect, as do we. Images of the men are sent among the Regions and handled with reverence. As a young girl, I collected trading cards with their information written across the back. Folsom was always my favorite: serious looking; his eyebrows angled in such a way that made him look both angry and wounded; full lips that never smiled. Not all of the End Men appeal to me, but regardless, they are gods and everyone wants their attention.

I want to tell Sophia that she probably won't get a chance to talk to him tonight, but knowing Sophia, she will. I don't want to dare her into something I'll regret. My sister is both shallow and determined.

To offset the color of the Region, the room where the Ball is held is entirely white: mother of pearl floors that swirl beneath your feet, walls cut from salt rock, and a ceiling of flecked snow. The overall effect of the white is dizzying; add a thousand women dressed in red and you have a slaughterhouse of silk and taffeta. I've joked before that every Ball looks like a murder scene, but no one finds it funny. We take ourselves very seriously in the Red Region.

We walk into the Ball as the band is playing something slow—a love song, which is ironic since none of this is about love. My mother and sister flitter off to be social, leaving me standing awkwardly alone with a champagne flute in my hand. I look around for someone I know from work maybe, but everyone I know is as antisocial as I am. They're probably all hiding in the bathroom. Good idea. I remember that the bathrooms are on the far wall, a trek away from where I'm standing. I'll have to enter the sea of women to get there. I'm four steps into the throng of bodies when I remember that there's a smaller bathroom on the second floor, one the staff uses on nights like tonight. I head there hoping it will be empty, but when I arrive, there is a sign on the door that says *Out of Order.* Glancing around, I make sure no one sees me before I push the door open and slip inside.

I only have to be here for two hours before I can leave, and I can kill at least twenty minutes in here. I plan on taking the longest pee of my life and then washing my hands fifty times, and maybe if I'm lucky this bathroom will have one of those sitting areas…

I stop dead in my tracks. At first, I see only boots, large boots, too big for a woman. He hears me come in and perches forward on the sink to peer around the corner.

"You can't read or you don't care?" he asks.

I'm too shocked to know what he's talking about, then I remember the *Out of Order* sign on the door.

"I can't read," I say. "I'm just another stupid woman trying to have a baby."

He laughs. It bounces across the bathroom walls and hits me in the chest.

"Well, at least you have a sense of humor, stupid woman."

I'm witnessing the very serious and stern Folsom Donahue laughing. I stand there staring at him, not knowing what to do.

And then I ask, "Are you hiding, too?"

"In plain sight," he says. "Who are you hiding from?"

"Everyone."

"How's that working out for you?"

I eye his casual stance, the large hands resting behind him on the sink, the crossed ankles. "Not well, since you're here."

He laughs again, this time just a slow rumble while he watches my face.

"I have to go," he says, pushing away from the counter.

He walks toward me, and my heart races. I've never been this close to a man. *He's just trying to get to the door*, I tell myself. But, then he stops so he's towering over me. I have to bend my head back to see his face.

"Have a good night," he says.

And I learn for the first time what a smirk is. Full lips, teasing. I blink at him, my lips parting to answer, but then he's gone and I'm not even sure it really happened.

I watch from the balcony above as he flows into the sea of women. He's fluid, a strong current. They have him for a moment and then he's gone. To have so many eyes and hands on you all the time…I shiver.

I'd not expected him to be so…likeable? Enigmatic? Human, maybe. He is a character in the story of our country, a prop in the news. To see him in person makes him real. I am transfixed as he works the crowd. Women clamor for his attention. He'll fuck them all, no doubt—they've paid for his services. I see my sister among them, her beauty only dimmed by her best friend, who pushes toward Folsom with determination. I feel a shelling of jealousy; I had him first. And then I laugh to myself. Stupid woman.

FOUR

GWEN

A noise in the hallway interrupts my tossing and turning. I can't believe I slept at all. I bolt upright in bed, staring at the door, trying to get my thoughts together. Today is my appointment with Folsom. I've been anticipating this day since my mother put the arrangements in motion when we found out that Folsom would be the next End Man sent to the Red. My treatments began weeks ago: booster shots, fertility drugs—all to increase my chances of conceiving. I was twelve when I had my first dream about a baby. I'd never seen one—I've still never held one—but my dream was vivid. I woke up and told my mother every detail.

"*We'll make it happen.*" She'd said it so matter-of-factly that I'd believed her.

Sophia heard me talk incessantly about taking care of a baby and decided she wanted one too. Of course that's what every girl wants nowadays, but Sophia didn't catch the bug until I did.

With the male population wiped out, we've been left with a society that has, for the most part, crumbled. It's all I've ever known, but my mother still remembers what our world used to be. A baby is a luxury only the very wealthy can ever hope to attain, and even then, it's more complicated than that. The End Men have been helping rebuild us, and their demand is something I can't fathom. Relentlessly, they move across the twelve Regions under the control of the Society: a group formed to save humanity from extinction. There's protocol to secure an End Man, and even after my mother became a representative for the Red Region, we weren't sure how to bypass some of that to get an appointment before we're grey. For that reason, my mother became Governor Petite's lover. I'm still unsure of whether my mother has genuine feelings for her or if it's still all a show. I have a feeling it's the latter, but I don't really want to know until this is over and I have a baby in my arms.

Maybe if we're lucky, we'll have two.

My mother knocks twice and opens my door, holding a large breakfast tray.

"I'm surprised you haven't been up for hours," she says, setting the tray down on the table and then moving to open the drapes. Sunlight streams in and I flinch against it.

"Sophia's already eaten. Well…she ate a grape, but I think that's her usual breakfast. You better hurry or she'll try to hog Folsom."

I laugh and step out of bed, making my way to the table. I take a sip of tea, scratching the back of my leg with my toenail.

"As long as I get my chance with him, I don't care who has him first," I say, waving my mother off. "A dick is a dick." I don't mean it. Folsom has always been my favorite End Man.

My mom pulls me from my thoughts when she sits beside me at the table. I can tell by her smirk that she knows exactly what I'm thinking.

"You put this all in motion, you know," she says. "Your dream begins today." She laughs and leans over to kiss my cheek. "Now eat up and Phoebe will draw your bath."

"Will it hurt?" I call after her. I don't know why I asked it, and my face grows hot as I wait for her to answer me.

She presses her lips together and glances up at the ceiling as she considers this. I wait with my hands clasped in my lap, flexing nervously.

"Depends on his size," she finally says. She seems content with her own answer because she leaves me alone then with my very conflicted thoughts.

I'm twenty-five and have never had sex, not even with a woman. I want a baby, and while all kinds of research and progress is being made in the Red Region, we still need a man to make a baby. The sperm banks dwindled long ago and our technology isn't as advanced as it used to be. Science took a backseat to war. We're doing the best we can with what we have left.

Phoebe comes in and applies a softening mask over my entire body. I try to relax, but I keep thinking of our exchange in the bathroom. It's been two weeks, but I can still remember how nervous I felt being so close to him. I wonder what he's like, what he cares about…

My skin is softer than velvet after the mask is thoroughly rinsed off. I put on a dress, nothing new and fancy like Sophia, who had hers made just for the occasion. But, it's attractive on me, hugging all of the right parts. Phoebe arranges a few sprigs of gardenia in my long, wavy hair. I'll take them out right before I see him, just to leave the impression of the scent.

And then I wait for what seems to be forever, but every time I check the clock only ten minutes have passed. Finally, after an eternity, my mother peeks into my room.

"He's driving through the gate now."

I walk to the window and see a dark car coming down our tree-lined drive. It's too far to see him right away, but I watch as it inches toward our estate. The driver gets out and smooths her hair before opening the door for Folsom. Resting my elbows on the sill, I watch with interest, as two long legs appear then the top of his dark head. He looks around, light glinting off of his sunglasses. When his head turns up toward my window, I duck out of the way so he can't see me.

I laugh at myself. "Stop it," I say out loud. "You're being ridiculous."

I step away from the window and yank the gardenia from my hair, tossing the white blooms in the trash before walking toward the stairs. My mother is waiting. She puts her hands on each shoulder and looks me over.

"You're beautiful. He may have had many, but he's never met anyone like you."

I smile at her gratefully, knowing she's supposed to say that. I have a great mother.

"Would you like to meet him in the foyer? Or shall I bring him up here?" she asks.

I don't know why I haven't told her we met at the Ball. I liked tucking away that moment with him and keeping it to myself. I wonder if he'll remember.

"The foyer," I say, decidedly. I want to greet him head-on, as an equal, not be a simpering girl stretched out on a bed.

We go down the stairs together. Sophia is already downstairs and ready to answer the door. The oldest and always letting me know it—I should've known she'd want to make sure he saw her first. Sophia is far more beautiful than I am with her high cheekbones, thick, blond hair that reaches her waist, and the legs that most describe as "endless." I see that her dress is tight and short. I try not to hold her body against her. She looks like an angel, but I'm not sure angels feel the endless need to compete as she does.

Mother puts one hand on Sophia's back and the other on the door. "Allow me," she says.

I laugh to myself. Until the day I die, my mother will be trying to practice fairness with her girls. I've tried to tell her it's a waste of time—I don't care. Sophia obviously does; let her win these small victories. Mother just shakes her head and forces equality between us. It's probably lost on both of us.

When the door opens and he's standing there, his hulking frame filling the space, I begin to rethink everything. How did I think I could go through with this? He's so much *more*…of *everything*. Introductions are made. His dark eyes do a silent assessment of my mother, move on to my sister, and then land on me. I start to shake all over and feel the heat rise to my face. And what he sees in me seems to amuse him. The corners of his mouth twitch as if he's suppressing a smile.

Great. Nothing like mortification when you want to appear sexy. Then I catch sight of his boots, and I'm completely distracted.

His voice is like raspy sandpaper dipped in whisky. It feels indulgent just to listen to him speak, though I don't know what he's saying because I'm still looking at his boots. And then I realize he was speaking to *me*.

His lips—oh his lips—curve up and he laughs. I feel the sound in my gut and drop my hand, teetering between laughing and crying. Normally the calm, laid-back sister, I've clearly lost it.

Sophia steps up to him and puts her hand on his shoulder. His laugh dies down and he slowly looks away from me, toward her. I feel the loss acutely and it unsteadies me. I back into the wall as Sophia runs her hands over his arm.

FIVE

FOLSOM

It's the little one who interests me, her hair more tangled than her sister's, like she didn't bother with it at all. I'm pleased it's her, a familiar face. Her eyes are curious and wild: brown, common and yet uncommon in the way they slant upward at the outside corners. She stands in the foyer, her hands clasped at her waist, but instead of studying my body like most women do, her head is tilted to the side, eyes fixed on my boots. I clear my throat to get her attention and she drags her eyes away from my feet and back to my face. She frowns and shakes her head like she's just realizing where she is.

"Your boots are beautiful," she finally says. From somewhere beside me her sister groans and her mother lets out what I take as an embarrassed laugh.

"Thank you," I say, unable to keep the humor from my voice. "I designed them myself." I don't usually tell people that, but she seems genuinely interested.

"You design clothes?" she asks, surprised.

"You're surprised that I'm good at something other than fucking?"

Her mother makes a choking noise, but we both ignore it, our attention solely focused.

"Yes, I'm quite surprised," she says. "Though I can't attest personally to the fucking part…"

"Yet," I say.

"Yet," she echoes, with a slight nod of her head. She's realized to some degree how derailed our conversation has become because her cheeks color and she looks quickly at her mother and sister in apology.

Her mother motions toward her. "This is Gwen," she says wryly then holds her hand out to the other girl. "And Sophia."

I'm entertained. Usually these meetings all go the same: I'm ushered into a large, affluent house, my hosts accommodating and well groomed. The conversation is a game of choreographed female entrapment—coy and polite. I'm asked question after question, the women pretending to be interested while counting down the minutes until they can lead me to their bedrooms. Where was I last? How did I like it? Be sure to eat at this and this restaurant—banal small talk. I think the exchange has come to an end and I almost feel disappointed when Gwen suddenly speaks up.

"Can I try them on?"

I raise my eyebrows. "Right now?"

"Yes, why not?"

I look around for somewhere to sit and spot a leather wingback chair near the door. Sitting, I begin to loosen the laces while Gwen's mother and sister insist that I needn't bother. I ignore them, watching her face until both boots are off and my socked feet rest on the wood floor. I hold out the boots to Gwen, who steps forward to take them. She sits directly on the stairs that lead up to the second floor, slipping off her own shoes and dropping her feet into mine. Her hair is even wilder than I thought, falling around her face and almost trailing the floor as she bends forward. Before I can say anything, she's standing up and walking over to a large gilded mirror; the boots clomping as she walks, several sizes too large for her tiny feet. When she reaches the mirror, she turns from side to side admiring her reflection.

"They're the best boots I've ever seen," she says over her shoulder. "Can you design something for me?"

"Gwen," her mother interrupts before I can answer. "That's enough."

She shoots her mother an apologetic look before returning to the stairs to take them off. I wink at her when she returns them, and she blushes and quickly looks away.

I know what it's like to be shamed out of your real personality.

"We've prepared lunch, Folsom, if you'd like to follow me into the dining room," her mother says. The perfect hostess smile has returned to her face and she's walking toward a doorway expecting me to follow.

I don't move. "Actually," I say. "I'd like to get started. I'll eat after the first appointment, that way I'll be rested for the next."

Gwen's sister—what was her name again?—smiles in my direction. Gwen, having returned her shoes to her feet, stands up and bounces a few times on her toes.

"I'm ready if he is," she says when her mother looks at her for approval.

"Well, there you go," she says. "You two can head right upstairs."

I follow Gwen up the winding staircase, thinking how cliché a winding staircase is. The End Men are told to read books, romance books are encouraged—a crash course in what women want. My personal favorite is *Gone with the Wind*, in which slowly winding staircases were a staple of Southern wealth. Rhett Butler's plight in life rang true for me, always wanting something he couldn't have. In Rhett's case it was the spiky Scarlett O'Hara, in mine…freedom. We reach a hallway of doors, each one heavy and old, paneled in oak. Gwen rests her hand on the third door down the hallway and turns to look at me.

"Is this awkward for you?"

"No more than for you," I say.

"I don't feel awkward," she says. "I've been waiting for this my whole life."

"You've been waiting for my dick your whole life, what an honor." I place my hand over my heart to emphasize my sarcasm. She rolls her eyes, undeterred.

"For the baby, Folsom."

She says my name like she's known me for years. A little chill runs down my neck. Familiarity is something I crave, a grown man looking for a security blanket. I admitted it once to Jackal when we were both drunk, and he laughed so hard he fell off the couch he was lying on.

"How do you know you'll get pregnant?" I challenge. It's a ridiculous question, but I want to hear her answer. There's nothing wrong with women's fertility, there's just nothing to fertilize them with.

"I just know," she says. "Ready?"

She opens the door before I can answer either way, and we stand at the threshold of a large bedroom, its walls painted white. I'm surprised right away. The room is minimalistic and modern compared to the rest of the house. A simple bed faces us, low to the ground, with a white, rectangular headboard. On each side of the bed are two simple nightstands, also in white. A large oil painting of tree trunks hangs on one wall, the leaves and branches not visible, and on the opposite wall is a simple gas-burning fireplace. The only cozy thing in the room is the rug, which is plush and royal blue.

"Not what you were expecting?" she asks. She's studying my face.

"Not what I'm used to."

I stride into the room and she follows, shutting the door quietly behind us.

"My mother hates it," she says. "But I find clutter distracting." She scrunches up her nose.

"I agree," I say.

She smiles and I notice there's a dimple in her cheek.

She touches a space on the wall and two panels move away to reveal a bar. "What can I get you to drink, Folsom?" she asks, looking over her shoulder at me.

This is not uncommon, a woman I'm about to fuck asking if I'd like a drink. They offer the type of things they drink: champagne, wine, vodka, and soda.

"Bourbon," I try.

She smiles her biggest smile yet and pulls out a bottle of bourbon and two glasses. She shakes it at me.

"You drink bourbon?" I ask, my eyebrows raised.

"Yes, and I like your boots." She uncorks the bourbon and pours two generous portions into glasses. "Are all the women you meet the same?"

She hands me a glass and drinks hers down in seconds, flinching when she comes up for air.

"Nervous?"

She shrugs. "I've heard that it hurts—the first time."

"Many women prepare for this with toys to avoid the pain."

She scrunches up her nose. "I didn't."

"Then have another drink," I suggest. She moves back to the bar hiccupping.

To the left of the bed and near the large bay window are three armchairs set in a semicircle around a table. I take a seat in one, sipping my drink slowly while I watch her. In every other woman's bedroom I've been inside there have been fresh flowers in vases. The absence of them gives the room a stark, cold feel.

"You don't like flowers?" I ask.

She laughs as she comes to sit in a chair near me, shaking her head.

"What makes you think that?"

I motion around the room. She sits forward in her seat suddenly fascinated.

"Tell me about the other women," she says. "Do they give you gifts, do they all have flowers in their bedrooms? What are they like?"

I laugh. "Don't you have friends?"

She slumps back in her chair. "No, I don't. I'm busy with work mostly. My sister does, but I hate her friends."

"What do you do for work?" I ask. The bourbon is relaxing me. I lean my head back against the chair as I watch her, my free hand drumming my knee. This is the first time I've accepted a drink for an early appointment. I like to be in control of myself, my mind clear, unlike Jackal who drinks both his breakfast and dinner. I save liquor for my free time, nights when I'm alone and I tend to think too much.

"I work for Genome Y," she says, plucking a stray hair from her dress. "We do research to find out—"

"—Why there is a lack of the Y chromosome in male sperm."

"Yes," she says, glancing up at me.

I take a sip of my drink. Normally women in her social position don't work. Not until they're past their childbearing age. "How's research going?" I'm goading her and she knows it. She looks at me, tight-lipped, an annoyed expression on her face.

"I'm sure you'd be the first to know if there were any breakthroughs," she says curtly. "You keep asking me questions, but you haven't answered any."

"I get a shit ton of gifts," I say. "Clothes, watches, money clips, money…and flowers—women love flowers. They're everywhere. Once a woman even wove them into her pubic hair before I fucked her."

"Do you keep the gifts?"

I shrug. "Some."

"You sound bored," she says, surprised. "It's an honor to do what you do. You're helping society. You're—"

"A sex slave," I answer for her. She looks away.

"I'm sure not all of you think that way," she says, uncertain. "Men have always been known to seek out sex above everything else."

"Maybe I'm not like them." I set my empty glass on the table and begin unbuttoning my shirt. Gwen's eyes move to my hands as they work at the buttons.

"So you don't want to be here?" Her eyes are intense, narrowed in what I take as shock.

"Would you?" I stand up to shrug off my suit jacket. My shirt is unbuttoned all the way down to my waist and I pull the tails of it from my pants as I watch her.

"I don't know. I've never thought about it like that. The other men, they seem to enjoy what they do. I just assumed…"

"Take off your clothes," I tell her.

I slide my belt from the loops, suddenly done with the conversation. I've never in sixteen years said these things to any woman and I don't like that I just said them to her. Gwen stands, her eyes locked on mine. Her dress is easy to get off, no zippers or buttons; she simply slides it down her shoulders and it falls around her ankles in a puddle. She's wearing a simple lace bra and panties in a pale pink. The color is attractive against her olive skin tone and dark hair. She's not trying to play the seduction games the others are taught to do, and there's no excited lust in her eyes. She's waiting to be told what comes next. This is a business transaction and she's treating it as such. She wants my sperm, not me, and that's what bothers me most. Jackal would be hysterical if he could hear my thoughts. I'd never fucking hear the end of it.

I kick off the boots she loves so much and step out of my pants. She's watching with curiosity, studying my body, not in a sexual way but with genuine interest. I mean to shock her when I pull down my boxers, the pill I took in the car having just taken effect. I feel a sick satisfaction when her eyes grow wide and her lips part as she stares at my cock.

"It won't fit," she says, shaking her head. She slides her hand up and down her forearm, looking worried.

"Oh, yes, it will."

I take a step toward her and all of a sudden she seems self-conscious of her body, crossing her arms over her chest. The bourbon has fully reached my head and I feel irrationally angry with her for making me say things I never intended to say.

"Turn around," I tell her. She does as she's told, spinning until her back is to me. I unstrap her bra, though she holds it there with her hands. Reaching my head down, I kiss the dip in her neck and work my way toward her ear. I like kissing her. I like the way she smells. She shivers and I see the gooseflesh break out across her arms. When I spin her back around to face me, her eyes are closed and her lips are open and wet. I kiss her, moving her hands away from her chest. Her bra drops to the ground and I reach up, skimming my hand over the cleft in her panties. She jumps but I move on, quickly taking her breast in my hand. She's kissing me back, mirroring the movement my lips make. When I suck on her lip, she sucks on mine. When I slide my tongue into her mouth, she slides hers back. A good student. I move us over to the bed until the back of her calves hit the bed and tell her we're there. Her knees buckle and she lands, sitting directly at eye level with my cock. I move my hand to her head and push her face toward it. Sucking my cock is optional, I never push the issue unless they offer, but I want to see what she'll do. She opens her mouth instinctively and now it's my turn to jump, my muscles clenching as she lets me slide into her mouth. She watches my face as I arch my back, sliding back and forth between her lips. Then she grabs my thighs to still me and moves her mouth over it without my help, surprising me with how good she is. The little novice has skill. I relax as I let her touch me with her tongue. When I want to be inside her, I push her onto her back.

"Lift your hips," I say. She obeys me and I slide off her panties. She's hairless; no flowers, only smooth olive skin.

"I read that you don't like hair," she says. "So I had it taken off." She's watching my face intently to see what I think. I decide to show her.

I dip my head down and kiss her right there, sucking. Her skin is soft. She buckles underneath me and I slip my tongue between her lips for added effect. The noise she makes is surprised, between a scream and a yell. This is not something I do, this is something women pay me extra for, but I want to taste her, and so I yank her thighs open and lick away the wet. She's loud, she's very loud. From experience I know that her sister is eavesdropping at the door, jealous that she's not the first one. I suck on her clit to make her yell louder, smiling when she does. It doesn't take me long to make her come, especially when I slide a finger inside of her. She grabs my hair and clenches my head between her thighs so that I can't breathe and then her body freezes and shudders. When I crawl up her body, her eyes are open and she's breathless.

"I didn't know," she says. "—That it would feel like that."

"Now comes the part that's going to hurt," I tell her. "Try to relax."

"It's not going to fit," she says again, lifting her head to get another look at it.

"I know how to make it fit, Gwen," I say, closing my eyes.

She's drenched and I find her without trying, pushing myself slowly into her. She moans, lifting her hips. I take one of her nipples in my mouth and suck hard.

"Am I hurting you?" I ask.

Her eyes open. "Yeah, but it's a good hurt."

That's all it takes. I work my way into her, thrusting a little bit at a time, breaking through her virginity. Her insides grip me and it's like sliding over warm silk.

Normally, I can last a long time, I give them their money's worth, but this time I feel myself hardening the way I do before I finally come.

"I want a son," she says, wrapping her arms around my neck and pulling me closer. "Give me your son."

And then I explode inside of her and the heat is almost unbearable.

SIX

GWEN

My eyes are squeezed shut, savoring this content, sky-high rush. When I hear Folsom roar as he spills into me, I regret not watching him. What does it feel like for him? Is he glad to be finished or did he take pleasure from my body? I open my eyes and watch as the storm crosses his face and eventually winds down. I think he liked it. I place my hand on his cheek and smile…grateful. He looks almost shy, his guard down for seconds; then he blinks and I think I imagined it. He pulls out slowly, placing a pillow under my hips to keep his seed inside me for as long as possible.

"It fit!" My attempt at humor.

"Yes, it did." He half smiles.

He's on his back now, looking distracted. Something monumental for me was just another day in his life. I'm surprised by how much it stings.

I look him over. Beads of sweat are on his chest and his waist tapers into a perfect V. He's still hard and wet from being inside me; his cock pulses a few times, like it enjoys my attention. My entire body flushes and I want nothing more than to start over from the beginning with him, instead of this experience already being over.

My mother often talks about how difficult life is now because she knows exactly what she's missing. She hopes it's easier for us girls to never have known the way it used to be. My mother went to a sperm bank for my sister and me, but she grew up with both a mother and a father. She was made in the traditional way. I've always loved hearing her stories despite not being able to relate.

Suddenly he's up and on his feet. "Keep lying there and I'll get a shower." He walks toward the bathroom and I lean up on my elbows to watch him. The muscles in his back roll as he stretches his arms above his head.

Where I am all soft curves, he is sculpted muscle. I want more time to study the intricacies of his body, more time to explore. I didn't expect him to make me feel so good. I push that thought aside and focus on the life that I hope is in the process of forming.

When the shower turns off, I sit up and put my bra back on. I'd like to shower too, but instead I keep still and squeeze, trying to keep every trickle of him inside me. He walks out minutes later, body dripping, and hands me a warm washcloth.

"Thanks."

His jaw ticks and he doesn't say anything. I run the cloth over my body and clean up as best I can, while he stands there and watches. I expect to feel embarrassed, but it never comes. Every nerve ending sparks under his gaze, my nipples tighten until they hurt, and I get lightheaded.

He bites the inside of his jaw and his eyes darken. I can't look away, but eventually he does, picking up my dress and handing it to me. I murmur my thanks again, but he still doesn't respond. I can't tell if he's uncomfortable with me, or if I've done something to upset him. I glance down at his cock—that seems to be an indicator of what he's thinking. It's standing at attention, swollen and angry. He gives it a few tugs.

I know I should look away, but it's too fascinating. "It just sort of bobs around," I say. "I'd play with it all the time if I had one."

He lifts his eyebrows, his lips twitching. "If you had one of these you wouldn't have time to play with it yourself."

"Right," I say, frowning. "How many times a day do you have to do this?"

Folsom shrugs. "Two or three…"

I balk. "Every single day?"

"We get days off."

"What do you do on your days off?"

"Not fuck three women."

Interesting. I'm doing the math in my head, counting the women he's been with just this year, when his voice makes me jump.

"I should go."

My face heats. I tear my eyes away from him and stand, stepping into my dress and pulling my hair over my chest. He picks up his shirt, and I admire the way it clings to his shoulders. He reaches into his small leather bag and pulls out new boxers. I don't like what I feel as he puts himself back together.

"I'll take you to the dining room. You must be starving." I walk toward the door and pick up his boots, admiring them one more time.

Once his pants are on, he takes the boots from me, and his lips curl up into a faint smile.

"Hold up your foot," he says.

When I do, he takes hold of my heel and aligns it to his boot. He studies it for a moment and nods, letting go.

"You have pretty feet."

"What constitutes pretty feet?" I don't think I care what constitutes pretty feet, I just want to keep talking to him.

He returns, bending down in front of me and lifting my foot from the floor. I sit on the edge of the bed and watch as he runs a finger along the inside from toe to heel. I'm too stunned by his touch to find it ticklish. This feels more intimate than what we just did.

"This arch," he says. "And the symmetry of your toes…" He touches the tip of my big toe with a fingertip, and then moves his entire hand to my ankle, and wraps his fingers around it. "Tiny ankles."

It's silly, but his praise pleases me. He doesn't seem to be the complimentary type and I'm not the type who needs to be complimented, but…this has been a day of firsts.

I grin. "I'll show you where lunch is being served."

As we walk through the narrow hallway, our arms brush against each other. I'm aware of how close we are to one another, how the heat of his skin transfers into mine.

Sophia and Mother are standing in the living room, attempting to appear casual but failing. Their backs are stiff, eyes are wide, and the curiosity is about to break them both in two. It would be comical if I didn't suddenly become overwhelmed with dread for having to share his company. He seemed in a hurry to leave my room, but I wish I'd found a way to stall.

"Done so soon?" Sophia's tone is mocking, as she puts her hand on Folsom's chest. I wonder if women just touch him like this all the time. He doesn't seem bothered by it; rather, he ignores her hand and looks at me.

My breath catches. His face is stony, as if a wall just went up. I wonder what he's guarding. Mother swoops between Sophia and Folsom and takes his arm. We walk to the dining room, where all of our best is out on display. She places him at the head of the table and motions for us to sit on either side of him. She signals to Phoebe that we're ready for the dining service to begin and Phoebe lets the kitchen staff know. When it's just us in the house, we're not nearly so formal.

Once the platters are brought out, my mother takes a seat next to me. I clasp her hand in hopes that she'll relax. She's making me anxious.

Folsom fills his plate with mostly vegetables and fruit, especially the raspberries. At the last second, he takes a large chicken breast. I file it all away, not bothering to take any food. He chooses lemonade, a favorite of mine.

"How is your schedule while you're here?" my mother asks. "Do you ever get a day off?"

Folsom sets down his knife and stops chewing. "I'm expected to attend the Region parties, which as you know are most nights, but I'm not always expected to impregnate someone at them, so…little bit of a break." He gives a savage grin and picks his knife back up. "I have an occasional Tuesday off. It just depends on how the lottery goes." He looks at me then, popping another bite of chicken in his mouth. "Do you work full-time?"

"She never stops working," Sophia answers for me. "Like a plebeian. You'd think she was born to the lower end."

"She's here today," he says, his gaze running over my face. "It seems we have the same work ethic, Gwen."

Sophia rolls her eyes. I pick up a glass of water and sip it, hoping it will cool me down.

"I enjoy my work," I finally say. "I want to be part of the solution. The world has enough people lounging around hoping things get fixed for them."

"Are you going to put me out of a job?" His voice sounds almost hopeful.

"Yes, actually," I say bluntly. "Not that you can't keep doing what you're doing, but it would be really great to not have to depend on the End Men to save us."

"It would be great," he agrees. "Not nearly as much fun as what we just did, though…"

I laugh then but don't respond. He waits a moment and seems satisfied with what he sees on my face. He's still smirking as he tucks back into his food.

Sophia scoots a little closer to him and runs her hands through his hair.

"Sophia, let the man eat," Mother says.

Sophia glares at our mother and puts her hand in her lap. "I'll be at all the parties," she says. Folsom eats a large handful of raspberries and grabs another spoonful. "I'll see you there," she adds.

He lifts his glass and gives her a mini-salute. She doesn't seem to realize he's not interested in anything but the food right now. He turns to me.

"I hope you find the answer," he says quietly.

It takes a moment for me to understand and then I know—no one wants to be done with his job more than he does.

All the preconceived thoughts I've had about the End Men and their glamorous life fades. It might be different for the others, but with Folsom, it's obvious that he's ready for his obligation to the Regions to be done. The problem is, with a good forty years or so left of virility he's not anywhere close to being finished.

I thought women had it rough, the few who can afford it getting one chance at a child, but I can't imagine being bound to the Regions' beck and call. It changes everything. I feel awful for him, but the point remains: I want a baby. So I've contributed to his bondage.

It's too much to think about…too much of a shift in the way I've always thought. I feel guilty and yet excited over the thought of what we did today. Mostly excited.

I stand up, nearly knocking my chair over in the process. "I have to go. Thank you, Folsom." I hold out my hand and he takes it in his. "I'm so glad it was you."

I pull my hand away and he looks stunned.

"Where are you going?" Mother asks.

"I have to get to work."

"Gwen, really, sit down. The next appointment isn't for another half hour," Mother says.

I leave before anyone can say anything else. I do want to work this afternoon, but more than that, I've felt entirely too many emotions today and I don't want to hear Sophia's cries of pleasure when it's her turn.

When I arrive at the lab, I throw myself into work, catching up on what I missed this morning. No one but my boss knows about my appointment with Folsom, and she has the grace not to ask when she sees me. I can still feel the throb where Folsom was inside of me. He invaded more than my body; I can't stop thinking about him.

SEVEN

FOLSOM

My job is simple. Intellect is not needed when you're fucking your way through an entire Region of women. There are days when I long to have a meaningful conversation, to discuss, and dispute, and have my voice mean something to this corroded world we're inhabiting.

I shower again before I meet Gwen's sister, Sophia, in her bedroom. The water runs over me and I'm given a reprieve from the constant looks and touching. There is a stark contrast between the two sisters. I wonder if they get along or if the tension I felt is real. Where Gwen is quiet and introspective, her sister is talkative and social. The type of woman you kiss just to shut up, not to actually enjoy it. A servant directs me to her room. I knock once and she opens the door wearing only her underwear and a pair of heels so high they look fucking painful.

"Come in, Folsom."

They like to say my name. It makes me feel like a fucking dog. *Come in, Folsom. Sit down, Folsom. Eat this, Folsom.* She turns on her heel and I'm given a view of the tightness of her body.

I step past her and I'm immediately hit with the heady smell of lilies. I smile to myself when I see the various flower displays across the room.

"It stinks in here," I say.

Sophia bats her eyes, uncomprehending.

"The lilies."

"Oh! Do you want me to have them removed?" She heads to the door to summon someone when I stop her.

"No, don't bother. I won't be here long." It's meant as an insult. I don't like the games she was playing with Gwen, but when she walks toward me, I can tell it's gone straight over her head.

"Well, I certainly hope you're staying for a little while at least…" She trails a finger across my chest as she heads for the bar. "A drink, Folsom?"

"No, I'd prefer to get started," I say.

I don't need to be drunk for this one. I drink when I feel too much—good or bad—and only then.

She looks mildly disappointed. I'm used to this—the women expecting to be entertained socially before we have sex. It's like a courting ritual I don't care to play. I'm here for one thing and one thing only. Sophia sets her drink down and begins to touch me. I stand still as she takes off my clothes, first unbuttoning my shirt and running her hands across my chest, then cupping me through my pants to feel if I'm ready. I am. The pill I took at lunch only needed an hour to stiffen me up again. The women are unaware that we take pills. It's a joke among the End Men that women think we are always hard and capable of fucking once an hour. Even Jackal, who brags that he hardly uses the tiny blue pills, laughs along with us.

Once Sophia has confirmation that I'm hard, she smiles slyly and leads me over to the bed. A bed covered and draped in silk. She makes a show of stripping off her clothes, running her hands across her bare skin to entice me, and then walking over to suck on my fingertips. I let her suck while I unbutton my pants and try to engage my mind in what we're about to do. *Focus, Folsom, fucking focus.*

"I've had female lovers," she tells me. "I know how to pleasure a woman, but I want you to show me how to pleasure a man…"

Jackal would be so much better at this than I am. I grimace when she turns her back, sashaying slowly to the side of the bed and beckoning me closer with her finger.

She is beautiful; her blond hair hangs across her breasts, which are full and perfect, the nipples a deep rose. I'm familiar with the shade of rose because of all the fucking flowers in all the fucking bedrooms. She stands on her tiptoes to reach my neck where she kisses me softly, moaning like it brings her pleasure.

"Get on the bed. On your hands and knees," I say, my voice low. She casts a coy look over her shoulder before doing what I say.

I take her with a singular anger that on any other day I would not have allowed to reach the surface. She seems to enjoy it, crying out in pleasure each time I slam into her, her back arching and her head twisting around to watch me. I can see every inch of her, the erotic folds of her pussy, the way it looks like it's grabbing onto my dick when I pull out, trying to keep me inside. But, I'm not thinking of her, I'm thinking of Gwen. Gwen, who wrapped her body around me like we were doing more than just fucking. I felt more intimacy in those moments than I have in years. I pull out of Sophia, moving her onto her back. She spreads her legs for me and I settle between them. I don't have to work my way in like I did with Gwen because she's already so wet. I move inside of her the same way I did with her sister, telling myself that the things I felt with Gwen were in my head. A moment of weakness brought on by our conversation. I could feel that way with anyone if I tried.

Sophia moans beneath me, repeating the same phrase over and over: "It feels so good, it feels so good…"

I let myself go rigid, pressing my lips against her mouth as I come, to shut her up. When I'm done, I remove myself from her lax body and walk to the bathroom without looking back. My job in this house is finished. Thank God for that. It was a strange morning and I feel off-kilter. I had to think of Gwen to come. That has never happened before.

Their mother is waiting at the bottom of the stairs as I make my way down. She smiles up at me as I'm straightening my collar. It's always an awkward exchange, seeing the parent when your dick is still wet from her daughter.

"Thank you, Folsom," she says when I pause in front of her. The sincerity in her voice throws me and I stand there for a full minute not knowing what to say.

"Your driver is waiting," she says, breaking the silence.

I'm at the door when she calls my name. I pause halfway out the door and see she's walking toward me.

She dusts some imaginary lint from the lapels of my coat. It's so distinctly maternal that a pang of something rips through me. I immediately want a drink. She folds her lips together and shakes her head sadly.

"Out of the two of them I'm pulling for Gwen," she says, softly.

I don't know why she's telling me this. I hold her eyes for a minute before nodding once and ducking out the door. The car is waiting just outside, my driver leaning against the front side smoking a cigarette. When she sees me, she tosses it to the ground, shrugging. Smoking is forbidden across the Regions. Anything that shortens the human lifespan or affects fertility is strictly forbidden. She holds the door open and I slide into the backseat, my eyes still on the house.

"Back to the compound, sir?" she asks.

"No," I say. "Take me to a bar. It doesn't matter where." She glances at me in the rearview mirror before pulling down the long drive.

"I have to remind you, sir, that you have your lottery drawing tonight and I've been advised that you should show up for the drawing sober…also, we don't have your security detail with us..."

"Take me to a goddamn bar and don't worry about my sobriety," I snap.

I see her nod once before I press the button to raise the partition between us. The End Men have very few rules we are expected to abide by, and those we do have are mostly ignored. If we do our job, they are willing to turn a blind eye toward our indiscretions. The more children you father, the more favor you receive, and I've fathered a lot of fucking kids.

When I step out of the car, I'm standing in front of a giant fish tank. My driver stares at me sourly.

"What's your name?" I ask.

"Sera," she replies curtly.

"I'm sorry, Sera. For earlier."

Her face relaxes at once and I smile at her, relieved that I didn't burn that bridge. A year is a long time to spend with someone who hates you.

"What is this place?" I ask, looking up at the glass walls. Large fish swim lazily around the tank, weaving between electric red coral.

"It's a bar. You told me to take you to a bar."

"Yes, I did," I say, glancing at her. I can't tell if she's being a smart ass, so I head toward the door, hands in my pockets. The door opens before I can reach it and two women spill out, clutching each other and laughing. Their jaws drop when they see me.

"A little early to be drunk, ladies," I say, as I walk past them.

One of them recovers quicker than the other. "Speak for yourself," she calls after me. They erupt in a fit of laughter, which is abruptly cut off when the door closes behind me.

Once inside I stop short to catch my bearings. The effect is similar to being underwater and would be peaceful if not for the thumping music pounding through the speakers. The light moves in blue and silver shadows around me as I walk toward the nearest stool. Overhead, fish of every color move gracefully through the water, fanning their paper-thin fins. The Red Region: the wealthiest have money to spare. I study the bottles of liquor in amazement. I'm surprised Jackal ever left this place. The last Region I was stationed in had one bar that served moonshine in glass jars. The roof was made out of tin, and if it rained there were a dozen spots you had to avoid if you didn't want to get wet.

The bartender is jarred when she sees me but quickly hides her surprise, ambling over while still polishing a glass. Her head is shaved, and her face pierced. I like her on sight.

"Well, well, what an honor," she says, dryly. "Welcome to our humble establishment."

"Bourbon straight," I say. "A not so humble pour."

She nods before moving away to locate a bottle. She comes back with a full rocks glass and I nod at her gratefully. I take out money to pay her, but she waves it off.

"We're just so grateful for your jizz, man. Don't worry about it." She does a little bow, and I can't help but laugh. "You made it just in time for happy hour." She points to the clock and I have to spin around on my barstool to see it.

"How bad?" I ask her.

She makes a face. "In about ten minutes at least a hundred women will be all over your dick. Lucky man."

She winks at me, and before I can respond she's moved away and I'm left wondering if she's exaggerating.

I find out ten minutes later when women start pouring through the door, stopping short when they see me. I move to the far corner of the bar, out of sight, and the bartender gives me the thumbs up like it was a wise choice. I have one sip left of my drink when someone slides into the stool next to me and picks up my glass, draining the last of my bourbon.

"Only sad people drink alone."

I turn to see Gwen grinning at me. She shakes my empty glass and says, "Buy me another. I lost my virginity today."

EIGHT

GWEN

"Should you be drinking?" he asks me.

"If I am pregnant, Folsom, all I have are a couple of cells soaking in your come. It won't hurt anything yet. Besides, I had a hell of a day, didn't you?"

"Same as any other day." He folds in his lips and nods. I find the expression endearing.

Just another day for him—meanwhile, my entire world has shifted.

My older friends from work talk about the romances they had with men…when there were men. It's a novelty for me imagining that once there were as many men as there were women, and they just walked up and down the street like the rest of us. When they talk about them they get these dreamy expressions, eyes all glassy, blinking slowly. Laura's stories are my favorite. Henry made her feel like the luckiest woman alive, like she was the only one he saw…he treasured her. And when they "made love" it was as if they were the only two people in the world, nothing else mattered but the two of them. *Making love*—that phrase doesn't quite seem to fit what Folsom and I did.

Maybe sex is one of those things that in memory looks one way, but in reality is just a whimsical fantasy. It's something I'll never know. The stories are nice, though.

Folsom motions to the bartender and she fills up his glass. You'd almost think they knew each other with how comfortably they exchange words.

"So do you feel older and wiser now that you've finally had sex?" he asks. He swivels slightly in his stool so that our knees bump.

"I feel more in the dark than ever." I pick up his glass and drain it dry again.

He laughs. "Easy, kid. I'll have to carry you out of here." He reaches over the bar top and gets a glass. He lifts it and the bartender ignores all the women clamoring for her attention to fill up both of our glasses.

"Would that be the worst thing?" I ask, turning to face him.

His eyes narrow on mine. "Did you follow me here?"

I scowl back, feeling the first blurring edges of the bourbon hitting me. "Are you always such an asshole?" I take another long swig and clank my glass down hard, making liquid drip down my hand. "Welcome to the Red Region, Folsom, and our one and only bar," I say, rolling my eyes. "I thought you had your fancy *party* to go to." I practically spit out the word "party" and wipe my mouth with the back of my hand, licking away the drops of bourbon while I'm at it. Parties are the foulest form of dim-witted entertainment. I was forced to attend them for most of my adolescence, and the minute I turned eighteen, old enough to make my own decisions, I refused to tag along with my mother and sister, the Ball being the exception since Folsom was there…

He doesn't say anything for a moment, just studies me until I get itchy.

"What?"

"Are you normally such a mess?" he asks.

"Define 'mess.'"

He faces forward again, narrowing his eyes and smacking his lips like he's thinking real hard about it.

"Oh God, that bad?" I ask.

"It's the look in your eyes mostly. Crazed. Like you're ready to bolt at any moment."

"Yikes."

"You don't even try to hide it," he says.

"Should I?"

Folsom shrugs. "Wild eyes, wild hair…makes you interesting."

I look away. Two girls are making out next to me. One of them accidentally bumps into me and calls out "Sorry" over her shoulder. I sigh. "It's hard losing something you never really had." I turn to him. "You know?"

"Can you try again in English?"

"I'm not attracted to women," I blurt. I widen my eyes, expecting him to understand, but he just stares at me. "So if I'm not attracted to women, and there are no men, it means I'm going to be alone for the rest of my life."

"Aloneness sounds pretty good to me," he says, looking away.

"You don't really want to be alone," I tell him. I'm feeling loose-limbed and bold; blame it on the bourbon. He looks shocked that I've said this, so I expound.

"You said it yourself earlier today, you've been forced into this life. But no one wants to be alone. We all want to be understood by at least one person. You just don't get to choose one person to be with."

"You're attracted to me," he says.

I laugh and then look exaggeratedly around the room.

"Everyone in this bar is staring at you, Folsom. We're all attracted to you."

Even the two girls who just had their tongues down each other's throats keep shooting him looks. I see a few of the bouncers, women well over six feet with plenty of muscle, holding back a few dozen women. Trans, DSD, and straight alike…they all want him, they're all trying to get to him. If nothing else but to say they've experienced an End Man.

"But if there were many, many other men—you'd still be attracted to me," he says.

I consider this. He's probably right. Something about the moodiness...and the boots. I'm not going to give him the satisfaction of answering.

He pries my glass out of my hands and sets it down, shooing my hand away when I try to reach for it again.

"I'm going to miss doing...what we did. But, it was worth it," I say. "It was. To have a baby will make it all worth it."

"You liked fucking?" he asks. "Which part?"

He's teasing me. I don't like how vulnerable it makes me feel.

"The part where you put it in all the way to the part where you took it out. Well, I didn't like the part where you took it out, but you know what I mean."

He has a weird look in his eyes as he watches me. A little smile plays on his lips.

"The women are starting to circle," I say suddenly. "I'm surprised they've been as accommodating as they have, but it's going to blow in a moment, mark my words."

Folsom glances at them warily.

I look around and ask, "Is it like this everywhere you go?" I'm shocked he seems so calm. I'd lose my mind if I were being stared at like bait all the time.

"Normally it's much worse. There's more restraint in the Red Region than I've seen in a while...maybe ever. I don't want to push it, though. Walk me out?"

"Hmm. I might be wobbly." I shift my legs to the side of the barstool and set my feet on the ground. It swims a little but then goes into focus. "Not bad."

He shakes his head and holds out his arm for me to take and I grip it hard. Jo, one of the bouncers I know, motions for us to follow her. We go out a side door and walk down the long hall. Jo points to the exit sign above the back door and Folsom thanks her.

The sun is just starting its descent and the night sky is blue slashed with pinks and purples. I twirl around in a circle, taking in the color.

"Don't tell me you're dancing now," he says.

"Look up," I tell him, pointing at the sky.

He does and stops walking, making me barrel into the back of him. He steadies me and then drops his hand to his side, still looking at the sky.

"It's beautiful here," he says quietly. He turns to me. "You're fortunate to be here. Are you aware of what it's like in the other Regions?"

"Only what I've heard. I haven't been anywhere else…I pretty much live in the lab. Tell me what it's like."

He shakes his head. "And further wreck your 'hell of a day'? I might be an asshole, but I'm not that bad," he says.

"Ready to go, Mr. Donahue?"

I turn around and notice his driver for the first time. She looks nervous and I wonder if he's supposed to be here—better yet, where is his security?

"Five more minutes, Sera," he says.

She nods and walks back to the car, pacing with her hands in her pockets.

He turns to me. "Come to the party with me."

"What? No. Are you serious?"

"I'm always serious."

The laughter bursts from my throat before I can stop it.

His eyes roam down my neck and to the cleavage that shows when the wind catches my dress just so.

"Let's go," he says like it's already decided.

It's probably asking for more anguish to get to know Folsom any better. Nothing good can come out of it, only more confusion. But how can I refuse him? I get into the back of the car with him.

"I wish I could at least freshen up," I say, looking down at my dress.

He's sitting surprisingly close and when he turns toward me, my eyes are drawn to his lips. My face flushes when I think of all he did with that mouth.

"Did you shower after I left?" he asks, voice low.

I swallow, unsure for a moment that I heard him correctly. He stares at me, waiting.

"No."

"Why not?"

I squirm in my seat. Suddenly I don't want to be so close to him.

"I couldn't wash you all the way off just yet," I admit. "Is that weird?"

"Yes," he says.

I want to die. I want to die a thousand deaths. I wish someone would let me out of this car so I can die…

"But, I like it."

"Oh." I get comfortable in my seat again.

His pupils dilate, pulling me in deeper. I gasp when his fingertips trace from my neck all the way to the dip between my breasts then lightly tweak my nipple. I hold my breath, unwilling to move an inch for fear he'll stop. His other hand travels down my stomach to my thigh and rests there. I want to beg him to claim any part of me he wants. Right here, right now. I don't care who sees or hears, just to have him inside me one more time will be enough.

I lean my face into his and brush my fingers across his lips. His tongue flicks out and licks my finger. He inches closer to my face, his lips hovering over mine, our breath searing into one another. I close my eyes and wait for his kiss.

It never comes. My eyes flutter open and he pulls back, scoots over in his seat, and runs his hands through his hair. His breathing sounds heavier, but that's the only sign that I might not have dreamed it up.

I look at him and he stares steadfastly out the window.

"I know you want to take all you can get while you have a man around, but I'm all used up today," he says.

My mouth drops. "You act like I asked for any of that."

A lump gets lodged in my throat and I swallow hard a few times trying to get relief. I square my shoulders and scream inside to not let one tear fall over this man. I meet a man and in one day he makes me cry? I don't think so.

"I can take you home if you'd rather not go to the party," he says.

"No, I've changed my mind. I *want* to go to the party," I tell him.

He looks irritated and I don't care. It's been a long time since I've stayed out late anywhere other than the lab. I'll go and enjoy myself just to spite him.

We're getting closer and closer to the oceanfront, and the sun takes one last dip into the water. The hotels and high-rise buildings that used to line the sand are few and far between. Most have been torn down and sleek glass, dome-shaped buildings take their place. We turn in the parking lot for the Council of Affairs and are driven all the way to the entrance.

"I don't want to walk in with you. Can you have her just drop me off and I'll walk in somewhere other than the red carpet?"

The car stops and he shoots an annoyed glance my way. "We're here already."

Are all men this infuriating?

Sera lifts the divider and turns to face me. "It'd probably be best if I take Miss—"

"Gwen," I respond.

"Thank you, Miss Gwen, I'll take you around to the side entrance after Mr. Donahue exits. I didn't want him to be late; otherwise, I would've dropped you off first."

I gloat while he steps out of the car. And then watch as not one but two women grab his face and kiss the hell out of him.

NINE

FOLSOM

Different night, same party. I'm pushed and prodded down the red carpet, dozens of hands reaching toward me. They call my name—"Folsom, a picture!" "Folsom, we love you!" I stop to take selfies and sign the printed photos of myself that they shove into my hands, each one more ridiculous than the last. A woman grabs my dick as I pose with her, and I let her because that's what I'm told to do. I am the property of the Regions; I belong to these women. I smile and move down the line, stopping in front of a girl who holds up a sign. *Give me a baby, Folsom! It's my birthday!* I give her a kiss instead.

Gwen was taken around back and I wonder if she's made her way inside and is watching the shitshow unfold. When all of this started years ago—the End Men commissioned to save the dwindling population—it had been flattering to attend events like this. I was young and saw the lifestyle as a game. Any party I attended would turn into an orgy with me at its center. And then when I reached the age of twenty-nine, something changed. The sex became contrived, and the women desperate. I longed for a familiar face to wake up to every morning; I missed being known. Unhappiness settled over me like a stifling blanket. Where once I found freedom in my ability to have any woman I wanted, I now saw the truth of our situation. We were property, and they would milk us until we were dead while fooling us into thinking we were enjoying ourselves. I would never know my children, never see them walk, or laugh, or play. I was sent yearly updates on them, all lined up on a spreadsheet in order of their ages.

Jaoxin, ten years old. Location: Blue Region. Mothers: Adeline and Garva Lutin. Health: Excellent. Excels in Math and Science. There would be a small photo of the child as well, something grainy I could barely see. My sons were not yet old enough to enter the End Men program. When I thought about the life that awaited them, it made me sick.

I turn around to face the crowd when I reach the end of the red carpet and wave once before going inside. The crowd screams their goodbyes, and then suddenly the noise is cut off, and a new, more sophisticated crowd greets me. The upper crust of the Red Region stands there, clapping politely. I spot Gwen in the back of the crowd talking to someone and then a familiar face is right in front of me saying something.

"Sophia," I say, once I remember her name. It takes me a minute to recall the woman I fucked not even five hours ago.

"Let me introduce you around," she says, taking me by the arm. I notice that her dress is less revealing than the one she wore this morning, the hemline reaching her knees. She really shouldn't cover up; her body is the only thing she has going for her. She guides me through a throng of people all with drinks in their hands; they watch us curiously as she stops in front of Governor Little…no, what was it…*Petite*! Goddamn, I'm bad with names.

"Folsom! Welcome, welcome," she says jovially. "Get this man a drink," she calls over her shoulder.

Gwen's mother stands off to the side smiling at Petite, and I wonder what the nature of their relationship is. I am introduced to a dozen women, all who work in various branches of government. I'm still buzzed from the bar, which makes all the introductions bleed together. Name after insipid name, broad smiles and blindingly white teeth. They're leading me off somewhere else, Sophia still clinging to my arm like a monkey, when I spot Gwen a few feet away.

"Gwen!" I call. Her head jerks up, her eyes large. She looks around like she's embarrassed at having her name called out so publicly. "Are you still drinking bourbon or have you switched to something else?" I wink at her just as she turns a deep red.

"Gwen and I had a few drinks earlier," I say to Sophia. "At that underwater bar."

"The Fish Tank?" Sophia looks stricken. She recovers quickly. "I didn't know my sister was such a lush."

"Sophia, stop hogging our End Man." A group of girls saunters up to us and I feel Sophia's grip tighten on my arm.

"This is Folsom," she tells them proudly. "These are my friends."

I'm introduced to a lineup of names I'll never remember. The most interesting of the group is a tall redhead in an emerald green dress. She's striking and sexy and she bites her lip when she catches me watching her.

"Folsom," I hear from behind me. Governor Petite approaches us, a benevolent smile on her face. It's time for the lottery drawing. I nod to the group of women and untangle myself from Sophia's fingers. Sophia's hand is replaced by Governor Petite's.

"It looked like you needed some saving," she says quietly as we walk arm in arm.

I glance at her. "Can you save me from all of these women, Governor, or just the one?"

She looks up at me, surprised. "Do you want to be saved? I thought that…"

"There it is," I say, interrupting her. I didn't want to hear her surprise about me not finding contentment in being an End Man. I approach the lottery draw and see that it's a giant fish tank, a miniature of their grand bar.

"Yes," she says, clapping her hands together. "We had it constructed just for this. You put your hand in and pull out a plastic fish. Inside each fish is one lucky girl's number."

"Brilliant," I say dryly. "Should we get started?"

Governor Petite mistakes my sarcasm for genuine excitement and she runs off to make the announcement that we're going to get started. I see Gwen out of the corner of my eye. She's standing nearby with a bottle of water in her hand. When I look over, she shakes her head at me, a small smile on her lips. She mouths the word "brilliant" and rolls her eyes up in her head. I stifle a laugh and turn my attention back to the fish tank.

Fishing the plastic molds of fish out of the water and calling the numbers out as the cameras stream it live takes less than ten minutes. I'm given a towel to dry my hands, and I'm told that a lottery winner is here, one of the women who waited to see me walk the red carpet.

They pull her inside for an interview and check her number against the one we drew from the tank. When all is confirmed, she starts to scream. I try not to grimace, especially when the camera pans in on my face. Her circumstance calls this a miracle. She is not part of one of the elite families, my fee too exorbitant for someone of her standing to ever afford. If she becomes pregnant from our coupling, she will be hailed a hero among her people. The Region will financially provide for both her and her child. She is led up to the stage where I wait with the governor, and when she reaches me, she throws her arms around my neck. She's a pretty girl, fair-skinned with long, auburn hair. Her dark eyes fill with tears when they meet mine.

"Thank you, thank you," she says so that only I can hear.

I lift an arm and wrap it around her back, breathing in the scent of her hair. When I open my eyes, I immediately see Gwen. She's standing stoically in the crowd watching me. Her eyes are the saddest eyes I've ever seen. Despite my own.

Her name is Audrin and she's twenty-four years old. We are to be taken to a room somewhere in the building. I'm guessing it's used just for this purpose. Before we go upstairs, Robin finds me in the crowd and discreetly palms me a little blue pill.

"I heard you had an exciting afternoon getting drunk," she says. Her face is stern, but Robin could never be truly mad at me.

I shrug. "You took the day off. I didn't have a babysitter."

She frowns at me. "It won't happen again. For either of us," she says sternly. "You know how they get. You could have been mobbed."

"Almost was," I toss over my shoulder. "See you later."

I pop the pill in my mouth and swallow it dry. Once we are alone in the room, Audrin looks ready to faint.

"Have something to drink," I tell her, motioning over to the bar. "Take a bath to relax if you like, we have some time." The bathtub was the first thing she noticed when we walked into the room, exclaiming about the size.

"Are you sure?" she asks shyly. "You don't mind?"

I shake my head. I don't blame her. I've seen the way some of the lower ends of the Regions are forced to live. Entire families crammed into tiny, one-bedroom apartments, sharing a bathroom with everyone else on the floor.

"I'll make myself a drink. Go ahead."

While Audrin runs the water, I fill my glass with bourbon and sit on the bed. I've had a buzz from the time I woke up until now. Robin would be pissed if she knew how much I've been drinking. My arms feel stiff and there's a dull ache in my head. I find some aspirin in a gift basket on the table and pop a few into my mouth. I'm already getting hard, I can feel it. The longer you're on the pills, the less time they take to work. I wonder if Gwen left after I came upstairs. Would she ride home with her mother and sister, or would she find her own way? If I've learned anything about Sophia thus far, it would be likely that she'd close out the party downstairs, being the last to leave.

When Audrin emerges from the bathroom a while later, she's wearing a silky white robe and the expression of someone who looks like they want to throw up.

"You don't have to be nervous," I tell her. How many times have I said that to a woman? I motion for her to sit next to me on the bed and she does, perching herself on the edge while I'm stretched out next to her. I kiss her softly at first, and she kisses me back, moaning softly into my mouth.

"Will it hurt?" she asks, looking at me with innocent eyes.

"Yes," I say. "But not much."

She nods, her expression determined. I unbuckle my belt and lower my pants while still spread out on the bed. My dick springs free and I pull her on top of me.

"Lower yourself onto it," I tell her.

She straddles me, doing as she's told, slipping the robe off her shoulders. She makes a tiny noise as I break through her and settle inside her warmth. Moving her hips, I lean back and close my eyes as she rocks on top of me. Her hands press into my chest and she starts moving on her own. It doesn't take me long. I pull her down hard on my dick and explode inside of her.

Afterward, I tell her to lie on her back while I get up to take a piss. It's when I'm in front of the toilet, dick in hand, that the pain shoots through my chest. I groan and lean my forearm against the wall, rubbing the spot. It's unbearable. I bend lower, squeezing my eyes closed. And then everything goes black.

TEN

GWEN

When Folsom invited me to come, it never crossed my mind that he'd be gone most of the time having sex with one of the lottery winners. I don't know what I thought—maybe that he'd find me after the formalities were out of the way and we could resume the push and pull that I've quickly become addicted to, or maybe I was holding out hope that he'd finish the blaze of his hands across my body that he'd started in the car. Both are so far-fetched it isn't even funny. I've been listening to too many stories at work, getting my head filled with romantic notions that died along with the last batch of men. I look around at the crazed women of all ages, all eagerly awaiting another glimpse of Folsom. He'll probably have sex with someone else before the night is over and it won't be me. I had my chance.

I find my mother in the crowd, standing next to Governor Petite. I make my way to her, barely avoiding getting doused with wine by one of Sophia's friends. I narrow my eyes at the girls surrounding Sophia. They're the last people I want to see right now.

I put my hand on my mom's elbow.

"Are you okay, love?" she asks, leaning into my ear.

"I'm not feeling so well. Do you think I could take your car?"

She feels my face, checking to see if I'm fevered, but her eyes center on mine. I look away when I see the flash of pity there.

"Oh sweetheart," she says, arms going around me.

"Mother, please, *don't.*" I pull away. I'll never hold it together if she hugs me right now.

"I'll walk you out."

She reaches into her clutch and gives me the chip for the car. She leads the way and when we get to the parking lot, I see Folsom's driver standing by the car near the entrance. She tips her head at me as I hurry past.

"Will you be okay to drive?" My mother fusses over my dress as the chip hovers by our car. The door opens and I get in quickly.

"Of course I will," I tell her. "Don't worry."

As soon as she backs up, I shut the door and get the hell out of there. Once home, I can't get out of my dress fast enough. I'll keep him on my skin a little longer. Tomorrow I'll have to wash all of him away. I crawl into my bed and lay on the pillow he used. That's when the tears come.

It's still dark when I get up early the next morning, taking something for my headache and showering quickly. By some sort of miracle, I make it out of the house without seeing anyone, not even Phoebe, who usually seems to sense when I'm awake before I make a peep. I make the twenty-minute drive to work on autopilot, my thoughts still full of the day before. I wonder how long the party went. I heard my mom come in but never heard Sophia. I try to avoid thinking about Folsom, but he's all my mind sees.

Genome Y is located near the lighthouse at Fort Story, once a beautiful naval base that overlooks the Chesapeake Bay. A few of the original buildings are left and have been lovingly tended to and restored. Genome Y is the only new building and of the same design favored for the past thirty years, only bigger; six small glass domes connect to one larger dome that hangs over the water.

The sun is just coming up as I make the final approach to the gate and see a long line of cars. Reporters are camped out near the gate. Officers are standing guard and one of them directs me through the women. Another guard lets me in the gate. One reporter tries to get through the gate and the officers swarm around her.

My heart is pumping with adrenaline as I hurriedly park. I groan. I should've had coffee before I got here. I can't imagine what has caused all this commotion. All was quiet yesterday and we're not *that* close to a breakthrough that it would happen overnight, not without me anyway.

Two of the guards I normally only see outside the gate are stationed by the door.

Our central receptionists, Jade and Himari, are both facing their screens, buzzing excitedly. Himari's eyes widen and she waves when she sees me.

"Can you believe this?" she mouths.

I hold my hand out and shake my head.

"We'll be holding a press conference when we hear more from the medical team," she says, and the Silverbook moves to the dock. "It took you long enough to get here!" She stands up and walks toward me, her long, black hair swishing in time with her steps. "Corinne has been checking every ten minutes for the last hour and a half to see if you're here yet."

"What is going on?"

She stops and puts her hand on my arm, halting my steps. "You don't know?" She shakes her head and nudges me to keep moving. "Corinne will fill you in. I have to get everything ready for the press conference, like, yesterday. How was he, though? That's what I'm dying to know. Did he ride you like a horse and then seem worn out?" She grasps my arm. "I hope it worked."

I scowl at her. "What are you talking about?"

She rolls her eyes. "Fine, keep it to yourself. I will get it out of you." She motions toward Corinne's office and backs away, pointing at me. "Lunch. You can't avoid this. I'm living vicariously through you."

My mouth hangs open. I want to go back and restart this day—I'm so confused—when Corinne walks out of her office.

"Thank God you're here. The team is here and we'll need you to do the MRI soon." She ushers me past the first two domes and I pause. I typically only work in domes one and two.

"I came in early and didn't expect to see so many people here." I barely get the words out when I realize she isn't listening.

We walk past domes three and four, and around dome five I see women in blue lab coats that I've never seen.

"Who are they?" I whisper.

I glance through the open door past them and see a boy. He looks young, a teenager, maybe fifteen or sixteen at most. He's in bed hooked up to our largest diagnostics machine. He glances up at me and I falter in mid-step. He's beautiful and afraid. I move toward his door, eager to put him at ease, and Corinne stops me.

"Not him," she says.

She motions down the hall toward the last dome of the building. I've never been in dome six, but I've heard the stories. It's where the most deaths have occurred, where the hardest procedures are conducted. Maybe I haven't been aware of it since I didn't know anyone was in dome five either, but to my knowledge, dome six hasn't been occupied since I came to work at the main branch five years ago.

Dread begins to fully set in, my concern for the boy pushed aside. There's only one man in the Red Region and it can't be good if he's here. I rush toward the next dome and ignore protocol, moving past the doctors attending him.

Folsom lies in the bed, all the color and life I saw in him yesterday now a dulled grey. His skin is damp, his hair wet with perspiration, and every orifice is filled with a tube. Electrodes line his chest. I move to his side, shaky but determined.

"What happened to him?" My voice breaks on the last word, but I look around, demanding an answer.

The doctor closest to me gives me a fleeting glance before turning back to him, tearing off the printout of his heart activity. She takes a long look and then speaks.

"Mr. Donahue suffered a heart attack sometime early this morning. We're not certain of the exact time because Lottery 607 failed to alert anyone until at least two hours after it happened, maybe longer." She purses her lips and flips through the printout. "I suppose she was right to be afraid—she'll serve time for withholding."

I cover my mouth with my hands and pace the length of the corridor, occasionally glancing into his room. I'm overreacting. I know I'm overreacting. I barely know this man, so why do I feel so sick? *The End Men represent hope to all of the Regions*, I reassure myself. Of course I'm upset. It makes complete sense. And he isn't just any End Man—he's the original, the turning point in which we placed our hope. There are news crews outside and the entire nation is on alert. I calm my breathing and press a hand to the glass that separates me from Folsom. It is our civic duty to care about him: Folsom Donahue is our future. Yes, that is all. My Silverbook hovers and I glance at it distractedly. I turned it on vibrate after I missed Corinne's messages, but when I see who's messaging me, I immediately switch it back to idle. Sophia is frantic, wanting me to sneak her into the lab so she can see Folsom. I roll my eyes. She's acting like…she's acting like…*me.* Corinne comes marching down the corridor at that moment and I turn to face her.

"Most of the staff are busy here with him," she says, jerking her head toward Folsom's bed. "I need you somewhere else." We start walking in stride and I resist the urge to look back at him one last time.

"Right," I say. "Where do you need me?"

She stops abruptly and turns to face me, looking around quickly to make sure no one can hear her.

"This is highly confidential. We have not made the information public…"

I blink at her, unsure of where she's going with this.

"One of Folsom's sons is here, the oldest boy…"

I think of the boy I saw this morning and stare at her in shock. The hair, the jaw, the naturally wounded-looking eyes…I'd seen them before on Folsom's face. In all the commotion I'd forgotten about him.

"One of the five?" I ask, breathless.

She nods. "He was the first male birth the Regions had in twenty years. His mother won't let us even see him until he comes of age." She pauses. "And even then she's tried to hide him. We had to go in and remove him from the home."

"You kidnapped him?" I ask in disbelief. "He's just a kid."

Corinne shoots me an annoyed look, and when she speaks again, her voice is cold. "Gwen, in case you haven't noticed, men have been nearly extinct for the last fifty years. If we don't do something, we'll follow right behind them. The End Men…this boy…they're our last hope. We've brought him here to learn more about why this has happened. He's less than three years away from joining the End Men himself. We need this time with him. Run the tests." She shoves a stack of papers into my hands and frowns at me. "Can I count on you to do this?"

I nod, though my insides are churning and I want to be sick. She starts to walk away.

"Corinne," I call. "What's his name?"

"Laticus," she calls over her shoulder. "Laticus Donahue."

ELEVEN

FOLSOM

I wake up alone and in a white room. I'm tied down. No, I'm attached. Machines beep incessantly behind my shoulders, cords and tubes needling into my skin. I can feel the *pump, pump, pump* of the liquids, the cold chill as they creep through my veins. I try to remember how I got here, but whatever they're feeding me through these tubes has made my brain languid. *How did you get here*, I ask myself, but my thoughts have no cohesion. Then I see Gwen's face; she materializes from a door. At first I think I'm dreaming because she looks like a floating head, but then I realize she's wearing all white and blending in with the walls.

"What happened?" I ask. Fuck, I still sound drunk. Her lips tighten into a stiff line.

"The doctor will be here in a minute to talk to you." She looks over her shoulder then leans over me and quietly says, "You had a heart attack, Folsom."

I try to sit up, but she places a hand on my shoulder and pushes me back down. "Don't you dare," she warns. "Idiot man."

I smile at that one. So rarely do women insult me. What a treat. And then I remember the lottery and the girl. We'd gone up to the room. Had I fucked her? Yes, I recall something about that. I'd gone to take a leak and then…nothing.

"The girl," I ask. "Is she okay?"

"What girl?" Gwen snaps. Suddenly her facial expression changes. "Oh," she says. "She's in a bit of trouble. She didn't call for help right away."

"She was probably scared," I say. The door opens and a woman with grey hair walks in frowning.

"Folsom," she says. "You gave us quite the scare. I'm Doctor Hunley."

"Sorry to give you trouble, doc. That's what men do."

She glances at me from where she's examining one of the machines, not sure how to take me.

"A joke, doctor," I say, leaning my head back against the pillows and closing my eyes. There's nothing worse than someone not getting your humor.

She raises an eyebrow. "Glad to see you're well enough to joke."

"I feel like shit actually. Can I have something to drink?"

She nods to Gwen, tells her to bring me water. I'd meant an actual drink—the type grownups use to deal with difficult life situations. Apparently, I'm not funny anymore.

"You had an ST-segment elevation myocardial infarction—or in layman's terms, a heart attack. We've been notified that you take medication to help you perform your duties." She pauses to look at me over the file she's holding. I nod slowly, confirming my little blue pills, and she continues. "Combined with daily alcohol usage and a history of high blood pressure, it most likely contributed to a blockage in your arteries."

Gwen walks back into the room carrying a pitcher of water and a glass. She sets them down on a table and wheels it over to me. I make a face to let her know that's not the kind of drink I want, and she rolls her eyes. I notice that she looks worried and for a minute I wonder if she's worried about me. No, I remind myself, none of them are worried about me as a person. They're worried about me as an End Man. I return my attention to the doctor who is talking about my recovery.

"I can't stop taking the pills," I interrupt. "If you want me to impregnate three women a day, the pills are necessary."

"Mr. Donahue, I don't think you understand the gravity of this situation. Your life is at risk. If you continue to live the lifestyle you have been living, I guarantee you'll have another heart attack, and next time we may not be as successful in saving your life."

"My life is less important than that of the well-being of society, is it not? In fact, my life becomes completely useless to all twelve of the Regions if I cannot produce children. But go ahead, check with your superiors and see what they say. I guarantee *you* they won't advise taking me off the pills." I settle back against the pillows and accept the glass Gwen holds out to me. As far as I'm concerned the conversation is over. The Regions would never so much as allow a leave of absence. They'll expect me to be back on my feet and fulfilling my duties in less than a week.

Doctor Hunley considers me for a moment, a deep frown on her already worn face. "As my patient, you are my absolute priority, Mr. Donahue. Your health takes priority over any agenda the Statehouse may have. I will speak to them."

She leaves the room before I can reply and I decide that I like her.

"You take pills to…" Gwen's voice cuts through my thoughts. She's been so quiet I'd almost forgotten she was here.

"Yes," I say.

"With me…?" She's standing stiffly in front of my bed, and I get the feeling we're in a showdown.

"With everyone," I tell her.

She's pressing her lips together so firmly it looks like she wants to be sick.

"Of course," she says, finally. "Of course." She looks over her shoulder then quickly back at me. "They're bringing you dinner. I'll be back to check on you in a while. There's also something I need to talk to you about—" She's cut off when the door opens and a nurse wheels in a cart. It looks like she wants to say more, but she clears out of the nurse's way, wringing her hands near the door before she calls out "Later" and darts out of the room.

Later that evening I hear a commotion in the hallway outside my door. There is the crash of metal hitting the ground and then the door bursts open, followed by the booming of a familiar voice.

"Folsom, you son of a bitch. I'm out there working my ass off and you're lying around on vacation." Jackal strides into the room, his imposing presence immediately making me sit up in bed. A smile breaks over his face when he sees me and I think he's going to hug me when Gwen charges into the room behind him.

"Don't you dare!" she says.

He turns around suddenly, looking half-shocked and half-amused by the commanding tone in her voice.

"Tiny woman!" he says. "Are you this man's bodyguard?"

Gwen looks around the room like she can't tell if this is really happening. I smile from where I'm watching them and wait to see what she'll do.

"He's just had a massive heart attack…" She takes a step toward him and Jackal backs up. "If you stress him out, touch him, or upset him in any way I will throw you out of here myself."

"Noted," he says, this time more subdued. When she leaves the room, he turns to face me, an evil grin on his face.

"You fucked that one, didn't you?"

"Why are you here?" I ask.

Jackal, used to my bluntness, takes a seat in the chair beside my bed. He makes a face like he can't believe I'm asking that.

"Foley, you almost died." Jackal runs a hand across the stubble on his face, suddenly looking very tired. He must have jumped on the jet right away when he heard.

"You're my best friend," he says. "Why wouldn't I be here?"

I raise my eyebrows. He's never used the words *best friend* before. When you are an End Man, you learn to not put labels on things. You will never have a girlfriend, or a wife, or be around somewhere long enough to make friends.

"I'm glad you're here," I say, honestly. "Do they know you're here or did you jailbreak?"

His smile answers my question, and I laugh. Typical Jackal with no regard for the rules.

He suddenly grows serious. "I spoke to Kasper on the ride over," he says quietly. "He wanted you to know something."

I narrow my eyes. Kasper is the third End Man, joining just a year after me at barely nineteen. We've never seen eye-to-eye on issues and tend to stay out of each other's way. There's something about him that I don't like.

"He's in the Black Region right now," Jackal said. He closes one eye and makes a face at me.

"What is it, Jackal? Just fucking say it."

"He came across some information. Look man, I don't know how to tell you this, but they took Laticus. They have him."

"They have him where?" I bolt upright in bed and the sudden movement causes the machines behind me to go crazy. I'm forced to stop talking when three nurses come pounding into the room, panic in their eyes. Jackal keeps eye contact with me while they check my vitals, quizzing me on what happened. As soon as they're gone, Gwen walks into the room, eyeing Jackal suspiciously.

"What happened?" she snaps.

Jackal smiles at her when he shrugs.

She lifts her chin defiantly when she looks at me and says, "I've been told that I have to stay in the room for the duration of your visit," she says. "It appears Mr. Emerson didn't let anyone know he was leaving the Green Region." She glares at Jackal who winks at her. "His exit has caused quite a stir. The Statehouse has contacted us, and we've let them know he's here."

"You can say the rest of what you need to say in front of Gwen."

Jackal turns his body back to face me, and I see Gwen's face tighten over his shoulder.

"We don't know where they've taken him. But, Folsom, there are only two Genome Y labs on the continent and you're lying in one of them."

TWELVE

GWEN

"Laticus," I say. Both of their heads swivel toward me, and I can't believe I blurted that out. I could be fired. Corinne distinctly said it was to remain a secret that he was here.

"He's here?" There's bite in his voice and I shrivel back, desperately wanting to rewind time by thirty seconds. *Stupid, stupid Gwen.*

Folsom starts trying to undo all the leads that connect him to the various machines. I rush forward, holding his hands down.

"No," I say firmly, looking into his eyes. He stills and I feel mildly victorious. The furious protectiveness I feel over him has consumed me since I saw him lying in this bed.

I get right in his face, so close that our foreheads touch. "You don't want to set off the alarm again. Breathe. Okay? Just breathe. I'll tell you what I know—which isn't much at the moment."

He blinks and gives a slight nod, settling back into the bed, though his shoulders are tense like two invisible cords are holding them rigid. I stare at the peppery stubble on his jaw, tiny daggers that turn to smooth skin on his neck. What to say, and how much?

"Can I trust you?" I ask, my hands still clamping down on his.

"No," he says.

Jackal laughs and I throw a scowl his way. That man is entirely too pretty for his own good.

"I wish I knew more, but it's what I wanted to tell you earlier. He's here," I say quietly. "They wanted to test him, evaluate his health, but he fell asleep, so someone is assigned to do it later. I've been a little…tied up with seeing about you. When your alarm went off…" I flush and hope he doesn't notice. From the sound of Jackal, it doesn't get past *him*. "And then I was assigned to watch over this twit." I point my thumb toward Jackal.

"Is he…okay?"

"He seemed…scared," I tell him honestly. "But he's been through a lot. We'll take care of him. *I* will," I say, resolute.

His face doesn't relax; he actually looks more worried than he did a minute ago.

"He's only fifteen, Gwen."

In the Regions, eighteen is considered an adult, and some families give their daughters over to the End Men at sixteen, the chances of pregnancy seen as higher the younger you are, but the men have all been at least eighteen. Men have to earn their place in the world, but this is much too soon.

"I understand," I assure him.

"Is his mother with him?"

"She was not complicit with him coming here," I say quietly. I still haven't come to grips with what that means. Was the boy really kidnapped? "From what I've surmised, he was taken without her permission."

Folsom's eyes fly to Jackal's, the alarm in them making me take a step back.

"Find her," Folsom tells Jackal. "Let her know…" His voice cuts off and he looks tormented. He turns to me. "Go be with him, Gwen. Please. Make sure they don't…"

He tries to sit up again and I put my hand on his arm. He gives up and leans into the pillows, his face dark.

I clasp his hand in mine and squeeze. "I'll take care of him. You just worry about getting well."

I walk toward the door and Jackal follows behind me.

"Thank you," he says when we're out of earshot. "For helping him. He's a good man. The best man I know."

"You only know eleven," I smart off.

A smile breaks out across his face. "That's ten more than you, smart ass."

I narrow my eyes at him, shaking my head. "Will you try to contact the boy's mother?"

He looks away distractedly. "Yes. I'll find her."

"Good," I say, thinking about how awful it would be to give birth to a child and then have him ripped from your life. Absently I touch my belly and Jackal notices the motion.

"We don't belong to each other anymore," he says. "Be careful what you wish for." And then he's gone, striding down the hall away from me. I sincerely hope he can find her.

There's a flurry of doctors and attendants outside the domes, reading over the graphs and studying the screens for minute-by-minute updates on the two patients. I walk briskly past as they're consumed by their data.

I move to the Silverbooks that suspend in every central area and select Hamari. Her face fills the screen, looking harried.

"Are you busy?" I ask.

"Are you kidding?" she says. "We have two men in the building…"

"Right," I say. "I need all of the printouts you've collected for Laticus so far."

"Sure," she says. "I'll have them on your desk in ten."

"Thanks." I release the button and hurry back to dome five. Corinne is standing outside Laticus' door. She sees me walking toward her and stands straighter, hands moving to her hips.

"Where's Mr. Emerson?"

"He's left the building," I tell her. "I'd like to take over the patient's care."

Corinne nods. At times like this, it's helpful being the boss's pet.

"Fine," she says. "I trust you the most anyway."

I feel a pang of guilt at her words. I have every intention of breaking her trust and taking information about the boy back to his father.

"May as well get a start before this afternoon's filing is due." She hands me his file and I tuck it under my arm.

Since my promotion a few months ago, every afternoon at two and five, I conduct an extensive report for every test run in Genome Y. Some days it takes fifteen minutes at the most. Days like today have never happened since I began working here, so I can't imagine how long the report will take today.

"You go do what you need to do," I tell her. "I've got this."

"We still have a few labs to do on him, and so far we've been unsuccessful in getting a sperm sample…"

I struggle to not let my eyes widen. "Okay…how do you want me to—"

"You hand him a dirty magazine and get him to ejaculate into a cup," she says quickly.

"Got it."

"I'm just going to remind you that everything we find in the tests is classified. The only ones privy to this information are the doctors on the case, you, me, and the few designated in the Society. No one else can know the contents, including the patients themselves. Laticus is asking a lot of questions, if you could just put his mind at ease. You're good at peopleing." She opens his door and I follow her in, mouthing "*peopleing?*"

I am absolutely not good at peopleing. I hide from most people.

Laticus is watching the Silverbook hovering high on the wall across from him, and when I hear Folsom's voice, I follow the sound. It's live footage of the party last night and Folsom says "brilliant" before picking the lottery number. Another shot flashes across the screen of Folsom getting his picture taken with a group of women. I see Sophia in the background and inwardly groan. She's going to be furious with me for avoiding her all day.

Laticus glances over at me with an expression of boredom and fear. I try to look comforting and safe, but I probably look more manic than anything. There's no reason he should trust me.

"Hi, Laticus." I flinch at the sound of my voice, so unsure. I clear my throat and force my next words to sound more confident. "I'm Gwen," I say. "I'm here to make sure you're comfortable." He just stares at me so I continue. "Have you eaten? Are you hungry?"

He shakes his head.

"I'm hungry," I say. And it's true. I realize I haven't eaten at all today. "I'll just order something up in case." I pull out my Silverbook and send a message to the cafeteria. Assuming teenage boys eat the same things we do, I order half a dozen dishes and then switch the Silverbook to idle.

"Your father…?" I ask, nodding toward the Silverbook on the wall. He nods.

"I've never met him." Those are the first words he says to me and I sigh, relieved we are on speaking terms.

"I have," I say brightly.

Laticus sits up straighter in his chair, his eyes suddenly interested. "Is he here? I saw about the…"

"Yes, he's here. He's doing okay," I reassure him.

He settles back down, returning his eyes to the screen. "What's he like?"

I study his face and am struck by how similar his facial structure and eyes are to Folsom's. His hair is lighter and he's not as muscular, but he looks how Folsom must have looked at his age.

"Well, the two of you favor one another a lot," I say quietly. "Mind if I sit?" I motion to the chair next to the bed.

"Please," he says, his curiosity chipping away at his reservation.

"From what I've seen, he's dedicated to helping the Regions to the best of his ability, even if it means he suffers in the process." I shake my head, as it registers how awful he must have been feeling yesterday, even when we were together, to have had such a massive heart attack by last night. "He's serious, even though he's capable of teasing." I grin and Laticus grins back faintly. "And he's kind."

"Is he tall?" he asks.

"At least 6'3" maybe more." I nod.

"There's hope for me to get there still then." He smirks and I swear it's like Folsom all over again.

I groan. "The girls are going to *love* you."

"Isn't that how it's supposed to be?" he says, just as there's a knock on the door.

Vera pushes a cart filled with trays and starts unloading it on the table. "I might have to leave the cart here. There's not enough room on the table for all of this food!" She lowers her eyelashes at Laticus and smiles shyly, while I move closer to him, folding my arms over my chest. I dare her to flirt with him on my watch.

"Thank you, Vera. We'll take it from here," I tell her.

I uncover the trays and Laticus' eyes grow wide when he sees the array of seafood, baked potatoes, two salads, fruit, and an assortment of desserts.

"Anything look good?" I ask.

He laughs. "Uh, yeah." He reaches for the lobster tail and takes a bite, his eyes rolling back in his head. "Oh my God, what is this?"

"Lobster? Have you never had it?"

"Never. It's so good." He then stuffs five pieces in his mouth at once.

I laugh at him. "I take it you *were* hungry."

"Always." He motions to the shrimp. "Is it okay if I eat that too?"

"You can have all you want. I'll just take this baked potato and salad. Have at it."

"When can I meet my father?" he asks, mouth full.

I spend extra time chewing while I try to think of how to answer him. "Well, technically, you're not really supposed to know he's here, and vice versa, but I couldn't lie to you when you asked."

"Oh. Does he know I'm here?"

"Yes, he does," I say quietly.

"Is he dying?" He sets the fork down and wipes his face with the napkin, his eyes searching mine.

"He's in critical condition, but I have every hope he will recover. Just trying to keep him relaxed and—"

"I have to see him," he says. "I can't believe we're in the same place. I've always wanted—"

Corinne knocks then peers through the door. "Got that sample yet?" she asks.

"He's eating. We'll get to that after he's done," I tell her.

She nods and backs out of the room.

"What's that about?"

I look at the ceiling and hate my life right about now. "I'll work out a way for you to see your father, I give you my word. I'm sorry for how awkward this is, but…as soon as you're done eating, I need to collect a sperm sample from you." I point to the magazines on the table next to him. "If those aren't satisfactory, let me know. I can get more."

His cheeks darken and he looks down at his empty plate. He points to the brownie covered with ice cream and hot fudge. "Is it okay if I eat that first?"

I feel a pang in my chest and want to cry. He's just a baby.

THIRTEEN

FOLSOM

The days drag by, molasses days. They need me to heal, but they constantly prod me about how I feel like I have the ability to speed up the process on my own. The Society is not pleased. Good fucking days gone to waste.

"They are, of course, deeply concerned about you, Folsom," Robin says, and I want to laugh. "It's just that you only have a year here and you're already behind schedule."

"Simple solution, Robin, we can line them up and I can fuck them all the way down the line. Just bend them over. It'll be better than one of Jackal's orgies."

Robin stares at me, undeterred. I've always admired that about her. Nothing shocks her.

I hear a couple of the staff arguing in the hall about who will bathe me. Two or three of them have a habit of getting handsy. Essie wins and comes in the room, quickly undressing me and getting to work with the warm water and soap. Her hand wanders lower and lower even though I assure her I can find my way around washing my own dick.

She finally gets the nerve to cup my balls when the door flings open and Gwen appears like a bat out of hell.

"Essie!" she yells, stalking toward us. "I'm pretty sure Mr. Donahue is capable of taking care of that. You can stick to general bathing…shampooing his hair perhaps."

I put my hands behind my head and watch both of their eyes travel down my body. The flush in Gwen's cheeks grows darker, and fuck, if I don't enjoy making her squirm.

"Why don't you take over?" I ask, and she blinks rapidly.

"I'll take it from here, Essie," she says, shooing her out with her hand.

When she comes to me, she lifts the washcloth and hands it to me. "I'll do your hair, but you'll have to do the rest."

"I thought we'd gotten past these formalities," I tease her.

"You're too weak to be dealing with that." She points to my dick and I look down. Well, shit. I think this might be the first time in at least a decade that I've gotten hard without the appropriate drugs in my system.

"Essie was on a mission." I shrug, not wanting her to know that she's the one who seems to turn me on without even trying.

A pained look crosses her face and I immediately regret saying it.

"Lean back," she says curtly.

She comes behind me and I tilt my head back, but she still catches me by surprise when she dumps several cups of warm water over my head. Water drips onto my shoulders and into my eyes, but I don't complain—I deserved it. I like this flurry of emotion she brings with her every time she enters a room. She lathers shampoo into my hair and I enjoy the feeling of her hands massaging my scalp. She takes her time and when she rinses it out, I catch her eye and smile. She doesn't smile back, her bottom lip between her teeth while she focuses on getting all the suds out. When she's satisfied, she leans back and I grab her hand.

"Thank you," I murmur. And under my breath, I add, "It wasn't Essie..."

Her small intake of breath lets me know she heard me. Her eyes warm and she smiles.

Late one afternoon Gwen marches into the room, stopping in the doorway when she sees the two nurses standing around my bed. Her eyes narrow.

"Shouldn't you two be working?" Her voice is terse. She holds a stack of papers to her chest, lips pulled into a tight line. I watch in amusement as they look at her over their shoulders then exchange a glance, rolling their eyes.

"Our jobs, Gwen," one of them says. "We're checking on our patient."

The dark-haired one smiles at me reassuringly and I smile back. Gwen bristles in the doorway.

"Folsom doesn't mind us being here, do you, Folsom?" the girl asks.

I've seen Gwen's fury. I wouldn't mess with her if I were them.

"You two get out." Gwen walks toward us and I have to work hard to keep my face still. They seem flustered by her tone. I think I am too. I watch as they head for the door, shooting Gwen a nasty look.

As soon as they're gone, I bite the inside of my cheek and watch her.

"They shouldn't be in here...exciting you."

"Exciting," I repeat. "I assure you I'm completely flaccid right now, both in pants and mind."

She makes a sound of pure exasperation and I grin.

"You're very possessive," I note. "We have sex one time and you're chasing every female in a mile-wide radius away."

She looks so annoyed that I've said this, I laugh.

"I—I'm concerned about your health."

"Of course," I tease.

"I have to go." She storms out without another word and I close my eyes satisfied.

This is the way it should be. Men allowed to hunt.

The proximity to Laticus affects me in both a negative and positive way. The Society does not forbid us from meeting our children, though it is highly discouraged. They believe it removes our focus, personalizes what we're doing in an unhealthy way. Five sons and he is my oldest. I knew this day would come, when the work of the End Men would start paying off and my offspring would be handed over to a society of piranhas.

Jackal left two days after he arrived, being summoned back to the Green Region by the Society. But before he left, he contacted the boy's mother to let her know he was safe. He gripped my hand before he left and very seriously said, "If you need me, I'll come back. Fuck the Society."

I believed him.

Gwen is the face I look forward to seeing. She comes in multiple times to check on me, sweeping through the door and bringing with her the scent of outside and citrus.

"What shall we read today?" she asks, waving some kind of medical journal, a worn novel with a bare-chested man on the cover, and a copy of *Moby Dick*.

I point to the man with better abs than mine and frown. "Who is he?"

"*Ride Me Harder* it is," she says and I swear she nearly skips as she sets the other books down.

I scowl harder when she starts to read and the guy in the book is demanding that the woman get on her knees while he fucks her from behind.

"You said you were a virgin when we had sex," I interrupt.

"I was!" She holds her place in the book and looks at me.

"Not if you've read this trash," I tell her, indignant.

She rolls her eyes and keeps reading, a little bead of sweat appearing over her lip when the heroine is having multiple orgasms.

I'm frustrated when she leaves, and the feeling is foreign to me. It must be the long dry spell…who knew I could ever miss sex? Or it could be Gwen. Maybe this is what it's like to want a woman.

The next time she comes she shows me a picture of Laticus on her Silverbook. I see my brother straight away in his face and the way he holds his shoulders. Laticus is just two years younger than my brother was when he died. I stare at the photo, washed in emotion, not wanting to speak for fear of my voice cracking. Gwen removes the photo from her screen and stares at me hard.

"I'm sorry, I never thought about how hard it must be for you to see him. Someone you've never been allowed to know." She swallows hard. "I didn't mean to—"

"It's fine," I say quickly. "You learn to get used to it. All of it. It becomes a lifestyle. Most of the younger guys have never known anything different: family and the idea of marriage…"

Gwen looks bothered by my words. More and more in the last few weeks, I've learned to read her facial expressions, which in turn has caused me to pay more attention to her face. Her upper lip is an arched bow, fuller than her lower lip; when she doesn't know what to say, her lips say it without words. They are too sensual to go unnoticed. She is not typically beautiful like the women in the Regions who alter their faces and bodies toward perfection. Her face is untouched, odd in its striking beauty.

"I don't see how that's fair," she says finally. "I…I know that we need you desperately. But when what is right for the whole world becomes wrong for an individual, what is to be done?"

We sit quietly for a long time after that, our eyes the only thing communicating, finding each other every few minutes. There is intimacy in quiet, in being with another person and not needing to say anything. Gwen and I learn this together as the days go on and she comes to sit with me for a while each day. On most days, she has news of Laticus—he is healthy, and smart, and charming, and everyone in dome five is taken with him. On others, she brings me something sweet from the cafeteria or a book from her collection, and she is melancholy. I don't ask her what's wrong; I don't believe I've earned that right. On those days all there is to do is watch each other from across the room, asking questions in our mind. On one of her quieter days, she suddenly stands up and walks quickly over to where I'm lying on my bed. She lowers her face very suddenly to mine and I think she's going to kiss me, but instead, her head veers left and I feel her lips graze my ears as she speaks.

"I'm pregnant," she says quietly. Her face lingers next to mine and I can feel her heat. I have the urge to turn my head a degree so our faces will touch.

There is no joy in her voice.

"That's what you wanted," I say. I could use the same words of comfort for every woman across the Regions. She straightens up and stares down at me as if she's contemplating if she wants to say more.

"When did you find out?"

"Just yesterday. I'd forgotten…things have been so busy I hadn't even been thinking about a pregnancy until they called me in for my test."

I nod, knowing she has more to say.

"The baby is a boy." Her eyes fill with tears and she turns her head away so I can't see.

"He…will be celebrated by everyone in the Red Region and every Region," I add. But there is a catch in my voice—we both hear it. I grab her wrist and pull her down on the bed so she's sitting facing me.

"He will be taken from me," she hisses, "—like Laticus was taken from his mother."

It's true. It is what having a boy means. But most do not consider that, they only think of the prestige that comes with giving birth to a male child. The heartache and realization would come many years later.

"He's not even in your arms yet and you're already thinking about that?" I try to distract her, but she shakes her head.

"We don't belong to each other anymore. Be careful what you wish for."

"Who told you that?"

"Jackal. He said it to me before he left that first day. I hadn't known what he meant. But now I do."

"He shouldn't have said that." I pivot her chin upward so she's looking me in the eyes. Her eyes are wet, like they've been licked by an awful sadness, and I feel an inexplicable need to be this woman's comfort. It's not something I've felt before.

"You asked for a son, and I gave you a son," I say firmly. "Don't be an ungrateful brat."

She laughs, but she also starts to cry, and on impulse my hands wrap around the back of her head, tangling in her hair, and I pull her mouth toward mine.

Her eyes open wide when I kiss her. I grab onto that top lip I've been eyeing for weeks and suck on it gently. And then her lips part and we kiss softly until I slide my tongue into her mouth, at which point Gwen wraps her arms around my neck and pulls herself as close to me as she can. I touch her through her clothes, my hands groping and tugging, fingers trailing across the small patches of exposed olive skin. I rest my thumb in the dip at the base of her neck, and then slide my hands into her hair and down her neck. Her breath hitches when my hand slides into her shirt and I cup a full breast. There is lace between my hand and her skin. I yank it down, hearing a rip before her skin is warm against my palm. I break free of her mouth and lean my head back as I hold her in my hand, kneading.

"Take them out," I say.

Her eyes are glassy, but they never leave mine as she unbuttons her shirt, exposing the ripped black lace bra. I can see her pink nipple through the unripped side and I place a thumb over it, rubbing circles, while I bend my head and suck her free nipple. Gwen moans and laces her fingers in my hair. I switch to the other side, trying to figure out how to pull her pants down while she's still sitting, when suddenly she pulls away from me.

"Your heart rate," she says, out of breath. "They're going to come rushing in here in a minute." She backs away from the bed, quickly buttoning her shirt.

I prop my hands behind my head and watch her, amused. Her hair looks wild, like it was caught in the wind and whipped around for ten minutes. Just as she predicted, the door bursts open two minutes later, and the doctor and two nurses charge through the doors. Gwen busies herself with my water jug, looking up in surprise when the room is suddenly full.

Doctor Hunley looks from me to Gwen, her eyes lingering on Gwen's hair for longer than what is comfortable.

"Mr. Donahue," she chides. "You've been instructed to relax. We need that heart of yours beating nice and steady, no strenuous activity."

"As you can see, Doctor, there is nothing strenuous about lying in a bed." I smirk at her and she looks flustered.

"I see many things," she says slowly. "Gwen, if I can have a minute with you outside…"

I watch Gwen follow her wide-eyed, while the nurses fuss around the machines. When the door opens again, Doctor Hunley is alone.

After she dismisses the nurses, she takes the seat Gwen was sitting in earlier.

"I've been putting off coming to talk to you all morning." She smiles sadly. "The President has ordered that we discharge you."

"That's good. Great. I feel ready," I say. The thought of getting out of here is making me sit up straighter in bed. I look around for my boots.

"But the truth is you're not ready, Folsom. At least not to go back to work."

We both fall silent.

"It's not your fault," I say finally. "I know what's expected of me. I wasn't thinking I was getting extended leave," I joke.

She ignores my attempt to make light of the situation. "I did everything in my power to convince them otherwise. In the end they took a vote…"

"A vote?" I say in surprise. "Was anyone on my side?"

Doctor Hunley nods. "Twenty to eighty." She tucks her lips in like the numbers embarrass her. Numbers that could inevitably be the cause of my death, but I don't think about that. I'm not afraid of death, I'm afraid to keep living this life.

"All right," I say encouragingly. "What's next? When do I get to leave?"

"We're discharging you tomorrow. They want you to get back to work the day after. No more blue pills," she says.

"Is that from you or them?" I ask.

"Me."

I sigh, leaning my head back against the pillows and closing my eyes. It reminds me of just a few minutes ago when I had Gwen's tit in my hands.

"I strongly suggested that you stick to one, and only one, appointment a day."

"And…?"

"And they agreed to that…for now."

I nod, grateful for her effort on the matter.

"Small victories, eh?" She pats me on the leg before she stands up.

She's at the door when I call her name.

"Did you tell Gwen?" I ask. "Just now when you had her outside…?"

"Yes." She looks like she wants to say more, but then she quickly leaves.

FOURTEEN

GWEN

I grab a printout to look busy while I pace outside Folsom's room waiting for Doctor Hunley. Her words had been direct, but her eyes were kind in the delivery: *He's leaving tomorrow, Gwen, and as much as I don't feel good about discharging him yet, it appears to be precisely the right time for you.*

Those words play over and over in my head with each step. I look around at the team assembled in dome six and want to shake them. *He's not ready*, I want to scream at all of them.

When Doctor Hunley steps out, I'm ready to pounce. "Can I have ten minutes?"

She tucks a file under her arm and nods. "Let's go to my office."

We walk through the long corridor to dome three and stop at the office at the end. She unlocks the door, holding her arm out to allow me in first.

"Have a seat," she says. She points at the plush white chair across from her desk, which is tidy, but her bookshelves are not. The middle shelf sags under the weight of all the books shoved in haphazardly. She sits down and slips off her shoes, sighing when she stretches out her toes.

I can't be still, so I don't sit.

"He's not ready." I cut to the point.

Her gaze is razor sharp on me then. "I agree."

"I know the Society is breathing down your neck and even most of the team in dome six, but you're his primary doctor; can't you prolong his time here any longer?"

Her eyes are pained. "I have given them all of his data and spoken about my concerns until I am blue in the face. He's been here this long because of me. Trust me, I've tried every reasoning and they cannot be reasoned with—especially now with the news of your Y pregnancy."

"He can't go on those pills again. His heart isn't up to it." I lean my hands on her desk. "He'll die." My face crumples and I back into the chair, covering my face.

She comes around the desk and hands me tissues, leaving her hand on my back.

I take the tissues gratefully and wipe my face.

"He's agreed to not take the pills," she says. "And his schedule is greatly reduced." She walks back to her desk and looks out her window. "I've seen the way you look at him, the way he watches you…I can't in good conscience say that he's ready to be released, but I know the longer he's here, the worse it will be for you to let him go."

The tears keep streaming down my face and I angrily swipe them away. "He wants no part of this life. Did you know that? He feels like a slave, and seeing him in here, nearly dying, and knowing they only care about him getting back out there and meeting his quota…it's *wrong.* Our work is to preserve life, not extinguish it…"

She blinks rapidly and looks away. Finally, she moves toward me and takes my hand. "You love him?"

"I don't know. I think so." I exhale, the relief of admitting it almost making up for the pain of feeling it.

"I'm so sorry," she says, but she says it in a way that makes me feel like a silly girl. *I'm sorry you're falling in love with the only man you've ever met.*

"I'll do what I can to help him—but my hands are tied."

I stand, feeling hopeless, and walk to the door. "Thank you." As I open the door, I pause and shut it again, looking back at her. "There is something I need help with…"

I peek into Laticus' room, waving the mask to one of his favorite virtual games. I'm awarded with a huge grin. He hops up and takes it.

"If you promise not to stay up all night playing it, you can keep it in here," I tell him. I try to inconspicuously collect his sperm container, dropping it into a baggie and putting it in my pocket.

"Thanks, Gwen," he says. His face grows serious and I have a feeling I know what he's going to say. It's been a frequent topic between us. "I overheard the doctors saying Folsom's leaving soon. Is that true?" He fluctuates between calling Folsom by name and calling him his father.

"Yes, could be as soon as tomorrow. I just found out." I try to keep the emotion out of my voice, sure that Laticus will pick up on it.

"Do you think I can see him? Before he leaves?"

I'd hoped it would happen before now, but Folsom hasn't agreed to it yet. I can't tell Laticus that. "I'm still working on it. It might be the middle of the night or early morning…later tomorrow if he stays longer…but I will try to make sure it happens."

The adoration on his face kicks me in the gut all the way out the door. I hope I don't let him down.

At seven o'clock when Genome Y is usually still hopping, Doctor Hunley clears out all but one of the attending staff and assigns her to labs. Locked in an eight by ten windowless room, she will be secluded for at least an hour. Doctor Hunley buzzes me, and I quickly make my way to dome six. I see the doctor coming out of Folsom's room and going to the central desk, pulling out a few files and a book. She smiles when she sees me coming.

"I'm giving you time with him, not permission to exhaust him." She picks up her book and waves it. "I'll be right out here. Make sure he's rested. His meeting with the Society is at eight o'clock tomorrow morning."

"Yes, ma'am," I agree. "I won't be able to stay long anyway."

I might be back out in minutes if Folsom isn't in the mood for company. I tap on the door and then enter, holding up two glasses of lemonade.

"Sounds like you're skipping out on this place soon. Thought you might want to celebrate." I get all the words out without sobbing and wonder if that's what pregnancy will mean for me: constant emotion. Or maybe it's just Folsom's effect on me.

"No bourbon?" He turns to face me and reaches for the drink, clanking our bottles together. "The doc said I should get at least one good night's sleep in this place."

It registers then that he's standing by the window and doesn't have a machine or tubes trailing behind him. He takes a long swig of the drink as he looks outside and my throat burns.

"You seem happy to go. I thought you might like the peace a little longer," I say quietly.

He makes a face, wiping his fist across his mouth. "Peace? Being poked and prodded here, or poking my way through the female population out there…either way, no peace. I may as well get on with it. Live life to the fullest, isn't that the saying?"

I swallow the lump I've had in my throat since this morning and move next to him, watching the beacon from the lighthouse cast light across the water.

"I'll be sad to see you go," I tell the window. I can't look at him.

He turns my chin toward him. "You act like you'll never see me again."

"Because I most likely won't," I say. "I spend most of my time here and you'll be—"

He runs a finger across my top lip, smiling faintly like he's enjoying a private joke with himself.

He's looking at me with the same hunger as he had this morning… I haven't let myself think about that all day. He moves our glasses out of the way and takes my face in his hands. His mouth is on mine before I know what's happening, but I quickly respond, my tongue clashing with his. His hands are everywhere: my hair, my face, my breasts, my ass. My lab coat falls to the floor, shirt following, and he has my pants halfway to the ground before I can get his shirt yanked over his head.

"I want you right here," his teeth tug on my nipple, "against this window, with that light flashing across your skin…" His fingers move between my legs and when he pushes a finger inside of me, my head falls back against the window and I start panting.

"Folsom," I moan. "We're going to get caught…" He doesn't seem to care.

He draws his fingers in and out slowly and then gets on his knees. With his other hand, he spreads me wide and groans, watching his fingers disappear inside me. I'm so wet it's embarrassing, but he spreads all of my wetness across my clit as he looks up at me.

"You like that?" he asks.

I whimper out a yes, my legs trembling.

When his tongue flicks across my clit, I grab a handful of his hair and pull, anything to keep from screaming out. He goes faster, and I don't even know what he's doing with his mouth because it's all I can do to have a coherent thought. I shudder and convulse and he moans and bucks like he can feel everything I'm feeling. I clench around his fingers, coming so hard my knees buckle, and he holds me up, kissing up my body until he's standing over me, fingers still working me over.

He pulls out and puts my hand on his cock, which is hard and heavy, bobbing into my hand. He leans his forehead against mine as I fist around him and slide up and down. When I get a little braver, I swirl my thumb over the tip and his head falls back. He moves my hand away and plunges into me, deep. I cry out and he lifts his head and stares at me while we move together. I pretend we're two normal people falling in love and starting our lives together, rather than two splintered people saying goodbye. His eyes never leave mine and even when we both rush faster toward our finish, we ride out the pain, the fury, the ecstasy…together.

"Have you been sick?" he asks, when we're cleaned up and lying in bed.

"Too soon for that, I think. Maybe next week or the next the symptoms will start."

"Your sister?" he asks.

I grow silent. I haven't seen my sister in weeks. I've been so busy. It strikes me as odd that I don't even know if she's pregnant or not. Surely my mother would have said something…

"I don't know," I say honestly. Folsom nods.

I keep telling myself I'll only stay ten minutes longer, but we keep finding things to talk about.

"Yeah…" I trail off. "I have been more tired than usual. I guess this is why."

"Or because you work nonstop."

"That too." I smile.

I think about Laticus and the fun I've had getting to know him the past few weeks. He's such a good kid and I know Folsom would be proud of him. My heart starts pounding faster and I don't think, I just go for it.

"You need to meet your son."

Folsom turns to me and I see the resignation in his eyes. "Okay," he says quietly.

That was easy.

I get up and put my pants on, searching the floor for my lab coat. I have to hurry before he changes his mind.

"Does he want to see me?"

I pause in what I'm doing to look at Folsom. This is the first time I've ever seen him look vulnerable. His eyes are downcast, staring at his hands.

"Of course he does. He's a fifteen-year-old boy who's just been ripped from the only life he's ever known. He misses his mother, and I think it'll do him good to see you."

He nods.

"Folsom, if people knew…if they knew that you didn't consider the life of the End Men as…enjoyable… they'd—"

"They'd what?" he says, his head snapping up.

"The people should know. They should know how much they expect of you, how little they care about your well-being."

His eyes flash. "I don't need to be pitied. I'm doing what has to be done."

I straighten up and walk over to where he's sitting, then I bend down and kiss his forehead. "Thank you. It can never be said enough. For your sacrifice, for everything. Let's go, we don't have much time."

Folsom follows me silently through the hallways and waits as I scan my badge at each security checkpoint. I glance back at him once only to see that he's frowning. The lights in the building have been dimmed down, the brightness of the day gone. I've worked many late nights, often being the last to leave the building, but it feels strange to be creeping around with Folsom. When we reach dome five, I scan my card for the last time before stepping into the section where they keep Laticus. It's just a few steps now, and my stomach clenches uncomfortably. What if this was the wrong decision? Maybe seeing each other isn't good for either of them. Too late to turn back, we stand in front of Laticus' door and I glance once more at Folsom.

"Ready?" I ask. He nods.

I push open the door.

FIFTEEN

FOLSOM

The boy is awake. His face lights up when he sees Gwen and then his eyes slowly travel to where I'm standing. His expression changes, a shift in his eyes and mouth. He stands up slowly from the bed where he's been reading, and I move out from behind Gwen. His book slips from the bed and falls to the floor. He doesn't acknowledge it as he takes a step toward me, his bare feet hesitant.

"Folsom." He says my name first like he's trying it out.

I say nothing, taking him in. He is the spitting image of my brother, the uncle he will never know. I see the Donahue dark hair, glossy black/brown curls and thick, even eyebrows; underneath sit two blue eyes that are both honest and mischievous. All words catch in my throat as I look at him.

"Hello, Laticus," I manage finally, and he seems relieved that I've spoken.

"You look like me," he says. "More than on the news."

He glances at the Silverbook, which is on mute, a loop of my night at the party playing.

"I keep it on, makes me feel like I'm not alone in here."

His simple statement makes me hurt so deeply I have to turn my head away.

"What are you reading?" I ask, nodding to the book which lays open on the floor. It looks like a book shot dead and sprawled face down. Laticus bends to pick it up and hands it to me.

"I read that it was your favorite."

I take it from his outstretched hand, glancing at the spine. "*Gone with the Wind*," I announce. "It's definitely one of them."

"Rhett has some pretty good quotes about war," he says. I nod, unable to formulate words. I read this very book at his age and thought the same thing.

"Are you comfortable? Are they treating you well?" I ask him. He glances at Gwen then and smiles.

"It's okay. I'm bored mostly. Gwen is my new best friend."

"Yeah, that makes two of us," I say, glancing at her. She's standing with her back pressed against the closed door, trying to pretend she's not listening to us.

Laticus smiles and this time it's directed at me. "Want some candy?"

"Yeah," I say, my voice gruff. He walks over to a basket sitting on a desk and plucks out two large chocolate bars in colorful wrappers. He offers me one and I take it. We both tear open the wrappers, eyes on each other. We eat them mostly in silence, watching each other. I hardly taste the chocolate sticking to my teeth and the roof of my mouth, but the act of eating candy with my son is so significant that my hands are trembling.

"That's your favorite chocolate," Laticus says. "I've read everything there is to read about you. I kept a notebook and would write it all down."

I set my half-eaten bar down on the table, overcome with what he's saying. I've known his name, his age; I remember the night I took his mother and put him inside of her. She was one of my first and she'd been horribly nervous until I sang her my favorite song and stroked her hair. I'd meant it to be funny, but she'd told me that I had a beautiful voice and asked me to sing it again. After that, after I'd already moved on to my next station, they'd told me our coupling was successful and that he would be the first male child born to the Regions in twenty years.

"Tell me about you then," I say. "Because I don't know anything and I want to."

He pulls out the only chair in the room and I sit while he perches on the edge of the bed. He has straight posture, a strong chin. He bears none of the awkwardness I remember about myself at his age. I see what Gwen has been saying about him.

"What do you want to know?" he asks.

"What was your childhood like? How did you like where you lived?"

"The Black Region," he says. "It's all right. My friends are all girls…"

We both smile. "My mother, she's great. She never let me think I was special, while always making me feel special." He grins. "Like, you may be one of the only men on Earth, Laticus, but pick up your damn socks."

"Did you go to school?"

"The Society sent tutors. I'm fluent in six languages, and I have completed all of my University courses in mathematics."

"You have a degree in math?" I ask, surprised. He nods.

"I can also dance the foxtrot and cook a soufflé."

"Impressive. The perfect man."

"That's what they were aiming for, I think."

We grow silent. The Society's agenda has suddenly seeped into the room.

"They want me to join the End Men right away. I was supposed to wait another two and a half years, but they say I'm ready."

"You're not ready," I say quickly. I can almost feel Gwen tense up behind me.

"I want to help. I want to do what you do."

Anger clenches my insides. He's just a boy, but I have to warn him. I breathe deeply before continuing.

"The life I live is lonely. I have no home, I have no family, and I have no ties to any one place. What they make us do takes our souls; it turns us into machines that function without love. Every human needs love, Laticus. You have the love of your mother—your friends. But, they'll make you give that up when you join the End Men."

He's quiet for a long time, watching my face with something akin to confusion.

"I am your family," he says, finally. "You're not alone anymore."

It takes everything in me to not stand up and walk out of the room. His simple words crack open the resolution I try so hard to maintain. I think I'm having another heart attack and almost tell Gwen so, when I realize I'm feeling—feeling more intensely than I have in a very long time. I'm about to speak again when I hear Gwen's voice.

"Folsom, we have to go."

I look back at Laticus whose face drops in disappointment.

"So soon?" he asks.

"I'm afraid so." Gwen smiles at him gently and his shoulders sag.

"Can you come again?" he asks me.

"I don't know."

He nods and I can tell he's trying to be strong.

He walks us the few steps to the door and before I can follow Gwen out, I grab him, pulling him into my chest. He's still half a foot shorter than me. I feel his arms wrap around my back and squeeze. I hold him there for a minute before I abruptly let him go and push past Gwen into the hallway. I hear her say "good night" to him and then the door clicks closed, leaving my son in his prison.

The next morning I wake up with a terrible headache. Light streams into the room and I flinch against it, recounting the events of the night before. Gwen had led me back to my room silently, kissing me lightly on the lips before turning to leave. The knowledge that she is carrying my son while also taking care of my teenage son is something that makes me both relieved and unsettled. Before now, after impregnating a woman, I hardly saw her again. If I did, it was in passing: at a party, or years later when I returned to their Region and we ran into each other. I've seen Gwen more than I've seen any other woman, aside from Robin. My attachment to her has grown over the weeks. And Laticus, I'd not known what to expect when I saw him. Would there be a detachment, or would he feel like my son? But, the minute I walked into that room, I felt the connection. Maybe it had been his resemblance to my brother that caused my heart to immediately open to him. I want to protect him.

"Folsom," Doctor Hunley walks into the room, her face serious.

"Members of the Society have arrived. They're setting up for your meeting."

I nod. "I'll be ready in ten minutes."

The Society is a privately funded group, started by a man named Earl Oppenheimer just after the mumps epidemic sterilized the last of the men. He was eighty-seven years old when he called the first meeting, recruiting scientists, politicians, and doctors to join the organization as a way to find a solution to the universal problem of male extinction.

I was twelve years old when I first heard about it, my mother having received a summons to bring me to the newly founded Genome Y lab. Earl lived just long enough to see the birth of Laticus before he died, and his daughter, Milly, took over the organization.

Milly sits at the head of a large table when I walk into the room, her hands clasped in front of her. Seated around the table are ten other people, some of whom I recognize. They're all founding members of the Society.

Doctor Hildenburg, the head of the Regional research team, a fox-faced woman who keeps her grey hair in a long braid down her back; their lead scientist, a man in his eighties named Rolfston; and Rain Foster, who is the liaison between the End Men and the Regions. I nod to all of them as I take my seat opposite Milly, and then introductions are made around the table.

"We're delighted that you're back on your feet and feeling better," Milly says. "We've been in constant contact with your doctor here in the lab, and she assures us that you've received the best medical treatment they can provide. Can you tell us how you're feeling, Folsom?"

Such a loaded question.

"I'm all right," I say slowly.

This seems to satisfy her. "Good, good. Because we'd like for you to get back to work if you're ready."

I nod. I already knew this, but it's not why they've come. Ten members of the Society do not fly hundreds of miles to see how an End Man is feeling.

"There is something else we'd like to discuss with you. It's the matter of Laticus. If you recall he's—"

"I know who he is," I interrupt.

She glances at Doctor Hildenburg, and her next words are extremely measured.

"Of course you do," she says. "As you know, it won't be long before he turns sixteen and we've brought him in to do his initial testing. He's here at Genome Y at the moment." She pauses to see how I'll react, and when I don't, she continues. "We'd like to start him in the program, Folsom—"

"No," I say.

Milly looks irritated. It's the second time I've interrupted her.

"Marcus has not produced a pregnancy in one year. He's been removed from the program and is currently having testing done at the Genome Y lab in the Grey Region."

Marcus Welsh is the new guy. He came in about seven years after me at the ripe age of eighteen and has the lowest success rate of the twelve. I'd not heard that he'd fallen off in numbers completely.

"What does that have to do with me?" I ask.

"He's suddenly sterile, Folsom, and we don't know why. Half of what was left of the male population suddenly went sterile twenty years ago, the rest soon followed. We have twelve virile men in these Regions and we can't take the risk."

I lean forward, placing both of my elbows on the table. "You've put him in isolation?"

"Yes," she says quickly. "We had no choice."

"Neither did he," I say.

Milly's eye twitches. She sighs and then nods at Rain, who passes me a sheet of paper.

"As you know, each year we have a projected number of births we need to fill. The numbers are based on our estimation of stabilizing the population. With Marcus out of the picture, we fall behind. We need Laticus."

"He's fifteen years old. He's still a boy. The End Men don't start until they're eighteen, Milly."

She nods like she understands. "We know that, Folsom. We realize your concerns, but the boy is ready."

"His body is ready. God—" I run my fingers through my hair, shaking my head. "You people will stop at nothing. And if you want Laticus, why are you asking me?"

This time it's Rain who speaks.

"Laticus was the first male born in the Regions. Our protocol was not completely in place when he was born. Your name is on his birth certificate," she says.

I remember signing the paper when they brought it to me, my hand shaking when I saw his name written in his mother's handwriting as Laticus Donahue. At the time, I'd been surprised that she'd given him my name.

"And his mother? Her name is on the certificate."

"As you recall, Folsom, his mother was a lottery winner. She signed her rights to Laticus over to us before he was conceived. It is part of their arrangement. You, on the other hand, did not."

"You stripped a mother of her young son, took a boy from his mother all because in her desperation not to starve and to have a child of her own, she signed his life over to you?"

None of them say anything. But, I know. The pool of lottery winners come from the lower class, people who work long hours in service jobs. If they become pregnant after winning the lottery their whole life changes: money, a home, food—and they never have to work again. They sign their rights over willingly because they are accustomed to thinking about their lives in terms of tomorrow, not years into the future.

I sit back in my chair staring at each of them in turn. If what I am hearing is right, they cannot place Laticus in the End Men without my permission until he is eighteen.

"And my other sons?" I ask.

"The other boys were not born to lottery winners," Milly replies. "Their mothers will lose legal rights over the boys when they reach the age of eighteen."

For each of the male children, there had been a packet sent to me via courier. I remember signing what they asked without thinking too much about it.

"We need you to sign the release for Laticus," Rain says. She looks down at the paper sitting on the table in front of me as if she's prompting me to pick up the pen.

"No." I stand up and all of their eyes follow my movement. "If you'll excuse me, I have to get back to work."

And with that, I walk out.

SIXTEEN

GWEN

The next morning I leave the news station, blood pumping. My interview, the public announcement of Folsom's sixth son, is now playing on a loop on every station across the Regions. My hands are still shaking as I make my way across the parking lot toward my car. The fact that we were live was terrifying; all of those people watching me…I was terrified that I'd stumble over my words and say something stupid, but all had gone fine and now I'm on my way home. My feet ache, and I miss Folsom. If the Society had their way at his meeting this morning, I won't be able to pop in and see him anymore, and the thought of that is crushing.

I pull into our long drive and hope that everyone is out, but by the time I reach the house and see the rows and rows of cars I know I'm in for a long day. I'm not in the mood for company. I go in the back entrance and nearly run Phoebe over.

"Oh good, you're here." She looks so relieved, I move toward her.

"What's going on?"

She looks me over, assessing my wrinkled shirt and pants. "You need to go change into something nicer. You had to have seen the messages?"

I check my Silverbook guiltily. I've ignored Sophia's air messages and calls for weeks, only answering when it wasn't Folsom-related, but I didn't mean to ignore my mother. I didn't realize the sound has been off all morning. There are three missed messages from her, the words angrily flying out into the air, each with more caps than the last one. If I'd known what she was planning, I probably would've ignored her longer and stayed out.

I go up the back staircase and take a quick shower, avoiding getting my hair wet but scrubbing my face clean. I'll put my hair up, I decide as I zip up my dress. I pile it up, pinning my out of control hair into semi-submission. I hesitate to put makeup back on and decide to add mascara at the last second. Once whatever this is ends, I'll go to work and check on Laticus…and of course, dome six.

I take the staircase near the dining room and try to quieten my heels as I walk on the hardwood. I hear voices, but at least it doesn't sound like a massive party.

The chatter dies down when I walk in, but then my mom claps and everyone else follows politely. There are pink and blue balloons and flowers swallowing up the room. Sophia is dressed in a pink floor-length gown. She cuts her eyes toward me and I see the resentment. I should be relieved she's pregnant, but I'm the one with the boy and that will drive Sophia mad. She and her friends turn as one and stare at me until I feel the heat flood my face; one of them says something and they all throw back their heads and laugh. I swallow and make my way to her, stopping to hug my mother first then Governor Petite.

When I reach Sophia, I clasp her hands. "Congratulations, Soph! Can you believe it? Two babies in our family. We are so fortunate."

She shakes her hands out of mine and lifts her glass of sparkling water in the air. "To my sister who always gets exactly what she wants."

Her friends surround us and I back away, moving to sit at the table. Langley follows me and sits down, pulling her long red hair to one side. She's had it out for me since we were little girls vying for Sophia's attention. Out of all of Sophia's friends, she's the hardest for me to tolerate, but they're all vipers.

"Gwen," she purrs. "A boy, how exciting."

I nod, forcing a smile onto my face. I've heard through the grapevine that Langley has an appointment with Folsom. The thought of her touching him makes me recoil in disgust. I have to wipe the image from my mind before I can look at her again.

"Sophia says you've been taking care of Folsom all these weeks. Is he…is it anything serious?"

"He nearly died," I say. "So yes, rather serious."

Her lips fold into a sulky pout and she shakes her head sadly. "Terrible. Do they know…?"

"He had a heart attack," I say, not caring who she tells. Everyone should know. Folsom was being worked to death and it was our fault.

Langley gasps and clutches at the giant sapphire necklace that hangs between her breasts.

For a moment I think her concern could be sincere, but then she runs her eyes from my feet to my face, her distaste evident on her perfectly sculpted face.

"Just make sure he's out of there by next Friday." She leans into my ear. "We have an appointment and I'm going to fuck you right out of his system."

"That didn't even make sense," I tell her, standing up. I bump into someone and turn around, eyes wide. "So sorry, Governor Petite. I didn't realize you were there."

"It's okay, no worries." She laughs. "And enough with the formalities. For someone about to become my daughter, I insist you at least start calling me Pandora. We won't rush the 'Mom' title." She winks before smoothing back a curl that has fallen into my eye.

My mouth falls open. I glance around the room for my mother.

"Oh no, did I let it out before Diana could tell you? I've asked your mother to marry me."

I swallow and attempt a smile. "Congratulations."

"You're the one who needs the sentiment. A boy!" She puts her hand on my shoulder and squeezes. "He will be the salvation of his generation, the salvation of many generations. It is such a great honor. Born here to us in the Red."

I feel my stomach turn with her words and put my hand over my mouth. When she realizes I'm going to be sick, she backs up and I run past.

I barely make it to the bathroom and bend over the toilet, heaving up everything I've eaten in the last day—which isn't much. My mom comes rushing behind me and rubs my back. When I finally stand up, she hands me a cool washcloth and I wipe it across my forehead.

"This was too much for you to come home to," she says. "I've barely seen you and just wanted to celebrate your big news…and Sophia's," she adds, smiling. "Getting sick already?"

"This is the first time and maybe it's…I don't know, nerves or something." I pin a few strands of hair back and look at her. "When were you going to tell me you're getting married?" I attempt to sound joyful, but my mother knows me too well.

She frowns. "Did Pandora say something? I specifically told her to let me share the news with you girls first."

"Of course she said something. She came at me like she couldn't wait to spill the news. Is this what you want, Mother?" I lean against the vanity and face her. "You love her?"

"Sometimes we have to look at the bigger picture, sweetheart. I'm doing what I need to do for this family. And yes, I think in time I will love her. Romance is a thing of the past anyway," she says softly.

I reach over and hug her and we stand that way for a long time, until I lean back and look into her eyes.

"What's wrong, Gwen?" she whispers. "This should be the happiest day of your life."

"My son, Mother," I say, resting a hand on my belly. "They're going to take him from me eventually. I've seen what they're forcing Folsom to do, how they treat him like he's not a human, he's a commodity." I want to tell her about Laticus too, but there's a rap on the door and we both jump.

"Everything okay in there?" Governor Petite calls through the door.

I jump back, startled. My mom runs her hand over my cheek, concerned, and I smile.

"Better now," I say loudly.

"It isn't the way things used to be," she says sadly. "But it's the way it is now. Men serve their country in a different way, and it's their honor to do so."

I shake my head. "Have we ever asked them how they feel about it?"

"Shh." She glances behind her at the door.

A shadow moves across the bottom and I wonder if the governor is eavesdropping. That men are fulfilling their duty is something that's been drilled into us for years. Ceremonies at the Garden of the Dead, where statues are erected in their honor, the parades, and video clips, books, classes at school—we are conditioned to believe things, and until I met Folsom I never questioned a single one of them.

"We have to get back to the party," my mother says. "You are, after all, the guest of honor."

"Let's have a few more minutes, just us," I whisper and lay my head on her shoulder.

"I love you, sweetheart," she says.

We stand there like that long enough for me to feel vaguely human again. My mother has always been my strength.

When we step out of the bathroom, the governor is leaning against the window. Something about her expression makes me halt in mid-step. She moves toward us and puts her arm around my shoulder, leading me toward the door.

"Are you okay, dear?" Her face is the picture of supreme concern.

I'm not used to her undivided attention. Usually she greets me then sweeps my mother away.

"I'm much better," I tell her. I look over my shoulder at my mother who nods and follows us.

"You know I've been thinking, and especially after you were sick just now…with this baby boy coming, you really must do all you can to remain healthy, Gwen." She squeezes me closer and I turn to look at her.

"I'm fine, it was just—" I interrupt.

"I know you are now, but you overdo it. Your mom has been so worried about your long hours. I can have a talk with your superiors at Genome Y and have them give you a paid leave of absence."

I shake my head. "No, no, that's not—"

"Really, I insist. We have to protect this boy, and that means looking out for you while you're carrying him." She smiles sweetly and gives my cheek a pat.

I look at my mother, horrified, and my mother steps forward.

"I don't think that's necessary just yet, Pandora… really," she says.

"Well, if you keep having these bouts of sickness, I'll have to step in and make sure you follow a stricter regimen. We don't want anything to happen…" She leans forward and the light hits her eyes, making them gleam.

I feel a chill crawl down my spine and look at my mother. She's smiling at the governor fondly, as if she's grateful Governor Petite is looking after my best interests. I exhale and relax my shoulders. It's been a long day and I'm getting paranoid.

We walk into the party and my face is projected on the wall at the end of the room. Everyone's watching, listening raptly as I spill my heart out on the Regional news. Governor Petite's hand tightens on my shoulder and she leans into my ear, teeth gritted.

"You pull a stunt like this again and I will make your mother's world a living hell. You're an embarrassment to the Region." She pulls away and smiles at me like I've just said something precious and then she clears her throat and grabs a glass of champagne. "To Sophia and Gwen and the little miracles they're carrying in their bodies! Sophia will bring another beauty into the Red Region, and Gwen will bring our salvation! We must never forget that the End Men have willingly committed their lives for the good of the people, forgoing themselves at any and all cost. We can never allow ourselves to lose sight of their sacrifice."

She looks at me: her eyes hard and lips in a tight line, and I look at my mother, wondering if I've unknowingly sealed her fate.

SEVENTEEN

FOLSOM

The rain hits my face when I climb out of the car and make my way to my apartment. I'd crashed earlier before I could take a good look around.

My security detail does a quick sweep of the place and then leaves me to it. Robin already briefed me on the car ride over. Tomorrow is twin sisters. They've already forgotten about the one-a-day rule and gave me a new supply of the little blue pills. I eye the bar. An unopened bottle of bourbon sits on the console, a rocks glass positioned next to it. I walk to the kitchen and peer inside the fridge instead, it's stocked with all of the things I like to eat: greens for smoothies, fresh fruit, grilled chicken. Absently, I rub at my heart. I've been instructed to keep exercise to a minimum, nothing too strenuous—they suggested walking for now. Ten more weeks of living like my heart is going to stop working at any minute. Doctor Hunley suggested that for sex I stay on my back, let the women do the work. I'm fine with that; relieved I have a doctor's note that allows me to underperform.

I wander into the living room and turn on the Silverbook, sinking into the first chair I see. Gwen's face fills the screen and then the camera pans out and I can tell that she's on a stage, a podium in front of her. At first, I don't know what's happening, but then I remember: a press conference would be held to announce she's carrying a boy.

One of the head scientists from the Genome Y lab stands next to her, staring on proudly like she's the one responsible for the baby. She introduces herself first.

"I am Corinne Gonzalez, I am one of the lead scientists here at Genome Y. Today we very proudly confirm that one of our employees, Gwen Allison, is carrying Folsom's sixth son, the first boy to be born to the Red Region. I'll let Gwen take your questions…"

Corinne steps aside and Gwen stands at the center of the podium as reporters shout out questions.

"How do you feel?"

She makes a face and I smile at the screen.

"Good so far. No morning sickness yet."

"How far are you?" someone else calls out.

"It's still very early," she says. "You won't be seeing a belly for a while."

"Does Folsom know he's going to be a father again?"

Gwen nods, her lips curling into a sexy smile. "He does. He's very happy for the Red Region."

The next voice I recognize. Her name is Isolda Clark, a rogue reporter known to ask controversial questions. She's gotten into a lot of trouble in the past for it, once having to pay a huge fine to the Statehouse after questioning where Regional funds were going.

"Miss Allison, how does it feel knowing that when your son comes of age, he will be an End Man?"

There's a long pause. Gwen ducks her head to look down at her notes and then seems to disregard them altogether. Her face takes on a hardness and I know she's about to say something she shouldn't.

"I would like for my son to have choices in life, to be able to decide who he wants to be, to have a marriage and a family of his own, to not be forced into sex slavery as the End Men are. Our society has become lax in the nature of basic human rights. I would ask you this, when what is right for the whole world becomes wrong for an individual, what is to be done?"

There is a pregnant silence in the crowd and then noise erupts as dozens of questions barrel toward Gwen. She very quietly gathers her things and walks offstage, disappearing through the doors behind her. The camera pans to the group of Genome Y employees who are standing frozen in their spots.

They cut to the commentators and by this time I'm pacing the floor. How could she be so stupid? She can't possibly know the trouble she's unleashed. I grab my Silverbook and say her name; it connects before I've thought about what to say to her.

She sounds shaky when she answers. I don't bother with small talk.

"Forty-nine Cardinal Drive. When you reach the guard, tell her your name. I'll call ahead to let her know you're coming."

Forty-five minutes go by and I haven't been notified that she's here. I read the comments underneath the video of the press conference, which is on a continuous loop. Most are outraged by her words; I am surprised to see a few that agree with her. I drag my hands through my hair and step to the bourbon, pouring a glass and lifting it to my nose for a long sniff. No, I need to be fully cognizant for this conversation.

Another fifteen minutes pass and I hear the intercom beep.

"Gwen to see you, sir."

"Let her through," I say.

I'm standing, waiting for her when she walks in, all dressed up. I hesitate for a minute, distracted by evening-gown Gwen, which is significantly different than wild-haired Gwen and lab-coat Gwen. I shake my head trying to clear my thoughts. A party, the Region would have thrown a party in her honor, mother of the Red son.

"What were you thinking, Gwen?" I say between my teeth. I shake my head, wanting to shake her. "You do know you were on the news, right?"

She glares at me, folding her arms across her chest. "Don't talk to me like that. I'm not an idiot, Folsom. It needed to be said."

"What exactly did you hope to accomplish? Were you trying to put a target on your back? Do you think having a boy can protect you from the Society?"

"It was the truth! For the truth to make a difference, it needs to be said by one person at a time, until there's a noise loud enough to make a difference."

I want to kiss her and spank her all in the same minute. Her words are shockingly powerful, which makes me afraid for her.

"This is what life is. It's what my life is. I accept that."

She steps past me and looks around. "This isn't too bad. Are most of the places you stay like this?"

"I've stayed in some that aren't this nice, but yes, it's usually decent. See? Not so bad." I lift a shoulder and she narrows her eyes.

"Can you come and go as you choose?"

"I have a driver and security. Every place I go has to be thoroughly checked prior to me going there. The other night at The Fish Tank was a little off the beaten path. I only got minor correction for that. It probably helped that I had a heart attack that night."

"Can you say no to one of your…appointments—if you didn't like the girl, or didn't want to have sex with her?"

I stay silent.

"So the answer is *no* then."

"There is no right or wrong in this world. There is simply a matter of what must be done."

"Bullshit," she says.

I've never heard her curse and I try not to smile. I walk over to where she's still standing, wrapped in her own arms, bitingly angry. I speak gently to her because I need her to understand.

"They can take him from you, Gwen. Do you understand me? They can call you crazy, radical, mentally unstable, and they can take your—our—son. Say you're not fit to raise him."

Her face pales, the fire that was in her eyes just moments ago suddenly dims in realization. She starts to cry. I pull her to me and hold her against my chest. Her hands are fisted on either side of her face as she cries into my shirt, the warmth of her tears and breath dampening my skin.

Our son. I'd said those words and now the full impact hits me. What would it be like to raise a son with her? It's foolish to even consider it. I manage to keep my voice rough with her, but I can't help but be moved that she's willing to defend me, to take on the Society and the Regions. This one, tiny wisp of a woman.

"I'm glad you called," she finally says, coming up for air.

Her nose is red and her eye makeup is smeared across my shirt.

"Sorry," she says sheepishly, touching the spot with her fingertip. "I thought last night might be the last…" She looks down at my boots and smiles. It's gone by the time she glances back up. "Sophia is having a girl."

I make a face.

"What?" she says. "Just spit it out."

I walk into the kitchen and she follows me, bumping into me when I open the fridge.

"Governor Petite and your mother…" I say.

"They're together. They're getting married."

I pull containers from the shelves, stacking them on the counter as she watches me impatiently.

"She asked your mother to marry her after finding out that two babies will be born into your household?"

Gwen frowns. "I don't know the details exactly. The news was sprung on me tonight."

I spoon food onto plates and pull two forks from the drawer.

"Hmmm. And when is she up for reelection?" I slide a plate of food toward her. She only hesitates for a moment before pulling it toward her and sitting on a stool.

"Next year," she says, softly.

"Right."

"How'd you know I was hungry?" She frowns.

I shrug. "You've been causing too much trouble to remember to eat."

Gwen rolls her eyes, but I can tell she's trying not to smile.

"Folsom," she says, putting her fork down. "Do you really think that's why she's marrying my mother?" She wipes her mouth with the napkin I pass her and then crumples it up in a ball. Her face is arranged in worry, lines creasing her forehead.

"Can't say anything for sure. Though the timing seems to work to her benefit."

Gwen looks sick.

"She threatened me—"

My head shoots up.

"At the party before I left to come here."

My fork clatters to the plate. "What did she say?"

"Oh, I don't know. She will not let me bring shame to the Region…blah, blah, blah…my mother will be the one to suffer." One corner of her mouth pulls in and her eyes fill with tears.

My heart pounds in my chest and I feel the slow climb of rage. As long as Gwen speaks the unpopular truth, everyone she loves will be in danger. But she's too hotheaded to hear that. Stubbornly naive. She has not felt the bite of the Statehouse, the control of the Society. And then there is the child. Another son born as leverage in a political tug of war. I think about the bourbon I left on the bar and groan.

"What? What are you thinking?" She walks around the table to where I'm standing and cups my face in her hands. "Don't focus on things that are bad for your heart," she says firmly.

"Like you?" I look down at her and her facial expression changes, starting at confused and ending in surprise. I dip my head down and kiss her hard, pushing my tongue into her mouth until she moans. Her hands have moved from my face to my hair, which she has corded around her fingers. She pulls away from my mouth suddenly and glares at me.

"Why are you just standing there?" she hisses. "With your hands at your sides?"

"You don't have an appointment," I say slowly.

Her mouth opens in surprise, and I start to laugh, my chest heaving in and out. I haven't laughed in, what—weeks? Months? Gwen punches me once on the arm, and then she's climbing up my body, her legs wrapped around my waist and her lips on mine. I lift my hands to cup her behind and I rub her against me so that we're grinding. She wriggles out of my hands gasping for breath.

"We…can't…do it like that," she says. "Your heart…"

"That's right." I eye her wet, swollen lips and grab her hand. "Come on, I'm going to teach you how to ride…"

EIGHTEEN

GWEN

Something has shifted with Folsom. I'm not sure when it changed, but I think maybe… I pound the steering wheel and groan out loud. It's crazy for me to be analyzing this, but it's what I do all day, every day…I analyze all the data. Here's what I know: when I left Folsom this time, he walked me to the door and gave me a long, lingering kiss. He held my face in his hands and told me to watch my back, to not trust anyone. He looked sad to see me go. That has to mean something, right? I wonder if he's ever had a relationship with anyone outside of his appointments. My little afterglow dissolves into a hard pang of defeat. His *appointments* put everything in perspective when I start trying to place us in a happily ever after.

I won't be getting a happily ever after with Folsom or anyone else, so I need to just enjoy whatever this is…or what it has been. I don't even know from one time to the next if I'm going to see him again.

Instead of going home to change, I head to Genome Y and grab the clothes I keep in my office. I change quickly and stop by the food machine since the cafeteria is closed. I get as much junk as I can carry. It's after hours, and now that dome six is empty, the only activity is in dome five. Only one nurse and a security guard are on the floor. When they see me, they wave and go back to reading.

I knock lightly on the door and open it. A cute, young blond dressed in the food service uniform, is sitting in the chair next to Laticus' bed, chattering happily, and he's staring at her with longing.

When they see me, the girl stops in mid-sentence, and Laticus swallows, eyes guilty.

Well, well.

"Who's this?" I ask.

"This is Charity. She started working here three days ago," Laticus answers.

Charity stands up and shakes my hand. "You must be Gwen. Laticus has been telling me all about you," she says. I look over her badge and memorize her ID number.

"I can come back later," I tell them. "Here, enjoy these." I unload the candy and chips onto the bed and turn toward the door.

"No, I have to go home. My mom will be so mad at me if I'm late again," Charity says, shyly. She waves awkwardly at Laticus and scurries out of the room.

Laticus sighs as she leaves. "She's so hot."

"How did I miss the fact that you have a new crush?" I clamp my lips together, grinning.

"Please don't tell anyone she's been hanging out after her shifts. She said we could both get into trouble." He looks so handsome, cheeks flushed and eyes bright.

"I won't tell, just be careful. I don't want your security amping up more than it already is."

"When can I get out of here, Gwen?" He walks to the window and stares out. "I'm losing it. I haven't even walked out of this room once." He pounds on the window and looks at me, his eyes bleak. "I miss my mom, my friends. There's not even the hope of seeing my dad, unless I become an End Man soon. He told them I'm not ready, but anything is better than this prison."

"You'd be going right into another prison," I tell him. "Folsom is right." I put my arm around his shoulder. "I'll get you outside—there's no reason for you to be cooped up in this room nonstop. I'll contact your team about it tonight. Okay?"

On my way home, outside the Red Region's offices, picketers stand outside the gate holding up signs that say: *Set the men free! End the Men's slavery! Enough is enough—we don't need more men anyway.*

Another sign catches my eye: *I'm with Gwen. Free the men.*

I laugh under my breath but then think about what this means. They're out here because of what I said. Governor Petite's threats seem very tangible now, and that makes me speed a little faster to get home.

Folsom doesn't need to see this on the news next or he'll think he's right.

There's a large van outside my house. What now? Just as I'm going to the front door, it opens and my mother and three large women walk out.

"Oh, there you are. I was hoping to tell you earlier, but you've been gone all day…" My mom motions for me to move past the women. One is carrying boxes and the other two are moving a couch.

Sophia walks down the stairs, holding some of her nicer dresses.

"I'm just going to drive these over. I can come back for everything else later," she says. She notices me there and stops. "Is Little Miss Perfect coming?" she asks.

My mother shakes her head. "Don't be like that, Sophia."

"Well, seriously, we can't even have a party without her ruining it and making it all about her." She walks out the door.

"What's going on?"

"We're moving in with Pandora. She has more room and we can plan the wedding better if we're together."

"Today? Why so sudden?" I take the box out of her hands and set it on the floor.

"Well, honestly, because of you," she says, her brows creasing. "Pandora says she can protect us better there, and I have to agree. She has twenty-four-hour surveillance and I'll feel safer there. Reporters have been calling here all morning. I think the only reason they aren't camped out here is because of the protesters at the Regional office. "

I get a sick feeling in my gut and clutch my arms around my stomach.

"Are you sick again?" She clasps my shoulder.

"No, I just don't like any of this. I didn't mean to cause trouble. I can't move into Pandora's, though, Mother. I don't trust her. Don't you think it's strange that she asks you to marry her now? You haven't even been all that serious, and as soon as Soph and I are pregnant, right before election time starts, she wants to get married? It just doesn't add up."

"I considered that," she answers. "But she's the reason I was able to line Folsom up for you girls…she pulled a lot of strings to get you on his schedule. We have her to thank that these babies are being born to our family."

"I don't want to owe anyone anything," I tell her emphatically. "Especially not *Pandora*."

"Too late." She shrugs and gives me a faint smile. "And you can't stay here by yourself. Too dangerous." She picks up the box and carries it out, just as the others are coming back in.

I follow her out. "We're not selling this place, are we? I'm twenty-five. I'll hire a guard of my own," I tell her.

"I have a meeting in an hour and need to get ready, but this conversation isn't over," she says.

The loaded van pulls out and she gives me a pointed look before going upstairs. I stay out of the way until I hear her leave and then I crawl into my bed. I can't seem to get enough sleep lately. I drift off and dream about Pandora and all the picketers. Something startles me and I wake up panting. My room is pitch black. The hair on the back of my neck stands up.

A low voice says: "Don't make a sound. I'm not going to hurt you, I'm here to talk about the boy."

The light clicks on and I blink hard, allowing my eyes to adjust. I have the comforter pulled all the way up to my neck, and below the blankets my entire body is trembling. A man sits in a chair, pulled up close to my bed, his wide shoulders blocking the light that filters in through the window. I sit up, pressing my back against the headboard and taking him in warily. He could snap me in two with one hand.

"Kasper?" I whisper, finally recognizing him. Of all the men, Kasper has the most unique style, choosing to wear bright colors and bold patterns. Whenever he's in a news headline, they spend more time commenting on his clothes than they do about him being an End Man. Tonight, however, he's dressed entirely in black and his face is somber.

"Gwen, Gwen, the Red Region shit-stirrer. I don't have much time, so shut that pretty mouth for once and listen."

I open my mouth, a retort balanced on my tongue, but then think better of it. It sounds like he's here to…help.

"I couldn't get to Folsom without them knowing I'm here. I need you to take him a message." His voice, even deeper than Folsom's, rumbles in his chest when he speaks. He's so different from the brightly colored man on the Silverbook.

"Your press conference lit little fires under activists' asses," he says. "They're trying to keep it under wraps, but when I left the Black Region this morning, the Governor's Mansion was surrounded by picketers."

I don't know what to say, so I look on silently and wait for him to continue.

"The Regions are trying to contain the protesters for now, but as soon as it becomes public knowledge that they took Laticus in the night and shipped him off to the Red Region, shit is going to hit the fan. He's sort of the Region darling, if you know what I mean. Excuse my language, Gwen. Do you mind swearing? I forget what a gentleman Folsom is."

I get the feeling that he doesn't mean this as a compliment to Folsom.

He crosses a leg over his knee and runs a hand thoughtfully across his chin.

"I wanted to thank you for what you said last night. It was a refreshing change to the normal pregnancy announcements." He grins at me.

"I can't tell if anything that comes out of your mouth is sincere or not," I say.

This makes Kasper's grin stretch into a smile. "You know, you're not nearly as dumb as you look."

My jaw drops at the same time as anger starts sizzling in my belly.

"I meant that as a compliment, Gwen. The pretty ones are always the dumbest."

"Get to the point, Kasper," I say between my teeth.

"Your governor…"

"Petite," I say, suddenly perking up at the mention of my soon-to-be stepmother's name.

"Yes, Petite," he says slowly. "She's working for the Society. The only reason they brought Laticus here was because of what she promised them."

I feel a lump form in my throat and try to swallow around it. "And what exactly did she promise?"

Kasper purses his lips, tapping his fingers on the arm of the chair.

"That, my dear Gwen, is for you to find out. Your boyfriend is defying them. The Society is grasping to regain their power with Folsom, insisting that Laticus be taken from his control."

"How do you know that?" I ask.

"Knowing things is my specialty, Gwen."

He stands up and I toss the blanket aside and scoot out of bed.

"Where are you going?" I follow him to my bedroom door. He turns around suddenly and I'm uncomfortably close to him.

"You're already pregnant, Gwen! There's nothing I can do for you."

I resist the urge to punch him in his cocky, arrogant face. "You said you had a message for Folsom," I say, exasperated.

"Oh, yes." He's taunting me and I hate it. "It seems that the Canadians don't agree with our methods. They focus more on research rather than whoring out their men. If Folsom can get the boy to the Green Region, we can get him across the border. Something to think about," he says.

He's about to walk out the door when he suddenly turns back.

"Here." He places something in my hand. "When Folsom wants to move forward with the plan, all he needs to do is push that button."

I look over the small black clip with the switch clicked off. It looks sort of like the devices we use at work, but sleek.

"We'll handle the rest."

I narrow my eyes at him. "You don't like Folsom."

He raises his eyebrows.

"Why are you helping him?"

"That's between me and your boyfriend," he says.

I contemplate calling Folsom to tell him about Kasper's visit, but the thought that anyone could be bugging our devices makes me set my Silverbook down. No, I have to tell him in person. Kasper said that my soon-to-be stepmother is involved. I glance at my Silverbook lying beside me on the bed with new suspicion. Would she?

Could she? I feel sick. Since I can't sleep, I decide to distract myself instead. I message the team about taking Laticus outside tomorrow and look up Charity's ID number. There's not much about her online, but she seems to check out. She and her mother live downtown. I make a note to ask around about her tomorrow. I'd just feel better if I knew a little more about her.

On my drive to work the next morning, I see even more protesters than yesterday, a few silver-haired men are scattered through them. Their cries are louder, their expressions more severe. There are news vehicles parked down the street, reporters aiming their cameras at the protest. I go so slowly to read all the signs that I almost miss the girl getting in the car parked next to me. Genevieve, Governor Petite's aid, pulls behind me. I don't think either of them notices me, and I look in the rearview mirror once more to be sure. Charity is sitting next to Genevieve, talking with her hands going every direction, and looking very different from the demure girl I saw in Laticus' room.

NINETEEN

FOLSOM

For the next week, appointments fill my days. It's an endless cycle of women and sex, questions about my health, and late, lonely nights back at the End Men compound. With the permission of the Society and recommendation of my doctor, my appointments are capped at two a day, during which time I abstain from drinking and only use the pills when absolutely necessary. The Society also deems the lottery as a risk and the weekly drawings are suspended from my stay in the Red indefinitely. I haven't spoken to Gwen in days, having tried to connect with her, only to have her tell me that she'd prefer to talk to me in person.

On the eighth day, I arrive at the Villanova house late in the evening. The estate sits on ten acres of rolling, green land outside the bustle of the city. My appointment is with their daughter and is to be followed by a party. The girl is a friend of Gwen's sister, Sophia; I recognize her from the night of the last party.

"Langley," she says, kissing me lightly on each cheek. Before I can respond, a toddler comes barreling into the room and grabs me by the leg.

"Are you my daddy?" she asks, looking up at me. She has Langley's red hair and a sprinkling of freckles across her nose.

"Ah, Folsom, meet my niece, Beatriz." She looks down at the little girl. "No, B, this is not your daddy. Your daddy's name is Jackal."

"Like the aminal," she agrees.

I crouch down on my haunches and look into the little girl's face. "I know your daddy," I tell her. "He's my friend."

It's the first time I've ever announced my friendship with Jackal, and saying it out loud gives me a sense of pride. She smiles so big her eyes disappear and then she runs off, her fiery hair trailing behind her.

"We're hoping to give her a cousin." Langley smiles. "Preferably a male one."

"It's safer to be born a girl," I say.

Langley frowns, a practiced gesture she's perfected. "But where's the glory in that?"

It strikes me then that Langley is the competitive type. With both her friend and Gwen pregnant, she won't be outdone.

"Twins would be ideal," she says. "Boy twins."

I flinch at the idea and Langley's laughter fills the room. "They run in my family," she tells me. "You don't have to worry about me, Folsom." She runs a finger along my jaw. "I'm no novice when it comes to men. I've had Jackal—a few times actually. Unfortunately our coupling didn't end in pregnancy." She frowns at that part and I wonder how hard she took it when her sister got pregnant and she didn't. I'd seen female disappointment turn into anger; it was a gale of accusations and blame.

After some light conversation, we make our way up to her bedroom where she offers me the obligatory drink. I accept it this time and wait in a chair while she mixes it. I expect her to take a different seat, but instead she straddles me, her own drink in her hand.

"I've heard that you can't strain yourself," she says, rubbing her free hand along my chest.

"We can do it like this…"

She puts on quite a show. Eventually I have to close my eyes or I'll laugh. She does this thing with her mouth that she intends to be sexy, but it's more like a horse baring its teeth. I'll have to ask Jackal if he remembers her.

"Look at me," she cries out.

I ignore her and nearly tell her to stop talking. I picture Gwen and wish I could suck her top lip right now. My dick pulses and I go faster, imagining it's her warmth that I'm fucking. Langley's braying brings me back to reality, but I'm close enough that I power through it.

She leans down and kisses me, still breathing hard. "That was incredible," she purrs.

I open my eyes and now all I see is the horse face. I smile. "You should lie down. I'll go get cleaned up. When is everyone arriving?"

"Oh, they're here already." She runs her fingers through my hair. "I'll join you in the shower," she says against my mouth.

I back away. "Go lie down." My tone leaves no room for argument.

"Fine."

She pouts as she climbs off of me then walks backward to the bed, rubbing her nipples. I walk to the bathroom and when she tries to get in with me a few minutes later, I rinse and turn the shower off.

"I don't think that time took," she whispers, palming my dick. "This time it will."

I brush her hand off and step out of the shower. Her arms wrap around my chest and I turn around to face her, pulling her hands off of me.

"I've fulfilled my contract and now I need you to back off and be respectful of my space."

Her mouth drops and her eyes spit fire. "Sounds like someone is an entitled bastard. Are you really buying into what all those protesters are saying? You think you have *rights*?" She laughs.

I put on my suit as Langley lies on the bed, striking another pose. If I grabbed her ass right now, she'd still beg me to fuck her, angry or not.

"Jackal was better," she says.

I nod. "That's because he enjoys it."

It is my duty to be charming to these women, have them believe I enjoy their sex and their company. But my patience is worn thin, and my mind is preoccupied with worry.

We make our way downstairs together, her arm clasped possessively through mine like we're a couple descending on our guests. And that's exactly what we walk right into, at least two hundred of Langley's guests, all sipping champagne and beaming up at us like we're the bride and groom. It's not lost on me that she chose an ivory dress, or that she has her hair braided, the long coil of it thrown over her shoulder and threaded with tiny white flowers, a customary style for brides. We near the bottom of the stairs and I see a familiar face in the crowd. I immediately jerk my arm from Langley's grasp. Gwen looks from Langley to me, a wounded expression on her face. I want to go to her, but people are saying my name and asking me questions. I catch her eyes, trying to communicate what I'm feeling. She turns and walks away.

Governor Petite finds me several minutes later. She has Gwen's mother on her arm and is looking pleased with herself.

"Hope you're enjoying the party, Folsom." She clinks glasses with me. "You remember Diana, of course," she says of Gwen's mother. I incline my head and Diana Allison smiles.

"Ah, here she is!" the governor says. I turn to see Langley approaching from behind. "I don't know of anyone more deserving of a baby than our Langley. She runs all of the Red's charity events and still finds time to volunteer at the home for the elderly. She's truly the best of us."

I glance at Langley, who blushes right on cue and leans in to give Petite a feminine kiss on each cheek. If Langley is the best, I don't want to meet their worst.

"Congratulations on your engagement," Langley says, addressing them both. "The wedding! I'm so excited for the wedding!" She clasps her hands together like a little girl as the two women smile on.

"Congratulations to you both," I say.

The smile clings uneasily to Diana's mouth, never reaching her eyes. Gwen appears behind her mother, and I break out into an easy smile.

"Mother of my son," I say, cheerfully. Gwen blushes all the way to her roots as she blinks at me.

"Hope that's water you're drinking." I wink.

Diana lets go of Petite to place an arm around her youngest daughter's shoulders.

"It's sparkling actually, your son refuses to let me eat."

I feel the eyes on us as people turn to watch our exchange. Petite's smile has stiffened and I can feel Langley's rage from beside me.

"Hopefully there will be more sons soon," Langley says, leaning toward me. "We certainly had fun trying to make one…"

Gwen quickly looks away, and I have the urge to tell her just how un-enjoyable it was for me, when Governor Petite taps her glass and calls out, "I'd like to make a toast!"

The room falls silent as everyone turns our way. Gwen glances at me, widening her eyes. I tilt my head to the side in question just as Petite begins to speak.

"First, I'd like to acknowledge our host, Langley Starter. We are all honored to share this exciting day with you. And though we don't have the results yet, we trust that Folsom's aim was true."

Langley beams as everyone stares awkwardly at her flat belly. It's like they're willing the child there.

"I'd like to raise a toast to Folsom. Our End Man, who in just a few weeks has renewed the Red Region's hope with the promise of three children!"

A cheer goes up among the guests, and I wonder idly who the third is. The lottery winner, I hope. At least that night wouldn't be a complete fuck up. It's when she continues speaking that a chill runs down my back. I clutch the glass of bourbon I'm holding tighter as she continues.

"Folsom, you live a most glamorous life. The Regions sing your praise wherever you go. You are a god among us," her voice takes a more somber tone, "and yet you've chosen to be here with us, and not only that, you've chosen for your eldest son, Laticus, to be here as well. You bring us great honor."

There is a murmur of surprise around the room at the mention of Laticus' name. I grow warm underneath my suit, my limbs prickling with anger.

"Thank you for your dedication to the End Men, for your service to the Regions. And for your son." She ends and there's a round of applause so loud I can't hear my own thoughts.

I feel Gwen's fingers dig into my arm and she leans up on her tiptoes to whisper in my ear.

"Come with me. We need to talk."

TWENTY

GWEN

I move quickly to the courtyard, Folsom following at a distance. Chandeliers light the way, but I find a dark area near the private lake on the property. Most are inside, just a few stragglers here and there, and I watch Folsom duck behind a tree when he sees a woman walk by. I laugh at how fast he dodges her.

He's smiling when he gets closer and I want to take him by the arm and drag him away from this place, away from this life. His expression clears, almost as if he can read my thoughts. I wonder what he wants, his deepest desires that have been shoved down and forgotten.

I don't know what to do with my hands, if he wants to be touched right now or needs his space. It was easy between us when I saw him last, but it's been over a week and he's slept with how many women since then? I've tried not to think about each and every one.

He reaches down and takes me by the hand and it feels sweet, shy almost.

"How are—" We both start at the same time then laugh.

I want to cringe at the awkwardness, but then he steps forward and wraps his arms around me, pulling me tight against him. And I breathe. I've missed him. I didn't want to…I needed a break from all the feelings…but I needed this so much more.

"Have you been hiding from me?" he asks.

"What? No," I say into his shoulder. "It's just been busy," I falter, hating how nervous I sound. "I've been staying at work most nights. Folsom, the governor's speech…"

"I know," he says. "She's trying to discredit what you said, making it sound like I enjoy this life."

"I think they put her up to it, the Society."

He nods. "You're probably right. They're trying to contain what you started."

"I haven't wanted to call," I tell him. "I'm worried the Silverbooks are bugged. And there's something I need to tell you about Laticus…"

He pulls away, both hands gripping my arms. "What's going on with Laticus?"

"There's this girl. I don't trust her. She stays after her shift and Laticus definitely likes her. I saw her in the car with Governor Petite's assistant, I don't—"

"Have you talked to him about her?" he interrupts.

"I've just tried to make sure they're not alone too long. I've become the third wheel. Listen though," I look around to make sure we're still alone, "we probably don't have much time. I need to tell you—Kasper came to see me."

Folsom's hands drop and he stares at me incredulously. "Kasper." He flinches, voice deadly. "Start at the beginning."

I falter at his tone but then take a deep breath and talk as quickly as I can. "He says the Canadians are sympathetic to the End Men. They're willing to help. He thinks you need to get Laticus to the Green Region and over the border. Soon. He says the Black Region will erupt when word gets out about Laticus being taken, which will be any day. Oh, and he confirmed that Governor Petite is working with the Society. He gave me a device." I shake my head in frustration. "God, I can't believe I don't have it with me—I've been too distracted over Laticus. I'll bring it the next time I see you. Kasper will help us, Folsom."

He turns, hands going to his head, and moves to the door of the gate, pounding it four or five times, hard, until the hinge breaks and it hangs skewed. When he turns around, his eyes are distant. I move to look at his hands and he holds one up, stopping me in mid-step.

"You're just now telling me all of this?"

If I didn't see his jaw ticking, I'd think he was calm. I swallow hard.

"Take me to him. *Now*," he says.

"We can't just leave the party." I put my hand on his arm. "Folsom, look at me. They'll come after you. Let's think about this."

"I'll deal with them when the time comes. I need to see Laticus."

I don't argue anymore but lead him along the water until there's an opening in the trees. My car is parked half a block from the house and when we reach the street, we only have a few feet left to walk. The house is shining like a beacon at the end of the street. Cars line each side of the pavement and the streetlamps flicker in the night sky. If only everything were as serene as it looks.

My car feels tiny with Folsom filling it up. I still get a rush being near him, even when he's angry, or whatever this is that feels like rage hopping off of him. I really want to know what the deal is between him and Kasper, but I know this isn't the time to ask.

I speed the ten miles to Genome Y, neither of us speaking, and when we're within range of the guard, I flash my badge. The guard flashes her light on Folsom and he stares ahead as if he visits Genome Y like this every night, nothing out of the ordinary.

"I'm running some tests," I tell her and she grins.

"Is that what we're calling it?" she asks. "Next time, put me on the schedule."

I glare at her and speed off when she opens the gate.

When we get in the building, Folsom waits in my office while I see who is on the night shift in dome five. As far as I can tell, only the guard and one nurse are attending. They're used to seeing me in here every night now. I've taken Laticus outside once during the day, and at night I have permission to walk with him around the inside of the building, as long as I never leave him alone.

He perks up when I come in the room. "I didn't think you were coming tonight..."

I smile and close the door behind me. "Let's take a walk."

He lifts an eyebrow. "You up for walking in those shoes? You look nice," he adds.

"Well, you certainly have the charm down." I nod toward the door. "Let's go."

"What's your hurry?" He smirks and each time I'm hit with how much he looks like Folsom.

"Thought you were sick of this place." I shrug.

I open the door and he runs and jumps, tapping the top of the doorjamb with his hand. The guard nods at us, and Laticus starts down the path we've gone the last few nights.

"Let's go this way tonight," I tell him, turning in the other direction.

He does an about-face, exaggerating his turn, and I laugh. Folsom and Laticus have become the closest thing I have to friends. I sober up, reminding myself that my time with both of them is limited. Maybe even shorter than I expected if we're listening to Kasper…which might be the real reason I didn't tell Folsom as soon as Kasper left, if I'm honest with myself.

We get near my office and I put my hand on Laticus' arm. "I don't want you to be alarmed. Folsom is in there," I tell him quietly.

His eyes widen and he barely nods, acknowledging he heard me.

When I open the door, Folsom is standing in the corner on full alert. Laticus walks inside and I take one last look around before pulling the door closed.

"You're looking well," Folsom says, giving Laticus a faint close-lipped smile.

"You too," Laticus says. They stare at each other for a moment before Folsom's gaze becomes serious.

He looks at me and his eyes soften before turning back to Laticus. "The Governor of the Red Region has announced that you're here. When word makes its way to your home, the Black will uprise, retaliate," he says.

I clench my teeth together and lean against the wall, stepping out of my heels.

"We need to get you out of here, out of the Red Region…out of the country," he tells Laticus and the room goes still. "Kasper will be helping us. You don't know me well enough to trust me yet, but I'm asking you to anyway. Can you do that?"

The boy nods. Folsom steps closer to Laticus and puts a hand on his shoulder. "Do you understand?"

Laticus nods solemnly. "I understand."

"Swear it."

"I swear," Laticus answers.

They clutch hands.

"We have to get back to the party," Folsom says, stepping back. "Don't forget, Gwen and Kasper…anyone else is probably working for the governor. That includes your new friend—" He looks at me.

"Charity," I finish.

Laticus' face pales and his Adam's apple bobs up and down. "Right," he says.

My heart hurts for him. I put my hand on his back. "I'll walk you back."

When we get back to the Villanova property, women are milling out on the front lawn, most likely searching for Folsom. I let him off a little further down than where my car was parked and he goes back the way of the lake. I park and walk barefoot to the house, hearing whispers wondering where Folsom is, and someone calling out that they see him. The crowd rushes to that voice and laughter rings out; it was a prank to see how fast the ladies would move. I go inside and Sophia is the first one I see. I groan.

"Where is he?" she says, face flushed.

"He's outside." I shrug like he's been out there all along.

She gets in my face, towering over me. "You've had your chance, now let the rest of us enjoy him. Why can't it be enough for you that you're having the boy of the Red Region? You're the most selfish person I know."

"Now that I know what *I* know, a boy is the last thing I'd wish on a mother," I tell her, opening the door and walking back out.

Folsom comes around the front of the house, surrounded by a flock of women. He makes eye contact with me, and Sophia huffs beside me. The smile suddenly freezes on his face as he looks at me. I blink at him, wondering what in the world is going on. The women who surround him turn to follow his gaze, their eyes landing on me. And then one of them starts to scream.

"Call an ambulance! Call an ambulance."

I shake my head, confused. Folsom looks down at my skirt and I do the same, my eyes growing large. My skirt has twisted around—the back of it now almost all of the way to the front—and there is a small stain of blood seeping through the pale pink silk. I reach down to touch it and my fingers come away wet. When I look up, he's walking briskly toward me across the grass, as people pour out of the house to see what the commotion is about. Then Folsom is in front of me; he's the only one. He scoops me up just as I hear the wail of the siren. I look over his shoulder to where my sister is still standing. The look on her face can only be described as hopeful.

TWENTY-ONE

FOLSOM

They take her from my arms and close the ambulance doors in my face. It all happens so quickly, me handing Gwen to the medic, the panic in her eyes. I want to go with her, but they shake their heads, one of them pushing me down when I try to climb in. As they're driving away, lights flashing, her mother runs toward me, holding her dress above her ankles.

"Did they take her? Is she all right?" Diana's hands reach out to me frantically.

I squeeze her hand. "Do you have a car?"

She nods, her eyes filling with tears.

"Let's go."

She leads me briskly toward the side of the house where Governor Petite's driver has parked the car. The driver is nowhere to be seen.

"I should tell Pandora," she says, looking around.

"Fuck Pandora," I say, getting in the driver's seat. She nods like it's decided and climbs into the passenger's seat.

Diana directs me to the hospital, bracing herself against the dashboard as I disregard every traffic law in the Red Region. We park the car and run toward the emergency room doors. Had Sophia really been smiling when I picked Gwen up and carried her to the ambulance?

I can't wipe the image from my head. My God, what is wrong with these women?

"Gwen Allison." Her mother says when we walk up to the desk. "They should have brought her in a few minutes ago. She was…is pregnant." She wrings her hands while she waits.

"She hasn't been brought here," the nurse says. "We'd know Miss Allison if we saw her."

"They must have taken her to the Genome Y lab," I say to Diana.

We run for the car. My Silverbook has not stopped buzzing since we left the party and it occurs to me that it could be Gwen. I switch off the idle mode before we turn out of the parking lot and glance at the screen.

"Gwen?" I say when we connect.

Gwen's voice fills the car and Diana lets out a cry.

"Folsom, are you with my mom?"

I glance at Diana. "Yeah, she's right next to me. We're on our way to you now."

"They have me at Genome Y…"

"We know. Are you okay?"

"I haven't seen the doctor yet, just got here. I'm worried." Tears fill her voice and Diana whimpers.

"We'll be right there, Gwen. We're coming."

I fight with the guard at the gate for ten minutes before Gwen calls Corinne and she lets us through.

"And here I was thinking you got special treatment by being a man," Diana says half-jokingly.

Corinne greets us and leads us upstairs, a somber expression on her face. She won't tell us anything when Diana presses her.

When we walk into Gwen's room, she's sitting up in bed, her hair piled on top of her head. She is more beautiful in a dull grey hospital gown with mascara streaking her cheeks than I've ever seen her look. Diana goes to her side and I stand back to let mother and daughter comfort each other while a sick dread hits my belly.

Doctor Hunley rushes in and barely pauses when she sees me in the room. "Folsom," she acknowledges, her gaze immediately shifting to Gwen. "Josie will be here any minute to do your ultrasound. I'll feel better taking a look, won't you?"

She barely gets the words out when there's a rap at the door and the technician rolls the machine into the room. She puts a blanket over the lower half of Gwen's body and lifts the gown up to expose Gwen's stomach.

She glances at me then and back to Gwen. "Would you rather do this privately?"

"I want him here," she says, stretching her hand out to me.

I take her hand and grip it, looking into her eyes rather than watching them prepare. Josie tells her when she's about to insert the device and we turn to the screen. She reminds us that it's early and we might not see much yet. I don't understand anything I'm seeing at first, but then Josie points out the gestational sac and the yolk sac and zooms in on it and I'm fascinated.

Everyone gasps when a consistent pulse is seen.

"Is that—?" I ask.

"That's the baby's heartbeat. We're definitely seeing cardiac motion," Josie confirms. "It will get even faster later, but this is completely normal for right now."

"I can't believe it," Gwen whispers.

Josie looks at the doctor and smiles then warns Gwen she's about to remove the wand. I carefully place Gwen's hand on her chest and back away, suddenly feeling out of place.

"Your baby looks fine," Doctor Hunley speaks up. "And it's normal to have some spotting throughout pregnancy, especially in the first trimester. We'll keep a close eye on you, though. Take frequent breaks, put your feet up, and drink lots of water. We won't give you any long-term restrictions now that we see how healthy everything is looking. Just pay attention to your body." She pats Gwen's shoulder and smiles at each of us before leaving the room.

"The baby is okay," Gwen says finally, looking past her mother to me. "It was just a scare."

Gwen and Diana start to cry, while I stand rooted to the spot, not knowing what to do. I'm not sure what I'm allowed to feel. Gwen is not mine, and the boy she's carrying will never belong to me, and yet I am relieved, so relieved that I want to hold her and touch her belly.

"Folsom," Gwen says. I stand to attention. "Come here."

I do as I'm told, my limbs rigid. I even remind myself of a robot. Diana excuses herself quickly to find a restroom and it's just Gwen and me in the room. She pats the edge of the bed and I sit. Grabbing my shirt in her fists, she pulls me to her and loops an arm around my neck. She holds my face against hers, our foreheads touching. I sit very still and try to memorize this feeling. No words, just touch expressing words. I wrap my arms around her slight frame and hold her tight.

"You can be like this with me," she says. "You don't have to be an End Man when we're together. Because no matter how many women you're with, or where they send you, I will always be right here belonging to you. I promise."

I pull away from her so I can see her expression.

"Do you understand what I'm saying to you?"

"Gwen…"

"—It's okay," she rushes. "You don't have to say anything. I'm happy to have you…as a friend."

"Friends don't fuck."

"Says who?" She grins.

I lean my forehead against hers and close my eyes.

"I can't say the things I want to," I tell her softly. "If I say them, they mean more. And nothing can mean anything. Not in my life."

She nods against my forehead like she understands. But how could she?

"I'm afraid visiting hours are over," Doctor Hunley says, walking into the room. "We're going to keep her overnight just so we can monitor the baby and you can pick her up tomorrow if you like, Folsom…"

"Right. Perfect," I say, standing up.

Diana inches back into the room to say goodbye to Gwen as Doctor Hunley hands me a clearance badge to get through the gate.

"Folsom has appointments. It'll be my mother who picks me up," Gwen tells the doctor.

"No. I'll come." All three sets of eyes turn to look at me.

"Are you sure? How will you—?" Gwen is shaking her head.

"I'm sure. I'll be here in the morning."

Diana informs me that Petite got a ride home after we stole her car, so I drive her back to the Governor's Mansion and arrange for Sera to pick me up there.

"How mad is she?" I ask.

"I don't really care, to be honest, Folsom." She sighs. "A parent never puts anything before their child. Pandora never had any, she doesn't understand."

"I have over two hundred children," I say.

She smiles sadly. "Yes, and you're creating a better world for them every day. A way for them to survive." Before she gets out of the car she grabs my hand and squeezes it. "Thank you for tonight. For being there for Gwen." She's about to say more, but the front door of the house opens and Petite's frame fills the doorway.

"That's our cue," I say to her.

We both climb out, and I raise a hand to the governor before making my way over to my own car. When I turn back, she has her arm around Diana's shoulders and is leading her inside.

Robin is waiting in my apartment an hour later when I walk through the door.

"I'm tired," I say when I see the look on her face.

"You've had a very busy night," she agrees. "The Genome Y lab twice in one evening, I see."

I look at her out of the corner of my eye. "You're tracking me?" I pull off my jacket and toss it on the back of a chair. Of course they would send Robin after me. She works for them not me, I remind myself.

"Well, when you disappear from your scheduled obligations, I'd say yes, it's my job to keep track of where you are."

"Speaking of those obligations, cancel my appointments tomorrow morning. I'll have to make them up some other time." I ease the buttons of my shirt out of their eyeholes.

"You know I can't do that," Robin says.

"I'm telling you to do it."

"And what am I supposed to tell the Society when they ask?"

"Tell them whatever you like. It doesn't matter to me."

I start walking toward the bedroom, but Robin calls after me. "You're playing with fire, Folsom. You have no idea what these people are willing to do to maintain control."

Her words lift the hairs on the back of my neck. I know exactly what they are willing to do. I've never wanted control. I gave it up years ago for the greater good. It wasn't until Gwen that the constraints I've lived with for so many years started to chaff. And why Gwen? Women have passed through my life; a running tap of names, and faces, and pussies, and no one—not one—has ever stood out. But I knew. The moment I saw her, I knew. A feeling, a draw, the smallest spark of kindling.

I want her. Oh my God, I want her.

TWENTY-TWO

GWEN

Folsom arrives bright and early the next morning smelling of fresh air and coffee. I'm not even dressed, and he looks like he stepped out of The End Men calendar, which I'm ashamed to say I own. He's carrying two cups: a smoothie for me and a coffee for him. There's a strange look in his eyes, and I wish I knew him well enough to know what it means.

"This is a nice change of pace," I say, as he hands me the cup. "What flavor did you get me?"

"I took you for a berry person." His step falters, like now he's not sure. I can't help it, I can't. He's always so serious that I have to take a shot.

"I'm allergic to berries," I pout and his face looks so crestfallen I burst into laughter. "Just kidding. I love berries." I take a sip to prove it to him. "You're the best man I know," I tell him, slipping my legs over the side of the bed and standing up.

"I'm the only man you know."

"Not true. Laticus counts, right? And I know Jackal and Kasper—I have nothing good to say about Kasper."

Folsom frowns. I watch his expression carefully, wishing he'd say more about his relationship with Kasper. They are about as different as two men can be: Folsom, dark-haired and light-eyed, and Kasper, light-haired and dark-eyed. Kasper's words are spoken with the intention of cutting, disguised beneath his charisma, while Folsom's words are careful…deliberate, even considerate.

They don't like each other, that is easy to see.

I untie my hospital gown and let it drop to the floor. I'm naked underneath, having removed my panties just before he came in. It was my game plan to tease him, but now that his eyes are on me, warming my skin, I feel as if I've lost control. I fumble with the clothes Corinne brought me, dropping the pants and then putting the shirt on backward, the heat of his eyes making me nervous.

Folsom never once looks away, and I want to snort with laughter at my attempt to be sexy.

When I'm dressed, I go over to him. He grabs my hand and places it on his dick to show me he's hard.

I kiss him softly and he cups my behind, pulling me into him.

"We're not allowed." I breathe into his mouth. "We're both broken."

He laughs and I lean my head against his chest to feel the rumble. And then he does something that really surprises me. He puts a hand against my stomach, holding his palm there.

"That's your son," I say, tilting my head back to look at him. "Not the Region's, not the people's. Yours and mine."

He pulls his hand away quickly and looks out the window like he didn't hear me.

I wish I knew what he was thinking. But, I'm learning, aren't I? I know that he tries not to feel anything. His only armor is the unfeeling way he moves through life. He thinks I don't understand, and maybe I don't, but I want to. If he'd just let me carry some of his burden.

I'm discharged and put on bed rest for the next week. That means no coming in to work. No keeping an eye on Laticus and Charity. Sera is waiting at the car for us; she smiles when she sees me, nodding her head in greeting. We've been on the road for no more than five minutes when I notice she's going in the wrong direction.

"Where are we going?" I ask.

"To the compound."

I look at Folsom curiously as he stares straight ahead. Am I imagining it or is he avoiding my eyes?

"Why?"

"Because your mother and sister have left your childhood home and moved in with Petite. I don't want you to be alone, and I don't want you at the Governor's Mansion. Neither is safe."

"Since when are you in charge of my safety?"

"Since I saw your sister smile when she thought you were having a miscarriage. Since Petite threatened you. Since you made that dumbass speech on the news with all twelve Regions watching you."

I blink at him. "Oh."

My sister, yes, I'd almost forgotten about that. A sick feeling takes root in my stomach when I think about Sophia. I tap my fingers on my knee, a dozen emotions competing for first place. Even Folsom noticed the look on Sophia's face. And did he really think I was a…dumbass? It's hard to tell if Folsom is angry or teasing. His facial expression hardly ever changes; the only way to know is to see his eyes, which are currently turned away from me.

"Where will I stay though?" I finally ask.

"With me," Folsom says simply. My eyes grow large.

"But, the Society…what if they find out you have me there? Are you…can I—?"

"I can entertain whomever I want. They encourage it."

"Right, but that applies to women who aren't already pregnant."

He looks at me then and his light eyes seem to be laughing. I look away when the butterflies come, ashamed at how quickly my body and mind team up against me. I reach for his hand. To my relief, he twines his fingers through mine and squeezes reassuringly.

When we pull into the compound, there are people milling about. A woman smiles at me knowingly and introduces herself as Folsom's stylist, Krystal. She is tall and long-limbed, her body a grid of lean muscle and feminine curves. I remember a detail he told me when we first met. "Does she help you design your clothes?"

"I give her the sketches," he tells me. "And she takes care of the rest." I look at him now, noticing the unusual cut and drape of his shirt. The long suede trench that looks like oil.

"I don't have any clothes here," I say.

"We'll have some made for you then." He holds the door open for me and I step past him. I want to shut the door quickly, block out all of the eyes watching us: stylists, and massage therapists, and bodyguards. They all look at me the same, with pity in their eyes. I'm falling in love with Folsom and soon he'll move on…with them…and I'll be left behind.

I feel an irrational spurt of jealousy toward Folsom's stylist. A woman who gets to travel with him, see him daily.

"I should be your stylist," I say as he leads me into the living room. Folsom raises an eyebrow at me.

"Oh, you should?"

"Yes. Absolutely. Then I can travel with you. Be with you."

"And what would you dress me in?"

"Well, I prefer you naked, but I'm sure I could whip some things up for you."

"Why this sudden interest in fashion?" He sits down on the sofa and I scoot next to him on my knees, my legs tucked under me.

"I'm jealous."

"Of?"

"Everyone who gets to be with you all the time."

"You're jealous of the women I *don't* have sex with?" He leans his head back and rubs his forehead in confusion.

"I'm jealous of everyone who gets to be with you when I'm not."

"But when I'm with them, I want to be with you," he says.

I'm so pleased I can't do anything but stare at him. Folsom, who doesn't seem to realize the effect his words have on me, gets up to go to the kitchen. When he comes back a few minutes later, he has a Silverbook in his hand.

"Genome Y has released a statement saying both you and the baby are fine," he says.

I nod. I expected as much. The news picked up the story of me being rushed from Langley's party in an ambulance and my Silverbook hasn't stopped vibrating since.

He sets his Silverbook down and looks at me with an odd expression.

"What?"

"I have something to show you. Do you feel okay?"

I crinkle my face at him. "I'm fine. What is it?"

"It's in the back room…I'm the *only* one allowed in there," he says pointedly.

He pulls me up and we walk past his bedroom to one of two closed doors. He opens the door and turns on the light. There are boots everywhere: some finished, some waiting to be stained, some in the beginning stages…and on the workbench sits the most intricate, stunning pair I've ever seen.

I move toward them and touch the soft, supple material. "I love them," I whisper. My eyes fill and I look at him. "You made boots for me."

"I started making them for you the night we met," he says.

"I can't believe you did."

"It wasn't all me," he admits. "While I was in the hospital Krystal worked on them."

He picks them up and hands them to me. "Do you need a pair in every color?"

"Yes! Yes, I do."

He laughs and pulls out the chair for me to sit and try them on. They slide on easily and he bends down to secure the clasps and tie the laces.

"Like they were made for me." I bite my lower lip, beaming. I tap the boots together and look up at him. "Thank you, Folsom. I love them."

"Your smile…" He taps his chest. I want to hear the rest of what he was about to say, but he bends down and kisses me instead.

When it quickly gets heated, he backs away and grins.

I'm about to suggest lunch when I remember he has to make up his morning appointments.

"You have to go soon, right?" There's a dread that follows those words, images of him with other women fill my mind. I hide my hands from him so he can't see them shake.

"Yes," he says simply.

Before he leaves, he sets me up on the sofa with snacks, drinks, books, and old movies playing on the Silverbook. I feel like a child being tucked into bed. But there's something about being taken care of by a large, unemotional man that touches me, and so I mutely accept. Robin comes to check on me during the day while he's gone, a stiff smile on her face. I want to ask her questions about him, but I know that Robin isn't Folsom's friend, she's his handler, the Society pimp.

I wait all day for Folsom to get home so we can have dinner together. Sometimes he brings food from somewhere: fried chicken from the lower end, biscuits that melt on your tongue like butter—and sometimes he cooks.

Since I have never cooked anything in my life, it fascinates me to watch him. Sleeves rolled to his elbows, he handles cookware with the same grace that I imagine he handles a woman's body. I grow jealous when he flips things in a frying pan. I inwardly seethe when the muscles in his forearms flex as he stirs. Everything is tainted. My jealousy is ridiculous, thickly cloying, and I acknowledge this. Folsom is not mine. We are not in a relationship. But I want to be and so I'm sick with insecurity. After a week of sitting, sitting, sitting, I am bored and restless. One afternoon, I'm tired of waiting for Folsom to get home. I search the house for the Silverbook and carry it back to my place on the sofa, my intention to read the news, but as soon as the headlines pop up, I freeze.

END MEN CRUSADER HOSPITALIZED AFTER PREGNANCY SCARE

WHERE DOES THE RED REGION GO FROM HERE?

GWEN ALLISON AND THE RED REGION'S SON

LATICUS DONAHUE TO SAVE THE REGIONS

The last headline catches my attention. My hands grow clammy as the article opens in front of me. I shake them out, already knowing that what I'm about to read is not going to be good.

> *Laticus Donahue, the fifteen-year-old son of the renowned End Man, Folsom Donahue, has spent the last two months in the Red Region, being tested at Genome Y. As Folsom's firstborn*

> *male, Laticus is the next eligible male who will join the End Men. The group, started seventeen years ago by late philanthropist Earl Oppenheimer, has become the Region's last hope, its sole purpose being to repopulate. Genome Y released a statement today.*
>
> *"After running extensive tests on the bright young man, we have found Laticus to be of extremely good health. His production of semen is high, and the Y chromosome is abundantly evident, more so than in any male currently living in the Regions. We have great hope in his future and the future of the Regions."*

I throw the Silverbook before I can read any more and bury my face in my arms. This is strategic on their part: Genome Y, the Society…even the President. They are aiming for Regional support, getting the private citizens excited and on their side. If everyone sees Laticus as a hero instead of a victim, they can quell the small pockets of uprising we're starting to see. They are also trying to strong-arm Folsom into allowing Laticus to join the End Men early. Good luck to them. If I have learned anything about Folsom thus far, it is that his will is unbending. And that's what scares me most. What will they do in order to make him bend? I sit for a long time, my mind churning until I finally make a decision. Retrieving the Silverbook from the floor, I reposition myself on the couch and start writing.

TWENTY-THREE

FOLSOM

If you were to ask me what I would remember most about Gwen ten years from now, I'd tell you that it's not her wild-looking hair, or her exotic cat eyes, or her perfect breasts and their rosy nipples, which balance perfectly in my hands…it would be her reckless defiance, which she displays any time she's angry. And though she doesn't get angry often, when she does, there are always casualties.

I am on my way back from my last appointment of the day. I showered while there so when I walk through the doors to Gwen I won't smell like another woman's pussy. I sip water in the backseat wishing it was bourbon as Sera navigates the car through the narrow streets. I want to be home, I want to see her, and touch her, and smell her. I scroll through the day's headlines, trying to distract myself. First I see the article about Laticus and suddenly my craving for something strong to drink increases. I burn as I read the words, my breathing ragged. But the headline that pops up afterward takes my breath altogether.

THE AGE OF WOMEN

When I look to see who wrote the article, I tell Sera to drive faster. I left Gwen for just a few hours and she's managed to trend online.

I quickly scan the words, my heart galloping faster the longer I read. The last paragraph, in particular, makes me afraid for Gwen's safety:

> *We are, in essence, nothing more than pimps whoring these men out to fulfill our cravings. It's one thing to ask adult men to sacrifice their lives…if it were really their choice…but is it? No. They have no say in who they see or when and where they will go next. And if we allow Laticus to start his "career" as an End Man, we will become a society who not only encourages but celebrates child prostitution. Would we do this to our daughters if the situation were reversed? Who are we? And what have we become?*

Holy shit.

Robin is waiting inside with a pale-faced Gwen when I walk through the door. They're sitting on opposite sides of the room, facing each other. The air between them is tight, filled with the things just said. Gwen won't meet my eyes, but Robin stands up straight away when she sees me.

"You have to talk sense into her," Robin says, motioning to Gwen. "If you care about her at all, Folsom. I can't seem to get through to her."

"And I don't know how you can stand idly by and watch him suffer," Gwen responds.

Robin stands up in a flash, while Gwen jumps up and stares back with her hands on her hips. I put my hands on her waist and look back at Robin.

"Do you mind giving us a few minutes?"

Robin nods and leaves the room. I wait until I hear the front door open and close before turning back to Gwen.

"Sit down," I say. "I need you to hear me this time."

Gwen flushes and backs away from me, standing defiantly. I step forward and pull her against me. My fingers trace her upper lip and I bend down and lick it.

"I've wanted to do that ever since I left you," I whisper in her ear.

She shivers and I spend a moment kissing her neck just to see what she'll do.

"I've never had anyone defend me the way you have, and I'm begging you to stop. Another first—me begging." I pull her by the hand and we sit on the couch facing each other. "I learned the hard way to not go against the Society. There was only one time I refused to comply with a scheduled appointment. It was a girl I grew up with, one of those cruel girls who mistreats everyone around her. I couldn't stand her. I'd started my career as an End Man and her parents paid for my services. When I walked in her house and realized it was her I walked right back out and refused. I was forced to do eight appointments a day for three weeks as punishment." I shake my head and grimace. "My dick was ready to fall off…"

I check to make sure she's listening. "There was a time in my early years of being an End Man that I wanted to see one of the children. I don't know if it was curiosity, or if I needed to feel good about what I was doing, but I broke an appointment and went to her mother's house. Her mother's name was Ella, and she was kind, probably too kind. She should have said no, but she didn't. She let me see Tessa, who was three by then. I gave her a doll and she loved it. I felt really good about going—Tessa was happy and Ella was a good mother. But the Society found out about it, and within a week, they'd taken Tessa from Ella and had her relocated to another Region…and another mother. They just took her child, handed her over to some stranger to raise. They have ways of making me pay, Gwen, even if it's through someone else. It's only a matter of time before they figure out that I care about you. And I'm afraid of what they'll do."

"You think they'll take my son?" Her eyes are big… watery.

"I think they'll do whatever they need to do to maintain control."

She swallows…nods…looks away.

I think the case is closed and I've sufficiently scared her enough to move on from this, when she clears her throat softly and says: "They'll take him anyway, just like they did to Laticus. And I'm not going to stand by and watch that happen."

"Focus on having a healthy baby. Finding a cure for this…this thing that's happened to us. That's what you can do to help."

Her face is hard when she says, "I'll focus on whatever I want to focus on."

She stands up with an air of finality and moves to a different room. I feel dismissed, a chastised child. My anger flares and I want to follow after her and shake her, make her see sense. Instead, I sit calmly and pull in a breath. Gwen will have to be dealt with in another way.

I move past her and go to the bedroom, taking off my clothes and lying on the bed. I have a couple of hours before I need to be ready for tonight's party and I feel like shit.

She comes in a few minutes later and I hear the sound of her zipper and material falling to the ground. She climbs on the bed beside me and lays her head on my chest, her leg wrapping around mine.

"Are we fighting?" she asks.

"I think maybe so." My voice comes out gruff.

"Time out for a little while, okay?"

She slides down my body and my cock stands to attention, the way it seems to now every time she's near. I groan when she puts her mouth on me…lose my mind. My hands find her hair and I let her win this battle.

I kiss her hard when I leave for the party. She's lying on her back on the sofa, one leg stretched out in front of her, the other trailing the floor, reading a book. There is something about the casual way she occupies this space that gives me a rush of longing so intense I have to look away. What would it be like to always walk into a room and see her? I find such comfort at the sight of her long hair, half straight and half wavy like God couldn't decide which to give her so he mixed it up. She's wearing one of my shirts and it falls off her right shoulder, giving me access to her skin. I kiss her there, and then on her neck. When she leans into me moaning, I head for the door before I can make myself late. It's a relief that she doesn't want to go, not because I don't want her with me, but because I think she'll be safer if she keeps her face out of the news for a while. She's full of things to say; I can see the opinions flashing across her eyes every time she looks at me. I can also see her bite them back, not wanting to be chastised for having them. In another world Gwen would be refreshing, in this world she is dangerous.

Protesters are lined on either side of the gate outside the compound and even more are outside of the Council of Affairs, where tonight's party is being held. Pictures of our faces are on their posters: I see one of Marcus and flinch. How long until the public finds out about what's happened to him and they start to panic? Would it aid Gwen's cause or harm it? Their demands for a replacement could place Laticus in danger.

I remember the honor I felt, the adrenaline of being the most famous human in the Regions. But the elation hadn't lasted. Year after year of meaningless interactions have left me dry on the inside. At first it felt as if I were cracking, the lack of life and warmth, and then it felt like nothing at all. I was relieved for the comfortable numbness, which was better than the alternative. And then a wild-haired girl asked if she could try on my boots and a crack appeared.

I sigh deeply as we drive through the gate, the parting of metal. I count twice as many posters extolling Gwen and her ideas than posters of the End Men, her quotes slashed angrily across the white backgrounds, slapping anyone in the face who dares to look. A truth of marker and poster board. There could be a torrential downpour destroying every single one of those signs, turning them into pulp, and her words would still live inside of the people who hold them. Words are a powerful weapon and they never die.

The party is held on a rooftop. The open air encourages some life in me, a change from the stifling bedrooms. I smile when I should, get groped, and try to be on my best behavior. Several times throughout the night, I catch Petite watching me. I'm about to excuse myself from a group that's been discussing the weather for fifteen minutes, a topic so banal I want to whip out my dick just to see what happens, when I feel a hand on my shoulder. I turn and see Diana standing behind me, wrapped in peach silk. It's the first time I've noticed a resemblance between her and Gwen. She smiles faintly and motions that we need to talk.

I excuse myself and follow her to a quiet corner. Crisis averted, dick tucked safely in my pants.

"Gwen says she's feeling fine, but I wasn't sure if I could trust her to tell me the truth," she says. "And that article she posted—Folsom…" She shakes her head, her eyes cloudy with concern.

I grit my teeth. "She doesn't quite comprehend the magnitude of what she's doing. Talk to her, Diana. She's not listening to me."

"She's staying at the compound with you. When the media finds out, they're going to—" She never finishes her sentence because we're interrupted by Governor Petite.

"May I request that you speak a few words tonight? To reassure the people after some of the rumors circulating."

"What rumors are those?" I'm baiting her, but the look on her face, the self-righteous air…I need to get away from her.

Her lips pull into a tight line and she glances at Diana. "I'm afraid Gwen has stirred some negative feelings toward the End Men with her recent writings. The Society has requested that you ease their minds. Reassure them that you believe in the cause."

Did they now?

"No."

Her head draws back as if I've slapped her.

"No?" she repeats. "Must I remind you that this is your job and—"

I cut her off. "If the Society wants something said, they can say it themselves."

I can feel Diana stir beside me. Her daughter's reputation and safety at risk, I wonder briefly if she will say something to defend her, but in the end, there is only silence. She's a coward, I realize. Just like everyone else.

"Folsom, don't you think it's in your very best interest to comply?" Petite tries to reason with me.

I smile stiffly. "I am here!" I spread my arms. Drink still in hand, several people pause in their conversations to look over at us. "Complying…" I give her a little bow before I disappear into the crowd, one thought repeating itself: I have to go home. To Gwen.

TWENTY-FOUR

GWEN

I tell myself to stay off of the Silverbook, but I'm getting dinged nonstop with notifications. When Folsom has been gone for close to two hours, I cave and open it up, reading some of them.

> *Thank you for sharing the truth with us. I knew there was something suspect about the way these men were kept isolated from the rest of us.*
>
> *Gwen, you are so brave to speak out for the rights of the End Men!*
>
> *The End Men fan club would like to extend an invitation for you to speak at our next meeting…please say yes.*
>
> *You should totally run for governor next election…or better yet, President of the Statehouse! I'd vote for you.*
>
> *Shut your mouth, you little whiny motherfucker. You forget you're one of the fuckers who is impregnated by this so-called slave. Guess that makes you the pimp, according to your logic.*

> *Ignore that person, Gwen. People who swear that much lack education. I think you're right.*
>
> *For thousands of years, men kept women in social and economical enslavement. It was about time they were endangered. Fuck them. They owe us this.*
>
> *Girl, preach. I been sayin this for years now and can't get nobody to listen. Finally! I hear you.*

I let out a long puff of air and look down to see how many comments have been left and my mouth drops. It says (526) COMMENTS in the lower-right corner. I keep scrolling down and the majority of them are supportive, a lot of them women who have been around the End Men and have had interactions with them. I'm still shocked people have latched onto this so quickly. When I hear the door open, I shove my Silverbook underneath a pillow and turn to face Folsom, a ready smile on my lips. But it's not Folsom who walks through the door.

Sera walks in nonchalantly, like she's been here many times. It makes me wonder who all has full access to Folsom's space. It's no surprise his room of boots is overflowing if it's his only escape.

"Hey," she says, holding up an envelope with my name across the front. "I'll wait outside while you get ready."

I point at my pajamas and double top-knots. "Do I look like I'm going anywhere?"

She waves the envelope. "I think you might want to after you read this," she says.

I open the note and admire Folsom's straight block letters before I start reading.

GWEN—DO YOU HAVE A MIDDLE NAME? JUST ONE OF THE MANY THINGS I DON'T KNOW ABOUT YOU. I WANT TO KNOW. I'VE NEVER WANTED TO KNOW BEFORE YOU…

YOUR WEEK OF IMPRISONMENT IS UP. GIVE ME TONIGHT. PLEASE.

NO SOCIETY. NO WOMEN. NO LABS OR PILLS OR ANYTHING ELSE BUT ME AND YOU.

FOLSOM

I smile and hold the note close. *Stop swooning*, I admonish myself. *Enjoy the moment and don't dare dream.* I hop up and rush to the bedroom, frustrated that I'm so excited and giddy with wanting to see what he has planned.

"You're ridiculous," I say to the mirror.

I put on a fitted blue dress and study myself to see if I'm showing at all. Still flat as a pancake. Bummer. I take my hair out of the knots and finger the waves then spritz on a pheromone spray. I grin, apply red lipstick, and rush out of the bedroom door.

Sera is blank-faced as she opens my door and I wonder if she could get in trouble for this. I climb in, half-expecting Folsom to be waiting for me inside.

She notices me looking. "We have to pick him up."

The drive to the Council of Affairs is brief and when Sera pulls around the side, my nerves build. I watch the women coming and going, and I wonder how many of them have had him inside of them. It's a dangerous road to go down. I avert my eyes.

The door opens and Folsom gets in.

"Are you wooing me?" I ask, waving the note and holding my lips together.

He laughs and looks away. "Is that what it feels like?"

I nod.

"Good," he says quietly then clears his throat.

"Am I embarrassing you, Folsom Donahue?"

"Maybe." He laughs again and I decide it's the best sound I've ever heard. Folsom laughing is my new favorite thing in life.

We're quiet the rest of the drive. He laces his fingers through mine and my heart does a little flutter. I'm midway through trying to shut down my excitement and decide to just go with it. It's one night. I want to enjoy it and go all in.

We drive out of the city, past the wealthier divisions. I watch in fascination as the scenery slowly changes, the buildings losing their slim lines and hard metals and morphing into something squat and colorful. They paint their walls! The artwork is so detailed and stunning that they'd be at home in any museum. I let go of Folsom's hand to turn sideways, my nose pressed against the glass. A girl's face fills an entire wall adjacent to a pharmacy. The colors used to fill her face and hair are jewel-toned. We don't have this color and emotion where I'm from, more's the pity. Sera parks outside the building with the sad girl and we get out.

Folsom holds my hand out and looks me over, smiling at what he sees. "I never know which Gwen I'm going to get," he says. "Each one is more interesting than the last."

"I think you're warming up to me, Folsom Donahue. And it's just Gwen Allison," I say. "No middle name."

I feel his ears lift with his smile and he whispers back: "Folsom Chase…after my dad and uncle."

I nod. "Very distinguished." I back up and laugh at Folsom's expression. "Where are we? You look excited. I didn't know you were capable of it."

He pulls me closer, almost playful. I like this carefree Folsom.

"You've never been?" He motions behind him and it's then I notice the word "SIMS" over a door hidden in the painting. From farther back the door looked like the girl's shirt. How do I tell him I've never been anywhere but my small, privileged corner of the Region?

"I've heard about this place!" I say excitedly. "I didn't know where it was."

"They don't put them where you are," he says, sadly. "Invented for the poor, by the poor."

"So how did a man with his own private jet discover them?"

"When you spend all of your time with the same type of people, seeing the same things, you venture out."

It couldn't be farther from the truth when it comes to me, but I don't say that. I follow him inside, my heart pounding with excitement.

Simulations were started a decade ago, usually in the rougher neighborhoods of larger cities. It's the way the ones who can't afford it live out their dreams. I've always wanted to see what it's like for myself, but I've also wondered if I'd ever want to go back to reality once I started a simulation.

A girl dressed in black nods when we enter and waves a scanner over us. She then hands Folsom a smaller scanner.

"Room four," she says, slipping her earbuds back into place.

We walk through the narrow corridor, the neon graffiti covering the walls lighting the way. It's beautiful and too much at the same time. My eyes hurt with all the color.

When we reach our room, Folsom holds up the scanner and a door slides up from the ground. We step inside and are enveloped in white. It's like the color was sucked dry. In the middle of the room sits a screen. Folsom places his handprint on it and a voice reverberates. "Hello, Folsom. Welcome back."

Folsom types "stupidwoman" on the keyboard and smirks, showing where I should put my hand. I act like I'm going to punch him in the gut and he swerves.

"You're in the system now," he says. "You should go first. Either type what you want and it will show its interpretation of what you write, or put the band on and it'll show exactly what you envision. Go crazy." He grins. "How would your life look if you could have exactly what you wanted? Are you brave enough to show me the truth?"

I don't hesitate. I put on the band and the entire room fills with me driving up to the Governor's Mansion. I walk inside and my mother lovingly greets me at the door.

"Hello, darling," she says and it sounds exactly like her.

I look at Folsom. "This is amazing."

He nods, eyes bright. We both turn and watch the simulated version of me walking down the hallway to the governor's office. The door opens and two large women drag Petite out of the room, bopping her on the head when she starts whining. They escort her off of the premises with her whimpering like a child.

Folsom's shoulders start shaking next to me, his fist going to his mouth to stay quiet. When I walk into the office, Sophia is in a maid's uniform and she curtsies when she sees me, a full tea service tray in her hands.

"Tea, beautiful one?" she asks timidly.

Folsom's roar bounces off the bare walls. I start laughing too, and when I glance at him, he's wiping his eyes.

"Sorry, keep going," he says, still laughing.

A man walks into the office and Folsom goes still. I decide to give him a dose of what it feels like and have the man kiss me on the cheek. Folsom's not laughing now.

"You are the sexiest woman I've ever seen," the man tells me.

"Do you really have to do this while I'm here?" he asks, teeth gritted and his jaw clenching.

I giggle. "Just kidding…now you know how I feel."

He scowls and I make the man disappear. I adjust the picture on the wall that says I'm the governor of the Red Region. And then I'm standing in front of a yellow Victorian with white trim and a wraparound porch that has a swing and rocking chairs by the front door.

"I thought your house would be white," he says. I shoot him a look over my shoulder. "I'll stay out of it now," he adds.

I step inside and the sound of laughter fills the room. A little boy and girl around the same size run into the room and yell over their shoulders, "Hi, Mama! Bye, Mama!" when Folsom comes chasing after them. He catches the boy and throws him over his shoulder, tickling him mercilessly. An older boy comes into the room then with earbuds in and hair hanging over one eye. He smirks at the chaos and gives me a quick hug before getting out of there.

I sigh and realize then that there are tears dripping off my chin.

In the simulation, Folsom puts down the boy when he sees me come into the door and gives me a kiss so scorching, my heart pounds. The real Folsom positions himself behind me, putting his arms around my waist. I can feel his warm breath against my hair and I shiver.

"That's more like it," he says.

"Your turn," I tell him, wiping my face and sniffling.

"Yours is not so different than mine," he says softly. "Watch." He types in "Foley97" and the view changes.

The scene I created melts away and now we're in his. We see a large log cabin in a field of lavender; it looks to be in the country somewhere. When we go inside it's sparse but beautiful, the walls roughly hewn from the logs. The sound of a woman laughing fills the house and Folsom walks right past us. This Folsom is different than the one standing behind me. His hair is long, touching the base of his neck in black waves, and his clothes are casual…untucked. I realize that the woman I heard laughing is me, and I feel such relief that it scares me. I look away from the picture to look at him and see the small smile playing on his lips. He's making this up as he goes along, adding me to his fantasy. I wonder if he's ever done this with another woman and my insides spark like a lightning storm. I grow stiff in his arms, afraid of knowing the truth. But then the scene changes and I'm lying on a bed naked, purple silk tied around my wrists and ankles and attached to the bedpost, spread-eagle. He has me bare, which makes me smile. He zooms in and I'm staring at my own waxed pussy. I turn my face away, embarrassed, and Folsom laughs in my ear.

"It's beautiful," he says. "I've seen thousands, trust me, it's beautiful." His arms get tighter around me as we watch him walk to the bed and run his fingers slowly down my body. He flicks my nipple and lowers his mouth to it, tugging it with his teeth and then licking the sting. The me in the simulation arches her back. My breath quickens as I feel his erection against my back and feel his hands wander down my body. I can't tell what turns me on more, seeing him touch me, or feeling his hands on me in real time; my senses are on overload. My lids lower when in the simulation his fingers reach between my legs. I stare, unable to tear my eyes away, when all of a sudden I feel Folsom's fingers reach underneath my dress. With one arm locked firmly around my waist, he strokes me through my underwear as we watch our simulated selves do the same. I can hardly keep my eyes open. It feels so good.

"Watch," he orders me. He finds the edge of my underwear and slides one finger underneath the lace. I jerk when we're skin to skin. I'm still not used to another human touching that part of me.

I force my eyes open and watch him lick me in the same place his finger is now snaking in and out of. I can feel myself grow tighter around him. "Folsom," I whimper. If he weren't holding me, I don't know that I could stand on my own.

The simulated version of me writhes on the bed, moaning, and I stare, transfixed. I remember when he did that to me on the first day we met. I remember the feel of his wet tongue circling me. I look almost feral in my want for him; I look the way he makes me feel.

"Is that really how you see me?" I ask.

"God, yes," he says, his dick pressing hard against me.

"Show me," I cry out when he slips in another finger, moving in and out, faster, desperate. Three fingers, I pulse around them.

In his vision of us, he unties the silk and moves behind me on the bed, pulling me onto my knees and shifting us so I can watch as he enters me from behind. The view of his cock pushing into me, faster, harder is so intoxicating that I'm drunk with what's happening both in front of me and to me. I've never seen myself from that angle, but I know he has, and I blush at the sight of myself so open and exposed. When his dick slides out it's wet, and when it slides back in, my skin turns pink to take him. It's beautiful, and erotic, and embarrassing all at the same time. The simulated me cries out, head falling back, and I match her…chasing my fall right behind theirs.

TWENTY-FIVE

FOLSOM

She asks to be fed after we leave the SIMS, dancing circles around me in the parking lot. She's wearing a dress and the boots I made her, and she looks like a fairy that can kick serious ass. She's high on life, her orgasm, and she's possibly in love with me. The sight of her makes my heart beat strong and steady. Sera looks on disapprovingly, and as we pass through the parking lot, people just arriving turn to stare. When they take out their Silverbooks to photograph me with Gwen, I grab her hand and move us faster. The fact that I'm out with her in public is going to cause a shitstorm in all twelve Regions. It's not the first time the media has caught me out with a woman; there were others I spent time with, friends. And in the end, it was always the same for them: public humiliation, ridicule, online articles that picked them apart and called them unworthy to be with me. It didn't matter who they were or what they looked like. In the end no one was good enough to spend time with an End Man, especially not the original one. I don't want them to do that to Gwen. I pull her close, and Sera opens the door for us. I practically toss Gwen inside and then we're driving haphazardly through the streets before anyone can follow us.

"What was that about?" Gwen asks.

"We don't need the paparazzi following us, or them getting too many shots of you out there. I should've waited until later to take you out."

"I don't want to be holed up like a prisoner. You should be able to live your life without always looking over your shoulder. So we went somewhere together, big deal."

I bite my tongue; I can try to explain it to her, but she won't understand.

"Are you always this difficult?" I ask her, legitimately wanting to know.

"If difficult means telling the truth, then yes."

It's dark but not too dark to see the storm flash across her face, and I know what she's thinking. Tonight was a step away from reality, hers and mine, but there will be tomorrow, and the next day, and the next, and we can't keep playing house like this without repercussions.

"What are you thinking?" she asks softly.

I shake my head, unwilling to share my thoughts with her. Not yet.

She curls her hands in my shirt and tugs me toward her. We're kissing with me leaning over her body, her back suspended above the seat, held up only by my elbow. With my free hand I press the button that raises the barrier between Sera and us, and then Gwen lowers her body onto the backseat, stretching out beneath me. I settle between her legs and she hooks them around me. Her hands are in my hair, damp with sweat; her chest rises and falls against mine, our breathing labored. I feel the kiss in my center, at the place where I keep my most private feelings. She's rustling around in my weakness and it's painful to let her do it. She reaches down between us and takes my dick in her hand, and as she does, she breaks free of our kiss and rolls her head from side to side, moaning, her eyes closed. I should be in on the moaning, I think. When she strokes, I throw my head back, my eyes rolling with pleasure, my dick thick in her hand. I'm pressed between her legs and when she lets me go, my dick drops and rubs against her wet panties; wet from before, wet from now—I don't know. I let her feel the full length of me as I pump back and forth across her clit. I let her know I want inside. She reaches down and yanks her panties to the side and now I'm rubbing against wet, bare skin as she shakes and cries out. Her noises are throaty, she doesn't try to muffle them as she calls, "I'm going to come," over and over. I want to sink inside of her, bury myself all the way to the hilt. My hand presses against the window above our heads, the glass cold against my sweaty palm. I can see the rosy glare of the streetlights as we drive.

"Please, please put it in…"

I glance out the window and lean my forehead against hers, still pumping against her. "We're almost there."

"Please…just once…"

I slide into her all the way and her legs stretch wide to take me. And then abruptly I pull out. Shuddering, I come on her stomach, sticky white against her olive skin. I clean her up and we kiss until we feel the car stop. I pull myself off of her and try to straighten our clothes, knocking heads and elbows as we do. When the door opens we fall out of the car laughing, and that's when the lights start flashing.

We run for the restaurant, her hand in mine. The buzz of excitement I felt in the car is gone, replaced with dread. I'd made reservations and the owner had assured me I'd receive the privacy I requested, but somehow things like this always leak. We are ushered through the doors while the press is forced to stay outside. We're shaken, but we have to gather ourselves quickly as we're being ushered to the table.

"Apologies," the owner says. He's a stocky man with stains underneath his armpits, no doubt from the stress of arranging five reporters outside. I stare at him but say nothing. I have no doubt he told them we'd be here. Good publicity.

"Where would you like to eat tonight?" he asks quickly, catching my look. He shifts nervously and I have the urge to send my fist straight into his face. "We have a lovely Riviera, and there's a charming bayou setting…"

Gwen gently places a hand on my arm and I'm jarred back to reality. We're here, and she is hungry. I shake off my anger and smile down at her.

"I sent it ahead," I tell him. A moment of confusion clouds his face and then he runs off to check. In the meantime, we are seated in the center of a white room, much like the SIMS room we just left. Seated across from each other I am given a view of Gwen's face, her messier than usual hair. I smile lopsidedly; she catches me and I squeeze my eyes shut because I know what she's going to ask.

"What? Why are you looking at me like that?"

"You're very pretty, Gwen. And your hair is crazy like you've been rolling around in the backseat of a car. And we smell like sex."

She opens her mouth to say something, but the lights dim and flicker, and for a few seconds we're left in darkness, and then we're not.

When they turn back on we're in a garden. The air is crisp and scented with the smell of cut grass and wet dirt. When I look up, wisteria hangs overhead and the scent of jasmine is cloying in the air. To our right is a white colonial with a wraparound porch and a bright blue door. It's sunset and crickets are singing from somewhere nearby. Gwen's head is straining around to see everything.

"Where is this?" Gwen asks, turning to me.

"It's my childhood home."

Her mouth makes a little "O" and she looks back toward the house, studying with a different set of eyes. Through the back window I can see the silhouette of a woman washing dishes at the sink: my mother.

"Is she—?

I nod.

"You wanted to show me…"

"I did."

"I didn't want to ask, but I wanted to know." She looks down at her stomach even though there's nothing to see. "For later…to tell him."

"Her name was Greer. She was named after her mother who had lavender hair…" I point to the wisteria above us. "She loved wisteria because it reminded her of my grandmother."

Loved. The odd thing of referring to your mother in past tense. I can still hear her laugh, feel the powdery softness of the skin on her arms. The wind blows and even though it's a simulation it feels real. The leaves of a nearby tree rattle, and Gwen's hair moves around her face like it has a life of its own. A server appears with two glasses of purple lemonade and a basket of rolls, placing it down between us.

"Your mother used to make these?" she asks, taking one from the basket.

"Yes. And this is Marionberry lemonade." I nod at the drinks. "She was a good cook. But the day my father and brother died she stopped. It was just the two of us then."

"What was she like?"

I don't have to pause here because I know what my mother was like; I've turned her over in my mind so often that even my memories looked frayed and worn. "She was simple. Good. She didn't ask for much. She put jam on everything: pizza crust, cereal, eggs…she salted her apples and wore socks to bed, even in the summer. We made fun of her for that. Sometimes my brother and I would sneak into their room in the middle of the night and pull her socks off while she slept."

Gwen laughs.

"Did she know it was you doing that?"

"She figured it out. She didn't say anything, but on the mornings she found herself without socks, she'd make liver and onions for breakfast. We hated liver and onions. We got the message loud and clear."

"She sounds fun. Tell me something else."

I search my memories for something else to tell Gwen. It feels good to talk about her.

"When she cleaned the house, she played Janis Joplin as loud as she could. If we didn't help, she'd chase us with a spray bottle of cleaning solution and squirt us with it. When my brother and father died, all of that stopped. She withered away like it was her fault."

"When did she die?" Gwen asks, and then she immediately places a hand over her mouth, embarrassed. "I'm sorry. I shouldn't have asked that."

"It's okay. She died about a year before I joined the End Men. Thank God for that."

"She'd be proud of you," Gwen says, shaking her head. "You're doing something for the good of everyone. You're a good man, Folsom."

I doubt my soft-spoken mother would be proud of her son being a prostitute for the government, but I smile gratefully at the woman who thinks so.

The secret to survival is to stay hard and focused, hard enough that the vastness of emptiness cannot live inside you. My life is a straightjacket, and if you don't want anything to hold power over you, including the straightjacket, you pretend you aren't wearing one. But, as I sit across from this woman, I feel it: every constraint, the painful tug of my conscience both toward her and the Regions. Before Gwen I did what I needed to do, I survived. But now I'm not so sure what that means. Our server returns with the main courses. The smells fill me with nostalgia, and for the time being I'm too distracted to think more about my mother. Gwen tries each dish, remarking about the tastes with enthusiasm. I'm happy in a way I've never been. Content to share this with her. That's how I know it won't last.

TWENTY-SIX

GWEN

I'm ready to get back to work. The days waiting for Folsom to get back from fucking everyone in town are too long and heartbreaking. It's best if I stay busy. God, the way he makes me feel. I can't stop thinking about last night. My hand flies to my neck, the heat alive in my cheeks.

Hamari is looking out the window when I arrive and does a little hop when she sees me. I hope she's just excited I'm back. I never know what her exuberance is going to mean for my day; it can be anything from the latest Genome Y gossip or that she has an extra stack of work that she wants me to delegate to someone else.

She claps her hands when I step inside and nearly barrels me over with a hug.

"I'm so glad you're back," she says. "Why do you hate me so much?" The words rush out, her laugh contradicting what she's saying. "You didn't tell me you were *in a relationship* with Folsom. That picture of you kissing..." She fans her face. "Oh my God. The two of you are so hot together—I can't even be mad at you for stealing him right out from under me. I can see now why you were saying all of those things on the Silverbook...I wouldn't want to sha—"

I hold up my hand. "There's a picture of us kissing?"

"Your hair looked so good," she gushes. "Out of control, but in a *good* way…how do you *do* that?"

I hold onto the counter and breathe. This won't go over well. "Thanks for letting me know. I need to get to work."

I head to my office quickly, glad that I got here earlier than most. I open the Silverbook and there we are, front and center. It's a picture of us through the back window of the car lost in a kiss that looks as passionate as it felt. The theories are swarming in rapid-fire. We're in love. We're conspiring against the Society together. I'm trying to steal Folsom from the End Men. I'm a man disguised as a woman and working for the Society myself...

I have to swipe it off before I lose a day reading it all. I work on some of the lab reports that have piled up and don't leave my desk until well into the afternoon. Hamari pokes her head in and hurries to the desk, setting down a thick file.

"Don't ask me where I got this. I knew you'd want to see it." She leaves the room quickly.

I flip through it, my outrage building with each document. I'm shaking by the time I make my way to dome five.

Laticus isn't in his room; Corinne, however, is outside his door when I come out, and she stalks toward me.

"We need to talk," she says, backing me into Laticus' room. She shuts the door behind us and folds her arms across her chest. "You wanna tell me what's going on with you and Donahue?"

"Not really," I respond.

"Well, here's the problem with that…we have a reputation to uphold at Genome Y and you have always exemplified the highest standards we require. But this…this is unacceptable. We work hand-in-hand with the Red Regional office *and* the Society. If they see our most trusted employee canoodling with an End Man—is it true you're living together?" She shakes her head. "You know what, don't answer that. You have to end it. Today. If you don't, the next conversation between you and me won't be this civilized."

I nod and move closer to her. "There's quite the pile of labs on my desk, as well as all the reports you weren't able to finish without me here…I'm sure you'll be able to find someone else with my qualifications who will be willing to put in the same kind of time I have, though. Right?" It takes everything in me to keep my tone low and balanced.

She purses her lips. "Are you being insolent with me, Gwen? What is this?"

I shake my head. "I'm all about telling the truth these days. Don't let Folsom hear you calling me insolent. He'll start trying it out on me." I walk toward the door. "Where is Laticus? I see that he's been tripling up on the sperm samples, some days even more than that? All under your advisement." I wave the file. "And did you notice that his sperm count has been lower the past two days?" I narrow my eyes at her. "You know you've gone against all kinds of protocol, Corinne."

She looks flustered. I've never loved my boss—we get along well enough, and until now I've always respected her, but the second I realized she didn't protect Laticus while I was gone, it was over.

"Give the boy a break." I leave all the threats unsaid. She knows the damage I can do. I open the office and leave her standing in Laticus' room.

I walk around the entire complex and even the places I've taken him outside—he's nowhere to be found. I start to get alarmed but quickly rationalize that I would know by now if something had happened. Hamari would tell me even if no one else did…if she was aware of it. I do another loop around and message Folsom, not bothering to worry if I'm interrupting an appointment or not. I tuck the files I can work on later under my arm to take with me, something I do at least once a week. I back my car out of the sparse parking lot. I haven't seen it this empty in months. Something must be going on in the city. There are picketers outside the gate this time, most of them threatening to shut down the lab, and a handful of posters with the picture from last night.

I speed to the compound, realizing halfway there that I'm being followed. I take a handful of wrong turns and go faster, losing them before I reach the gate. I'm out of breath when I walk in the door, the stress of the day catching up with me.

"Hello?" I call out.

Complete silence.

I take a shower and when Folsom still hasn't gotten back after I'm out and still no word from him, I venture into the other parts of the compound. Folsom needs to know what they've been doing to Laticus. Tears are just under the surface. I've got to pull it together before I talk to him...

Krystal is the only one I find. She's working on a red dress, hands around the mannequin's neck and sewing a small stitch to the neckline.

"Have you seen Folsom?" I ask.

"There you are! I'm just finishing your dress," she says, eyes focused on her stitches. She makes a knot with the thread and pulls it off. "There." She backs up. "What do you think?"

"It's beautiful on her."

She smiles. "Try it on and let's see if it works. You're already late for the party."

"I hadn't planned on any parties tonight," I tell her.

"Oh, but you have to." All humor leaves her face and she looks at me, eyes hard. "Don't fuck this up, Gwen. Folsom was just fine before you entered the picture, and he will forget you the minute we're in the next Region. Tonight you're going to the party and you're going to pretend Folsom doesn't exist. Be seen alone, like the pathetic excuse for a person you've always been."

Her features smooth out and she smiles again like she didn't just say the awful things she said. "That was a message from the Society. Sera will be here for you in fifteen minutes."

I take the dress she's now holding out and back away, turning around when I stumble. I get ready in a daze, Krystal's words on replay in my mind. I don't really know if I look decent or like the chaos in my chest, but I numbly walk outside when I see Sera pull up. We're at the venue in minutes, the historic concert hall decorated with twinkle lights for the party.

Very little fuss is made when I arrive. Most are inside. I realize why as soon as I enter the room. Women are swarming the center of the room, humming like a live wire. I walk toward the crowd and at the first opening I see him standing still, like a specimen under the glass... Laticus.

I push my way in, and when I'm finally in front of him, I reach out to touch his arm and other hands reach out to grab him, shoving me out of the way. He looks terrified.

"Laticus," I call out. His eyes search for me in the crowd. I press forward. "Laticus, over here."

A strong grip pulls me back and I turn around, ready to fight. My mother stands there, a strange smile fixed on her face. "Hi, sweetheart. You look flustered. Have you eaten anything?" She puts an arm around me and walks me away from Laticus.

"Let me go, Mother. I need to check on him. Do you see how scared he looks?"

"You're entirely too close to the situation, Gwen," she says in my ear. "Step away and have a bite to eat. You don't need to stress the baby."

I stare at her, trying to figure out why she looks so different tonight. I blink and look around the room. "Where is Folsom? He's here, right?"

"He's with a lottery winner right now, if you must know," she says. "A very beautiful one."

My mouth falls open and the tears instantly prick my eyes. "Why are you being like this?"

She gives a slight shake of her head. "Someone has to save you from yourself, darling. It looks like it's up to me."

I look around the room desperately, looking for my escape. Langley and Petite stand in the corner, watching my mother and me. My heart picks up its pace. I back away from her.

"What's going on, Mother? Are you mixed up in something you shouldn't be? I don't trust Pandora," I say between my clenched teeth. "And Laticus, they're trying to…"

She clamps her hand over my mouth. "There are ears everywhere. Stop. Talking."

Tears run down my cheeks. She drops her hand and dabs my tears with her lace-edged hankie. My mom has pretty linens for every occasion. She tucks it away in her pocket and looks at me with a concerned smile. I'm so confused.

"You need to leave," she says.

I shake my head. "I need to talk to Laticus and I want to see Folsom. I'm not leaving until I see him."

She frowns. "You have to—"

"Attention, everyone," Petite says in a microphone. "This is such a special night. We have Laticus Donahue in our midst, his first night at a party, and he's with us, the Red Region! We are so honored, Laticus," she says, beaming at him. "And we have a surprise for all of you here…step up, ladies…" Three young girls move next to her, one of them being Charity, who is in the most elaborate dress of the room. All of them smile proudly.

My heart sinks.

"Let's give a round of applause to our handsome, young Laticus. He has already successfully impregnated not one, not two, but *three* Red Regionals."

The crowd goes crazy, cheering, clanging glasses together. No one looks more surprised than Laticus. He meets my gaze across the room and his shoulders sag for a moment.

If the inseminations are working again and they've already started using his sperm to impregnate the young ones, it's only a matter of time before they send him out…with or without Folsom's consent. It's a well-documented fact that there's a higher success rate with the one-on-ones, and the Society—and the Regions—won't want to lose all the funding they get from the parties. The inseminations will help, but they won't put an end to all this hoopla. I jerk away from my mother and run out of the hall. I start opening doors…it's all offices and conference rooms. I have to find Folsom. I'll deal with the awkwardness of what I might see when I get there. He has to know what they're doing with Laticus. When the Black Region gets word of this, all hell will break loose. I hear steps scuffling behind me and turn around. Langley stands facing me, just the two of us in the room. She has something in her hand, but I'm too far to make out what it is. The look on her face terrifies me, though. She drops whatever it is and smoke billows around her.

"Fire," she yells, glancing over her shoulder. "FIRE!"

I stare at her, bewildered, and she drops something else before taking off toward the auditorium. Flames quickly engulf the space between the two of us.

"Fire," she yells into the room, turning once more to look at me, a smile on her face. "Security!"

I can hear screams in the main auditorium from where I'm standing. I run away from the fire, even though everything in me wants to run toward where I saw Laticus. I have to trust that the Region officials will see to him. For now, I have to protect my baby.

TWENTY-SEVEN

FOLSOM

I've been in a dark room most of the day, an IV in my arm, hopped up on whatever stimulant keeps me hard for days. It's been years since they've done this to me. I've learned to be cooperative. The last punishment was three days.

The effects of the drugs are erotic and torturous all rolled into one. They stimulate my brain to make me think I'm having sex, but I'm connected to a machine, my semen being harvested into little glass vials. My heart beats angrily in my chest, overworked by the drug. They'll use what they take to artificially inseminate women who are willing to pay for this second-rate service. It is considered a less prestigious route to pregnancy; the poor can afford it. My eyes are covered and my mouth is gagged. I hurt all over, and I'm hoarse from yelling at the guards, but my cock is working independently from my brain. In the early years, the men were given a choice: be harvested or fuck the way nature intended. They promised us every luxury, a life of extravagance. It was an easy choice. Our presence in society boosted morale, replaced panic with hope. The women had us as a solution to the problem, which stilled their panic. So the Society paraded us around, sold us in exchange for compliance and peace. Our compliance was not given any thought. We were the property of the Regions.

What would my mother say…my father?

The shame is a second skin. I don't know where it ends and where I begin; I've been wearing it so long. Gwen. I can't stand to think of her right now, when moans are grinding into my flesh like little pinpricks, but she's all I see. Her pink pussy taking in my cock inch by inch. I groan and pump harder. If I can come quickly, maybe it will be over. My head rolls side to side. God, please. I hope the sperm are alive today.

TWENTY-EIGHT

GWEN

I'm coughing by the time I reach Sera. She looks relieved to see me.

"Hurry!" I choke out.

She speeds out of the parking lot, leaving the mayhem in the dust. The compound is quiet when she parks, and I walk briskly through the courtyard. A wind blows as I pass the fountain and I feel the fine mist kiss my face. I walk through each of the rooms looking for Folsom, calling his name and already knowing he isn't here. And after searching most of the hall, I'm not sure he was there either. Hours pass and I stand in the upstairs window, watching the gate, one hand clutched around my belly, as if I'm trying to shield my baby from all of this. He hasn't responded to any of my messages. Something is wrong.

Around one in the morning, when he still hasn't come back, I find my Silverbook and start typing. By six, hundreds of people have responded and the outcry of a missing Folsom is growing with each minute. At eight, two police officers come for me, saying I have to go to the station. Sera, Robin, and Krystal stand in a cozy group, watching me go. They look relieved.

"Do you know where Folsom Donahue is?" I ask the officers repeatedly.

One of the officers finally speaks up when we pull up to an abandoned building. "This does not concern Mr. Donahue. Worry about yourself."

"This isn't the station. Where are you taking me?" I'm dragged into the dark building and taken to a sparse room that has a table, one chair, and a couch, and I'm left there to wait and wait and wait. I bang on the door to tell them I'm hungry and a guard gives me a banana muffin and sunflower seeds, which does nothing to abate the hunger. When the door is finally unlocked, my mother and Pandora walk in.

"Mother," I say, standing up, relieved. "Why am I being held in here?"

She looks at me sadly and I feel the panic build.

"I never dreamed you'd do such a thing," she says. "I don't even know what to say."

"What—what have I done?" I put my hand on her arm and she pulls away, moving closer to Pandora.

"We have a witness that says you started the fire at the hall last night," Pandora says.

"No! It was Langley!" I yell. "I *saw* her do it."

Pandora shakes her head. "Langley was with me all evening. I can testify to that when the time comes."

I stare at her, wide-eyed. "You're lying. Mother, she's lying. You know I wouldn't do something like this!"

"This…man—he's changed you, Gwen. I feel like I don't know you anymore." Her eyes are ablaze. She doesn't look like my mother. I glance at Pandora who stands back, a self-satisfied smile on her face. "You've become a zealot who is going against everything I've raised you to believe," my mother says. "I can't stand by and watch you become this person." She moves to the door and knocks twice.

"Don't leave me in here, not with her!" I plead with her. "I want a lawyer…"

The door opens and she walks out. I'm left alone with the governor.

"I have the right to a lawyer," I repeat. My heart is throbbing in my throat. I choke down my panic.

"No need for drama, you haven't been arrested. Yet. Here's what will happen," she says, leaning against the wall with her feet crossed. "I've managed to talk the police into letting you stay at the mansion while they conduct their investigation. It's an unfortunate thing, Gwen, that you can't be trusted with that precious, precious gift you've been given." She glances at my stomach, and my skin crawls. She scratches her hand and flakes of skin rain down like confetti. "But the second you start causing trouble again, charges of arson will be filed against you."

I slam my fist on the table. "Someone else started that fire. Don't you want to find the person who really did it?"

"Everyone thinks *you* set the fire in that ridiculous show of jealousy." She tsks at me. My cheeks burn and I fist my hands under the table. "Honestly, Gwen," she shakes her head, "—with your little schoolgirl crush. It's pathetic."

I want to jump to my feet and slap her in the face, but I know they're watching me. She doesn't know what she's talking about. I'm about to tell her so when she narrows her eyes, a cruel smile on her lips.

"Do you think that he loves you? He's an End Man. It's his job to charm women. You're no different than the rest of the little whores he fucks. That's what your measly followers will believe after word spreads about what you did…you're nobody." She taps on the door. "You're free to go and collect some of your things. You'll be expected at the mansion by this afternoon at two. If we have to come looking for you, you'll be arrested."

One of the officers drives me back, not saying a word during the drive. When we reach the compound, I walk into the bedroom I've shared with Folsom. I check the Silverbook and feel sick that he still hasn't responded. I write a note explaining that I'm being forced to stay at Pandora's and wish I could trust that he'll get the message.

I don't bother going online to see what's going on because I know the propaganda against me has probably already started. I'm beginning to see how it all operates. I wish I hadn't been so blind before now. How long has my mom been this deceived? Krystal and Sera and several of the others are watching as I take my things to the car. No one offers to help. No one says a word. Any generosity exhibited to me during my stay was contingent on Folsom being around. Without him, I am—as Pandora so kindly put it—nobody.

A couple of hours before I'm due at the house, I drive out to Genome Y and am denied entrance.

"I work here," I say to the guard. "You know me."

She shakes her head, but not unkindly. "I'm afraid you don't work here anymore. I can't grant you access without clearance."

Maybe they think stripping me of everything will shut me up. Maybe that would've worked on me a long time ago, but that girl is gone. My mom might have spoken the truth—I have changed. But it has nothing to do with a man and everything to do with fighting for what is right. I find a printing shop and make copies of the files I brought home from the lab yesterday and put the copies in a safe deposit box. After that, I drive straight to Governor Petite's mansion and submit myself. It goes against everything inside me to cave to Petite's demands, but I can't be any help to Folsom if I'm in jail. And I'm convinced more than ever that he needs me.

I'm escorted into the house, and a small group stands in the foyer, presumably to make sure I won't do a runner. When my mother sees me, she looks at me resignedly and backs out of the room. Governor Petite and Langley stand to my right, both smug. My eyes narrow on them and I hold myself as tall as I can. Why is Langley here? None of this feels right.

Sophia is given the task of leading me to my room. Always ready to play the big sister role. I remember following her when we were little girls, playing school and store and doctor and lawyer. Two years younger, I was the one who came up with the ideas, and she always played the most important role. I never minded so long as she was playing with me. I wanted to please her, but my very existence was an underlying aggravation for her. I learned early on that I would never be able to do things quite right for her, and eventually that need to please eased into independence. It seemed to annoy her further when we were in middle school and I no longer trailed behind, wanting her attention. By the time I went to high school, I stayed out of her way, and we've maintained a shaky peace for the past decade. That seems to be over. She's blatant with her disdain today. I'm kind of glad to finally have it out in the open.

"You've embarrassed this family. Keep your head down, Gwen."

"Which family?" I jump in. "Pandora's or ours? Because it seems to me a lot of things have changed lately, including you and Mother."

"You're the one who's changed," she shoots back. "It's like you care about those men more than the rest of us. The rest of *everyone,*" she emphasizes. "Don't forget, Gwen, that these men you love so much are the ones responsible for this mess we're in. They had control of this world for thousands of years and they didn't do anything but take from us, use us, and suppress us. 'The age of women,' as you call it, is finally here. And most of us couldn't be happier about it."

"You can't hold twelve men responsible for an entire gender, Sophia." Our faces are close now, our eyes trying to kill each other, though our bodies remain composed.

"We are. All twelve Regions and the rest of the world. They will give back what they took from us. Every single one of them, your precious Folsom included."

"What about my son? Your nephew?" I place a hand on my stomach to emphasize my point.

"You know this is the way it is. When the time comes, he will pay the price of being born a man." She begins to walk to the door. "Don't worry," she says. "I hear they're compensated quite nicely. Laticus has chosen black for his jet, just like his father's."

I stare at her, keeping the expression from my face. I don't want her to know how much I care. They'll use it against me.

"He will be taking over his father's appointments, by the way. Since Folsom is non-compliant, they've had to strap him to that harvesting machine."

I'm shaken. I feel like I need to sit, but I can't move my feet. All I can hear are Sophia's cruel words, meant to hurt me.

I stare around the room I'm to be a prisoner in, not really seeing anything. My mind is filled with Folsom. The machines, I've heard of the machines. They were experimental, used in the early days to check the remaining males for live sperm. They were deemed inhumane by all twelve Regions. I can't bear to think of him strapped to one of those.

"Why do you hate me?" It's meant as an honest question. Sophia stops, her hand on the door. I don't expect her to answer me, but then she does and her answer gives me chills.

"Because everything comes so easily to you. It's just not fair."

The door clicks closed and I'm left in my prison. Me and my son.

TWENTY-NINE

GWEN

During the next three months my son saves my life. A tiny unborn savior. I eat because of him, I sleep because of him, I do not throw myself from the roof of the mansion because of him. My stomach has swollen to a small round bump, evidence that the last five months have not been a dream. The torment of not knowing where Folsom is, or if he's okay, is almost too much to bear. I check the daily news reports for word of him, but they've restricted my Internet use so that I'm only able to view without commenting. Pandora wants me to see what people are saying about me after the fire. And some have said I'm guilty, they've called me all manner of names, and have accused me of being obsessed with Folsom to the point of endangering my baby. But, there are others, others who suspect the Society and the President have framed me. Websites have popped up, blogs, where people are still talking about both me and the End Men, calling for change. Sometimes at dinner I catch Pandora staring at me, a thoughtful expression on her face, like she's trying to figure out how to handle me. They thought that if they made me disappear, the uprising would disappear with me, but it has not.

I am treated as a prisoner, watched all hours of the day and night, if not by my sister and mother then by Langley, who clings to the walls of the Governor's Mansion like a house fly. I overhear my mother and Pandora talking about her as I pass the living room one evening, their voices thick from the wine they drank during dinner. Three glasses each by my count. Langley's night with Folsom did not end in a pregnancy. Pandora recounts this to my mother with sadness in her voice and I don't know if it's real; she is whoever she's expected to be. I feel sick when my mother tuts her sympathy. Langley is a snake; a baby increases her social standing. My relief that she's not carrying Folsom's baby whooshes out of me, and I shove a hand over my mouth, afraid they've heard. I've wondered at Pandora's attachment to Langley for a long time.

"She could try again," my mother says. "Now that they have a supply from him. The doctors might be more successful…"

Pandora doesn't say anything. I imagine her nodding, taking a sip of her drink thoughtfully. My back pressed against the wall, knees bending, I clutch at my chest squeezing my eyes closed. If I knew where they had him…

What? I ask myself. *What could you do?*

It's then that I remember the night in my bedroom; a stranger sitting on a chair at the foot of my bed. My mouth opens and I find myself nodding like someone has just suggested something to me. Kasper. The button. After the scare with the baby and then playing house with Folsom, I didn't remember to give it to him, and I was so shaken the day I had to come to the mansion, I didn't think about it then either. How could I forget? I'd left it among my things at the house. In a drawer or…under the mattress? It feels like a lifetime ago that he placed it in my palm. If I pressed it, would Kasper come? Would they do the same thing to him if he was caught helping Folsom? Pressing it would no doubt put him at risk. I have to be entirely sure it's something I'm willing to do.

The next day over breakfast I ask my sister to accompany me to our childhood home to pick up some odds and ends.

"Why? You can send someone to get what you need, or you can order it new." She's eating her usual breakfast of grapes and yogurt smothered in honey, her face resting on her hand. She's never been a morning person and this ritual of fruit and sourness is something she's done since she was a child. It takes me back to those early days when we were still friends.

"I miss home," I say. "Besides, I don't want people rifling through my things, you know how people steal..." This is a sore spot for Sophia, who complains to my mother every week about her things mysteriously going missing. I know I've hit the jackpot when her eyes light up.

"All right," she says slowly. "I guess I could grab some things too." I smile at her as sweetly as I can, my cheeks aching from the effort. We leave with one of the governor's escorts around noon. The air is humid, clinging. I fall into the backseat already needing a nap. That is what pregnancy is: napping, and eating, and throwing up. The house is a ten-minute drive from the Governor's Mansion; I open my window so the air can blow on my face. For the first five minutes, neither Sophia nor I say a word to each other, both staring out of our respective windows.

"I heard that Langley didn't get pregnant."

Her head swivels around to look at me, and then she slowly looks away.

"You heard right."

"She must be pissed that you're pregnant and she's not." I look over at her this time and find her looking down at her stomach. She is carrying smaller than I am, probably due to the fact that she hardly eats. She stares at it like she's never seen it before—an alien attached to her waist—and then reluctantly she shakes her head.

"She isn't happy about it," Sophia says. "She tried with Jackal too…a few years ago." She chews on her lip like she's said too much. I nod sympathetically.

"She's not been as lucky as us. It's no wonder she's hanging around you all the time."

Sophia shakes her head. "That's not the reason Langley is always there."

"No?"

"She's to be Pandora's chief administrator."

Well, there you go, just a little bit of poking and I got my answer.

I look at Sophia in alarm. "What happened to Damaris? She's served with Pandora both terms." I can't believe I haven't even thought of her until now. Timid and unassuming, Damaris is always tucked behind Pandora like an extra appendage. Except I can't remember the last time I saw her.

Sophia shrugs. "She got pregnant this season right behind us and didn't want to continue working. She transferred to the Green Region."

Another Folsom baby. I put my hand on my stomach and Sophia's eyes follow.

"That's really strange, don't you think?"

Each season with an End Man, all the successful lottery pregnancies move out of the Region and we get an influx of the other Regions' lottery pregnancies in an effort to prevent incest. It's rare for anyone in a powerful position to move out of a Region, though, especially while pregnant. The Region wants to hold onto all the babies.

"It's what he does, Gwen. You know that," she snaps, done with this conversation.

"That's not what I meant…" I shake my head and try to not outwardly shudder in front of her.

It's hard to think of Folsom having sex with beautiful women—any women, really—but Damaris…it's really hard to imagine him having sex with a woman who never looks quite clean and has long hairs hanging out of her moles. I cringe at my naiveté—I thought the men were just sex machines who were constantly turned on by the act of sex itself, no matter what the women were like. I remember my shock about the pills—the thought that they relied on pills had never crossed my mind. Hot and ready. That's how I perceived the End Men. But that's how we were taught to perceive men—the reason we are in this mess in the first place. For thousands of years, we were held beneath their thumbs and now we're liberated from them, while also desperately needing them. So stupid.

I put it out of my mind. I can't go down that train of thought today. Thoughts of Folsom and what he's going through, how much I miss him, and humdrum thoughts about one useless topic after the next have derailed me for entire weeks at a time. My brain has been mush while I've been locked away. It's time I pull out of this stupor. I can't afford to waste any more time.

We pull into the long driveway, and just seeing our house ahead makes me feel more alive than I have in months. Phoebe answers the door and pulls me into a hug.

"I've missed you," I tell her.

She holds my face in her hands and studies me like she's checking to see how bruised my insides are.

"You look well," she finally says. "I needed to see for myself. They're saying all kinds of things, you know…" She cuts off when Sophia clears her throat.

The three of us go upstairs and they follow me to my room.

"I'm not going anywhere," I tell them. "Where would I go? Can't I have even a minute to myself?"

"I promised I'd not take my eyes off of you," Sophia says.

My closet is inside of my bathroom. I pull a bag off a shelf and begin shoving things inside. Half of what I take wouldn't fit anymore, but I'm not here for clothes. I pull several bras out and set it all in the bag. I move to the cosmetics and go so slowly that Sophia's sighs get louder and louder. She plops down on the bed.

"Hurry up. God, you're taking forever."

"Feel free to go do something else," I call over my shoulder.

She scowls, and to my shock, eventually stands up and moves to the door. She's still wearing skintight dresses and from behind you can't even tell she's pregnant.

"We're leaving in four minutes. I'm going to my bedroom for some shoes. If you do anything that gets me in trouble, I'll make you suffer."

I roll my eyes at her and turn back to the drawers.

The minute she's out of the room I move to the mattress. My hand stretches so far under without feeling it that I begin to fear it's been taken. Suddenly, my fingers touch the metal. I close my eyes for a second and instantly breathe easier. Tucking it under my shirt, I turn to Phoebe.

"They're keeping me prisoner. I'm under constant surveillance, day and night."

Her mouth drops open and she grasps my arm. "What can I do?"

"Tell the people who are with me that I'm being held against my will. Tell them Folsom is being harvested. Demand that I'm—" I hear Sophia at the door and pull away, holding up my bag. "Just a couple more things from the bathroom and I'll be ready," I tell her.

Phoebe hovers next to me, but I'm not able to say anything else. Sophia looks at us suspiciously but doesn't speak either. We're pulling out of there a few minutes later, and I try to enjoy the moment of freedom. I feel a small hope that hasn't been there since Folsom went missing.

THIRTY

GWEN

A few mornings later, the sound of glass breaking wakes me up. I sit up and don't see anything out of place, but there's commotion in the library across the hall. Another shatter makes me jump and my mother comes through my door to make sure I'm okay.

"What's going on?" I ask her, following her into the library. A window is broken, and a maid scurries into the room to clean up the shards of glass.

My mother doesn't answer. She's mostly stopped speaking to me; other than the customary "how are you?" and "did you sleep okay?" we aren't diving into any real conversation. I walk to the next set of windows and see protestors lined against the gate, holding their signs high. The driveway isn't as long as ours at home, so I can read most of the signs clearly.

Some are chanting, "Free Gwen, free Gwen, free Gwen!"

My mother grabs my arm and leads me back to my room. "Stay away from the window—you could get hurt!"

"I'd rather be pelted with a rock than be a prisoner in this house one more day," I respond.

"You know you're not a prisoner here, Gwen…"

I turn and face her, hands on my hips. "Oh, I'm free to go then? Great, I'm leaving today."

"When that baby is safely delivered, you can move out." She smooths her hand down her skirt.

"I used to think you were doing all of this to give me the baby I'd always wanted…maybe even that you were with Pandora because of it…but I'm not so sure it hasn't always been on your agenda to be exactly where you are right now. Maybe I was simply the pawn that helped you put the pieces in place. Sophia would've been glad to get you here, though. Never mind, I still don't understand."

Her lips press together and she shakes her head, moving toward the door. "Nonsense. Pandora mentioned it last night and I think it will be good for you: tonight we'll go somewhere, get you out of the house for a little bit."

"If I say no?" I'm merely testing her for sport at this point. Of course I'll go anywhere just to be outside these four walls.

"You won't," she says, shutting the door behind her. She leans back in. "Oh, and your doctor's appointment is in an hour. You should eat something before she gets here."

Each appointment I've seen a different doctor, mostly doctors I've never met, but occasionally one I've seen through Genome Y, so I'm caught off guard when I walk into the living room and Doctor Hunley is admiring a piece of artwork with Pandora and my mother. She says hello but barely acknowledges me other than that. They talk about the colors a few more minutes and then she turns to me.

"We better get started. I'm afraid I don't have a lot of time. I have another house visit after this," she says with a smile. "Was the machine delivered?"

"It's been taken to Gwen's room," my mother says.

"Excellent. Lead the way, Gwen." Doctor Hunley motions me forward.

I take her to my room and am about to close the door when my mother steps forward to come in too. Doctor Hunley holds up her hand.

"I'll have you step in when I'm ready for the ultrasound." She says it with such authority that my mom backs up and nods.

Once the door is closed, Doctor Hunley takes my hand. "We don't have much time. I have a plan. How are you really?" she asks urgently.

"Sick with worry," I whisper. "Have you heard anything?"

"Get undressed and follow my lead. Okay?"

I quickly undress and slip on the gown she hands me while she keeps talking under her breath.

"I've heard a few things. Just this week, one of my colleagues flew in from Canada and I think if anyone knows, it would be her. I'll arrange a meeting with her. The Regions are fighting back, Gwen. Someone posted about you being kept here against your will and everyone is talking about it. A few of the vigilantes from the Black and Red Regions are talking about breaking you and Laticus out, if something doesn't change quickly. If Governor Petite knows what's good for her, she will release you. Or risk being overthrown." She grimaces. "She's not doing it fast enough for my liking."

I stare at her and hurry to lie down where she's tapping on the bed. My hands tremble as I pull the covers.

"Okay, we're ready," she calls out to my mother.

She gives me one more glance and pats my hand reassuringly before my mother steps in.

Mother stands where she can watch the screen along with me. Doctor Hunley turns the machine on and makes sure her tools are in order. Once she's ready, she looks at us and pulls the plastic gloves higher on her arm.

"You'd think technology would've advanced beyond this cold liquid…brace yourself," Doctor Hunley says, getting the wand in place.

As soon as the baby fills the screen, she starts taking pictures and logging things into her Silverbook. I stare at the baby and listen to the sound of our heartbeats. This will never get old.

"Hmm…this is…troubling." She frowns. "Are all your dates accurate?" She points to the screen and I nod, swallowing. Her concern is scaring me. I can't tell if she's pretending or if something really is wrong.

"The baby is not measuring what he should be for how far along you are, and I don't want to alarm you, but we need to do some tests right away," she says. She looks at my mother. "Can you make sure she comes in to see me this week?"

"Surely that's not necessary!" My mom looks at the screen. "Does the baby look healthy? Why does it matter if the measurements aren't quite matching up?"

Doctor Hunley shoots her a sharp look. "It could mean the baby has some health defects or that Gwen's not getting the nourishment she should be getting." She shakes her head. "You know what, no later than the day after tomorrow." She looks at me. "Eight o'clock on Friday morning, yes?"

"I-yes," I whisper.

"I assure you, we will keep a close eye on you," she says.

My mom and I stare at each other, and I start to cry.

"What if something is wrong with my baby?" The tears pour down my face. I don't know what's happening right now, but the thought that something could go wrong with my pregnancy is a fear I face daily.

"Just let me clear this appointment with Pandora," Mother says, clutching her handkerchief. She moves to the door.

In that moment I realize my mother is not who I thought she was. I wonder if she ever was.

The chants of the picketers down the street fill the air and I cry harder.

"I should've brought one of my more advanced machines." Doctor Hunley holds my hand and pats it. "Try to be calm. We'll find out more during our next visit."

My mother runs out of the bedroom door and Doctor Hunley and I don't speak at first. I think we're both in shock over my mother's reaction.

"Anything else I can do before Friday?" she asks.

"See that stack of books? The one on the bottom, flip open to the back and scan my notes…post it to every news outlet…please."

She hurries to the desk and does what I've asked, moving back to me quickly when she hears Mother coming back.

"Pandora prefers that you come here."

"Fine. I'll see you the day after tomorrow," Doctor Hunley replies, looking at me.

"Should we keep her on bed rest until then?" Mother asks.

"Feed this girl whatever she wants and get her in the sunshine. She's as pale as a ghost. The vitamin D will do her good until we can run more tests. I'd like to draw blood…the needles didn't get delivered with the machine, I noticed?" Doctor Hunley's raised brow is very intimidating. If I hadn't gotten to know her through caring for Folsom, I'd be terrified right now.

Mother stutters and makes an excuse to leave the room again.

I hear her telling Pandora about the appointment later that evening and Pandora tells her we'll get a second opinion. Mother doesn't say anything, but I hear her laughing about something a few minutes later.

The tears are legitimate. My mother's rejection will be something I carry the rest of my life.

The big "outing" Pandora has planned doesn't happen until the next morning and involves me walking on the front lawn and waving to the growing mass of people. I feel ridiculous, a growing clown on display. I haven't had a haircut since before I met Folsom and my hair is out of control. I don't like my clothes. The boots he made me are starting to feel tight. And I can't just go shopping for whatever I need…the seclusion is getting to me.

It does feel good to be outside. I step closer to the gate and Pandora puts her arm on mine.

"No, no, we're not talking to them. If you're going to be part of my family, you need to remember your place." She grins, gripping my arm until her knuckles turn white.

"Get your hands off of me, Pandora." I scowl at her and she grips me harder. "Let go and I won't scream for help."

"Where do you get your fire, little Gwen? Certainly not from your mother. She is so easy to keep under my thumb." Pandora smiles and waves and ignores some of the boos from the people. "It will be fun taming you." She turns and the gleam in her eyes is terrifying. "Okay, that should be long enough to satisfy them that you're alive and well."

I really don't expect to be allowed to see the doctor, but she is even bolder than I knew and shows up Friday and every few days after that with her equipment to do scans of the baby. With her comes news of what she calls the Rise of the Women, whispered in my ear as my mother waits outside the room.

"It's in every Region, Gwen," she tells me. "People are stirring and speaking out. A woman was arrested last week for starting a fire in the Blue Region on their governor's front lawn."

"Folsom…?" The same question I ask with every visit.

It gets the same answer. She shakes her head, unable to meet my eyes. "We're looking for him. But we have little resources, few options."

I nod. I know this, but every minute of every day I'm plagued with thoughts of Folsom. Worried sick. Thoughts of him lying in bed after his heart attack, skin grey, looking weak—make it hard to breathe. If he died, would they tell us? The Regions would grieve…riot perhaps. The Society and President would be blamed. They'd keep his death a secret for as long as they could. I shake the thoughts from my mind. I can't think about that. Folsom is stubborn… strong. He knows how to survive.

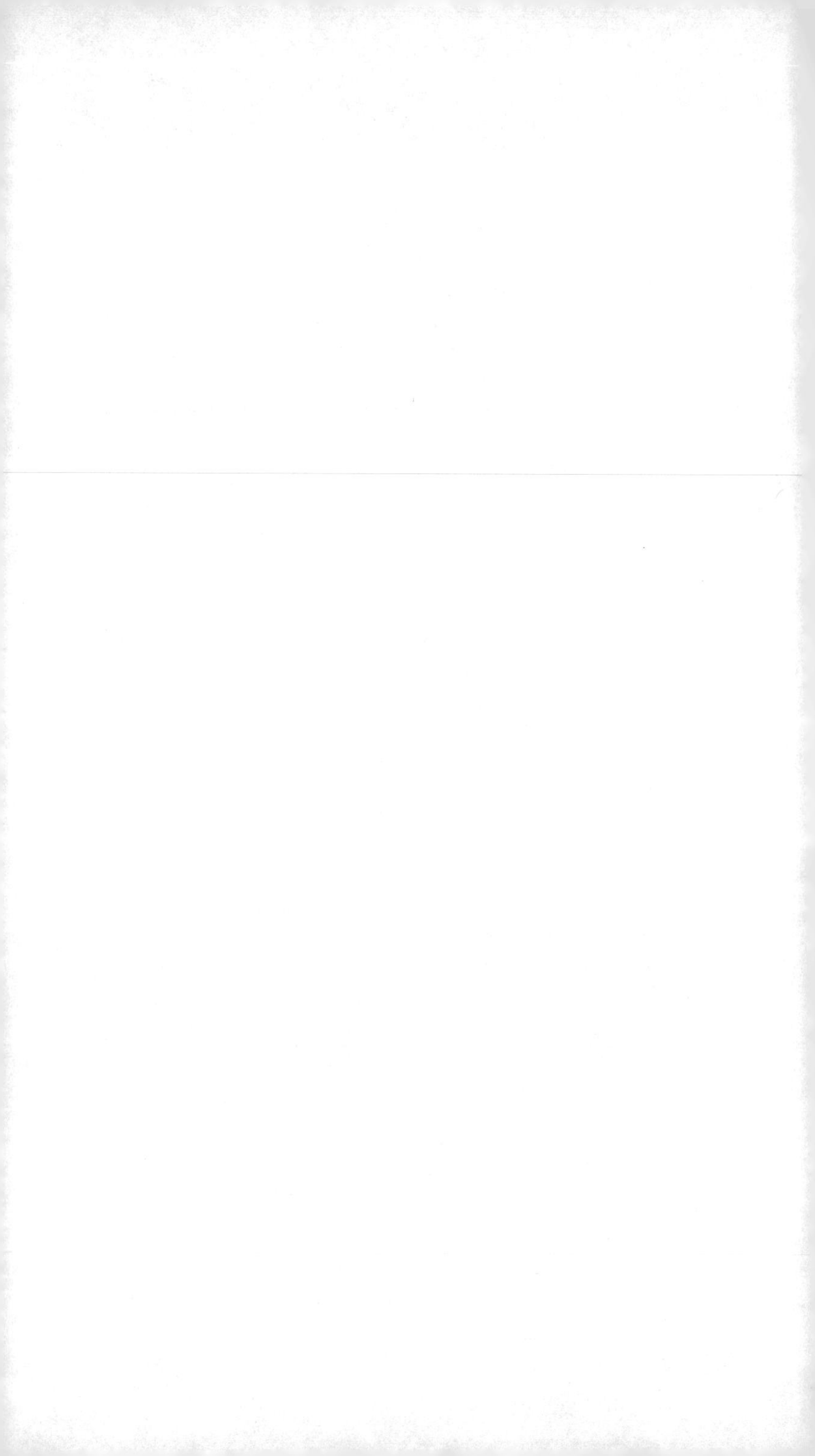

THIRTY-ONE

GWEN

Folsom's tongue works its way down my neck, to the nipples he's so fond of, down my stomach, dragging slowly, leisurely, to the spot that aches for him. I whimper and he…

There is a rap on my door and I keep pushing Folsom's head down. *Don't stop, don't stop.* A hand on my shoulder gives me a hard shake and I lean up on my elbows, glaring.

Sophia stares down at me, a slightly amused expression on her face.

"You look like shit," she says.

One thing that has been a pleasant surprise of pregnancy is all the sex dreams. I miss Folsom every day, with a longing I didn't know I possessed, and I wish we could be together now more than ever, but the dreams I have of us are so real that some days it curbs that craving. Some days when I'm not WOKEN UP MID-DREAM.

"Get out," I say dryly.

Sophia frowns and her mouth hangs open. Despite our tumultuous relationship, I never speak harshly to my sister.

"Gwen…"

"I mean it. I don't want to see you. I'm sick of this room, I'm sick of the games you people play, and most of all, I'm sick of your smug face. If you're going to lock me in here, give me some damn privacy."

Sophia's mouth closes and falls open again. "I shouldn't have…you're losing it, aren't you…"

"Why? Because I'm not taking your shit anymore?" I fling my robe over my shoulders and storm to the bathroom. "You'd have lost it the first time you didn't get your weekly manicure, or your monthly massage, or your daily shopping trips."

"Okay, point taken. You have been far more…tolerant than I would've been in this situation," she says. "But you also don't like massages, and pedicures, and shopping, and I do, so I'm not exactly a threat to the Regions like you are."

I throw her a dirty look. I don't know why she's being so accommodating; it all feels suspect.

"Why are you here? Are you paying a social visit, or did the governor send you for something?"

She shrugs. "Just feeling a little sympathetic, I guess." She bites her lip and looks outside. "And there's a lady here to show you some dresses to an event Pandora says you're attending tonight."

I freeze in mid-step. "What event?"

"I don't know. I wasn't invited."

I scrunch my nose. "She's here right now?"

"That's what I said," Sophia snaps. "She's waiting downstairs for you, whenever you're ready, Your Majesty." She walks to the door and looks back. "You don't really look like shit. It's just been a long time since I've pissed you off. I kinda miss it." She smirks and leaves before I can throw anything at her.

I wander downstairs still in my bathrobe, hair and teeth unbrushed. I don't care what the governor's people think of me. In fact, I hope to torture her with my morning breath.

"Gwen," she says when I walk down the stairs. Her skin is dark ebony and her hair is bound behind her and hanging to her waist in caramel-colored dreadlocks. She is wearing a yellow kaftan, and a dozen necklaces hang around her neck. She is not what I was expecting. I pause on the last step. She catches my hesitation, her face amused.

"Hello, Gwen. I'm Cardi." She smiles even when I stand rigidly in front of her. "I was sent your measurements and have five dresses here for you to choose from."

I follow her silently to a rack where she stands to the side, hands clasped at her waist. I eye her suspiciously as I flick through my choices. I choose one because I have to and hold it out to her.

"Let's try it on you, shall we?"

I'm unnerved by how unnerved she is. I'm trying my best to be rude to her, and she's the epitome of grace.

I stalk off to try the dress on, and when I come out wearing it, she nods approvingly.

"Very nice choice, Gwen. This dress is actually designed with your protection in mind…"

"My protection?" I ask.

"Not exclusively yours but any woman who chooses to wear it."

I nod, feeling silly.

She bends down in front of me and I get a whiff of her perfume, earthy and rich.

"Here." She lifts the bottom, catching my eye.

With a slide of her finger, she extracts a knife no wider than my pointer finger from the hem. The blade is charcoal black, and it glints in the light. There is an engraved number on the blade…I squint at it…ninety-seven.

"It slides right back into a sheath right here." She taps the place and puts the knife back.

I stare at the spot in fascination. Why put a weapon in a dress? How strange. I wonder if the others all had features like this and I want to ask, but Cardi has turned away.

"I'll just pack up while you change back into your robe," she says.

When I emerge from behind the screen she's ready to leave, a small case in her hands.

"Your ride will be here by six o'clock. I'm to tell you only one thing.

"And what's that?"

"There's a high price to pay for freedom."

And with that she walks out the door, leaving me glaring after her. I'm sick of the governor's threats.

At night the city is muted, the vibrancy of the day long past. I stare out at the buildings, their edges blurred by the streetlights. A fog brews on the asphalt, stirred by the cars that drive through it. The car stops in front of a skyscraper scaled in a moving advertisement. I watch as a woman in a purple dress tries to sell the entire city on auto eye color. *Change your eyes to match your outfit!* Every time she pulls off her sunglasses, her eyes are a different color. I look away ashamed. This is our priority. The human race is dying out, but at least you could die with a different eye color than the one you were born with. My door opens and I ease myself out of the car and into the heat. I stand on the sidewalk waiting for my next instruction, moisture gathering at my lower back. The driver is one of Pandora's regulars…Jane, I think? I take it that she trusts this one more than the others. I consider making a run for it. I imagine myself disappearing into the city, calling Doctor Hunley or Phoebe to come get me. But how far would I get being pregnant? And now that my face is plastered all over the news it is likely that someone *not* on my side would recognize me.

"Right through those doors," she says. "They'll be waiting for you.

They?

"Who is *they*?" I ask.

She stares at me blankly like she never heard my question.

"All right then." I sigh.

I march for the doors, which open before I reach them, a cold gust of air hitting my face, and a sterile computer voice greets me.

"Welcome, Gwen Allison. You are expected on the nineteenth floor…"

The door hisses shut behind me. There is no one else in the lobby. A neon artery appears on the floor in front of me, directing me to the elevators. I follow it, a growing trepidation clinging to my insides. My heels click on the marble and I wish I'd worn my boots instead. All the clatter is only making things worse. The elevator is waiting for me when I arrive; it carries me to the nineteenth floor, and when the doors open, I can tell why I was required to wear a dress. I am in the Society's Red Region offices; the black *S* logo set inside a circle rotates on the wall in front of me. I glance around nervously.

I wander past the empty reception area, toward the music I hear coming from the rear of the office. A wide hallway leads me to a banquet room where at least three-dozen people mill about in evening wear. I look down at my dress, which is a simple black with just enough room to accommodate my swollen belly. I'm underdressed for whatever this is…it reminds me of the Red Ball. I wonder if that was Pandora's intention—for me to feel out of place. No one turns to look at me as I step inside; no one seems to care that I'm here. I look for a familiar face, someone to tell me why I'm here, but I see none, not even the governor. A chime sounds on the hour. People move from their positions to an adjacent room set up auditorium style. Everyone knows where to sit and I realize they have assigned seats. I wait at the rear of the room, unsure of what to do, until everyone is seated. There is one lone chair left, right in the back. I slip into it hoping no one comes to claim it.

Petite suddenly appears through a door and walks to the middle of the stage, clasping her hands together.

"Our one and only item tonight is a very rare and special treat for all of you," the governor says.

An auction!

She casts a look over her shoulder. "Lift the curtain, please."

The red velvet lifts dramatically and Laticus is displayed in a glass case, dressed in a black suit. I search his face for signs of fear or distress, but he looks perfectly relaxed. He looks so much like his father that for a moment I have to look away. My heart begins to race. *Why is he here? What are they doing with him?* I glance around to see if shock is registering anywhere in the room, but everyone seems to know why they're here. I recognize some of their faces: Mrs. Doherty, who owns a chain of salons across the Red; her wife Deana, who is in charge of sustainable energy in all of the Regions; the Shaws, who have a shipping company that handles all of our international trade. Their daughters accompany them, sitting at attention next to their mothers, their eyes glued to Laticus.

The lust in their eyes repulses me. I turn to the woman next to me, grey-haired and regal. She sits with her hand on a younger woman's knee.

"What are they auctioning?" I ask her.

She looks surprised at the sound of my voice, like she didn't realize someone was sitting next to her.

"His virginity, of course." She turns back to the spectacle, not wanting to miss a minute of the action. I resist the urge to place my head between my knees.

I'm dizzy, my eyes wide with shock.

"We will begin bidding at—"

I don't hear anything after that but the roar in my own ears. I look around in a panic, searching their faces. There are at least a hundred people in this room…surely someone will say something. The vile nature of auctioning off a child's virginity. Each time someone bids, a ding sounds, followed by a number that appears on the glass Laticus stands in. I watch the price for him increase by the second; they're increasing it by increments of a thousand. I'm disgusted by what they're willing to pay for him, too scared to say anything in case they throw me out. By the final ding, his price is a small fortune. It's then that the words come back to me. Words from just a few hours ago. *There's a high price to pay for freedom.* The governor raises her gavel and before she can connect it to a final sale, I press the button on my chair. There's a pause during which time the room is eerily quiet.

"Sold to seat number ninety-seven," the governor calls.

My heart drops out when I hear the number.

The woman sitting next to me abruptly stands up, pulling the younger woman along with her. I realize that she was the last to bid before me. She shoots me a terrifying look before stalking out of the room, a sore loser.

"Seat number ninety-seven," the governor calls, her eyes searching through the faces.

I reach into the small clutch I brought with me, my fingers searching. I find it, small and solid. Gripping it between my thumb and forefinger, I flick open the cover at the same time that I stand. The governor finds me in the crowd, the smile dropping from her face. Her eyes register shock.

"Seat number ninety-seven," I call out.

I smile as I press Kasper's button.

THIRTY-TWO

GWEN

I'm escorted from the room and to a private area where I'll be asked to transfer the money for Laticus. The governor's eyes follow me out; her face is a mask, but I feel the rage spinning off of her body. My insides are thrumming, hairs on my arms standing to attention. It wasn't until I saw the shock on her face that I realized she had nothing to do with me being here. I think back to Cardi's words to me before I left the house. It hadn't made sense when she said it, but I thought she was one of Pandora's people. The knife in my hemline suddenly feels heavy.

I sign and wait as they draft the money from my account. The room is cool, but I find myself sweating. I have to sign a disclosure and a dozen other documents they pull up on a Silverbook. Finally they escort me to a private elevator.

"The lift will take you to your suite. The auctioned will be with you shortly."

The *auctioned?* I gape. He's not a boy; he's something to be sold. My heart beats out a tune: *Folsom…Laticus… Folsom…Laticus…*

There's no time to respond, the door is closing, moving up in a smooth motion. My feet ache in the shoes

I'm wearing. I wish I'd worn something more practical. I'm shaking so badly by the time the door opens that I barely register my surroundings as I collapse in the nearest chair. I don't have time to waste. I pull out Kasper's button. It's just as it was before. No magical light blinking. No message. Just a piece of metal that resembles trash. What if it had all been a joke, or the button has broken somehow? No. I can't think like that. Tucking it back into my clutch I look around. Someone orchestrated this. I'm in a large suite overlooking the city. I see a bedroom, small kitchen, and sitting area. I look around for stairs. There has to be stairs. The elevator dings and I freeze, my eyes on the doors.

Laticus. He looks around sheepishly, and I run for him, clutching my belly.

"You!" I say, taking his face in my palms. "Are you okay?"

He's grown an inch since I last saw him. And the way they've cut his hair makes him look older.

"I'm fine," he says, gripping my forearms. "My father…?"

I drop my hands. "I don't know. They took him. I don't know where he is. They were angry when he wouldn't sign you over to them…angry about me probably…"

Laticus' face turns hard. "He should have let them take me."

I draw back, surprised by the tone of his voice…was he angry?

"He's trying to protect you."

"I don't need protecting."

I swallow hard, swiping a loose hair behind my ear while I buy some time to think. I wasn't expecting this.

"Are you hungry?" I ask. "Did they feed you?"

"I'm fine, Gwen." He sounds almost impatient with me. Food had always worked with Laticus. Laticus the boy. This Laticus seems more like a man.

"You've changed," I say gently. "Just in the short time since I've seen you." I keep my voice light so he doesn't think I'm criticizing him.

"Why did you bid?" he asks roughly. "You're already pregnant..."

My mouth falls open. "I was trying to help you. I couldn't let them—"

"What?"

"Laticus—"

"This is what I'm supposed to do. It's no use fighting it. I was born for this purpose."

So matter-of-fact. I can't believe he's saying this.

"No," I say firmly. "The entire world cannot rest on your shoulders. Or on the End Men's shoulders. That's too much for anyone to bear."

"It's the only way," he argues. "We are the only hope."

His words make me sick. He's regurgitating the Society's rhetoric. They've brainwashed him.

Our eyes lock and I clench my fists at my sides. I'm having a standoff with a teenage boy. I drop my gaze, sighing deeply.

"Let's get some sleep, okay? We can talk about this tomorrow."

He nods once then marches to the couch. I remember doing the same thing to my mother when I didn't like something she'd said. It turns out teenage boys aren't so different than teenage girls. I use the bathroom, and when I come out five minutes later, I can hear his soft snores. I fall backwards onto the bed staring at the ceiling.

"Where are you, Kasper?"

I wake to a high-pitched trilling. It's so loud I roll onto my side and cover my ears. Disoriented, I look around. An auction...a suite...Laticus! I jump to my feet, careening toward the living room. Laticus is standing by the window, looking down. His hair is disheveled and he's shirtless. I have a brief moment of relief before I realize the noise hasn't stopped.

"Fire alarm," I say. "We have to leave."

He nods and I can see the fear in his eyes. Eyes so much like Folsom's. He's just a boy, and he looks every bit of it right now. The same voice that greeted me yesterday speaks through the walls.

"There is a fire in the building," it says calmly. "You must exit immediately. Please proceed to the stairs."

I look around frantically. *Where are the stairs? Where are the stairs?*

"Laticus, do you know where they are?"

He shakes his head. Before I can take another step, a neon light appears on the floor, running a line straight across the kitchen and ending at a wall. I grab his hand and we follow it. The wall slides open as soon as we approach it and we walk through. Laticus looks at me with concern.

"It's a lot of stairs."

"I can do it," I say, though I'm not sure I can. We're nineteen floors up. My heart starts to race.

"Here," he says. "Take my arm and hold onto the railing. We'll step together."

I have to stop several times to catch my breath. Laticus waits patiently for me while I close my eyes and try to ignore the cramping in my abdomen. We don't see anyone else in the stairwell, and I don't suppose we would since it's the weekend. I wonder if guards were sent to the suite and if they're after us now, but when I listen for the sound of footsteps, there are none.

When we finally emerge onto the street ten minutes later there is a crowd gathered on the sidewalk, their heads tilted up toward the building we just ran from. Flames burst from a window high above our heads, angry orange, flicking toward the sky like snake tongues. I count the windows until I reach the fire. Nineteen. Floor nineteen.

"It's the Society," I whisper to Laticus.

No one has noticed his presence yet; they're too distracted by the fire. He looks at me wide-eyed. My eyes travel around the street deciding what to do. I left everything in the suite, including Kasper's button and my Silverbook. I groan inwardly, kicking myself for my stupidity when I feel a hand clench around my forearm.

"Don't say a word. Come with me," a voice says in my ear. I reach for Laticus' hand as I'm shoved forward, away from the people, away from safety.

THIRTY-THREE

GWEN

We are taken to a waiting car, the windows so darkened there's no hope of anyone spotting us once we're inside. They shove Laticus in first, and when I hesitate, I'm pushed roughly into the interior of the car, scraping my knee in the process. A man climbs in after me, followed by a woman. The woman, who has a shaved head and eyebrows pierced straight across, sits next to me, while the man takes a seat across from Laticus.

"Where are you taking us?" I ask. "They'll know we're missing. You can't just kidnap us in the middle—"

"Never seen one of me, boy?" The man across from Laticus glares, his face a cocktail of contempt and aggression.

I press my lips together and place a warning hand on Laticus' knee.

"I haven't," Laticus says, honestly. "Your kind isn't allowed in the Black."

"Well, you're not in the Black anymore."

"He's just a boy," I say to the man.

He studies me for a minute before he grunts and looks out the window. In the Red, trans men are somewhat common, but the Black frowns on the change. Usually women who want to make the transition move to a different Region, typically the Blue.

The woman remains silent, her gun resting casually on her knee, staring straight ahead.

After several more inquiries of where they're taking us, with no answers, I fall quiet. Ten minutes later the car stops outside of an old brick building. We park to the rear of the building next to a yellow service door. As the car idles, the door opens and I see two figures step out.

"Let's go," the woman orders.

To my relief, several pairs of hands help me out of the car where I regain my balance, squinting against the sun and waiting for Laticus. When he's standing beside me, we move to the door, prodded along by the gun. It takes a minute for our eyes to adjust once we're inside. The smell of food is heavy in the air and my stomach rumbles. I reach for Laticus' hand and our fingers lace. We are led through a dank hallway, dimly lit; my foot catches on an uneven brick and Laticus catches me before I can fall. I stare at him gratefully even though he can't see my face.

We're taken down a flight of stairs to a basement. The woman steps ahead to open the door and ushers us inside. To my surprise, there is a large table spread with food. Laticus lets go of my hand and looks around.

I turn around to face our captors. "What is this?" But they're already gone, the door shutting behind them with a solid thud.

"Hungry?" I feign a smile.

I'd rather not eat, but I know I must.

"What if it's poisoned," Laticus says, studying a piece of fried chicken.

"Why would they poison two future End Men?"

He glances at my stomach and must like what I've said because he bites into the chicken.

I pick at the food, my stomach in knots, wondering what exactly they plan on doing with us. For now, we are safe for the exact reason I expressed to Laticus. Even in the womb End Men are valuable.

An hour later Laticus has fallen asleep at the table with his head cradled in his arms. I sit rigid, keeping watch. They've left us forks and knives. Weapons. This sets me at ease. If we were truly being held captive, why would they give us something with which to attack them?

I'm fighting off sleep when I hear the lock turn and suddenly the door is flung open. Gripping the sides of my chair, I stare at the figure standing in the doorway in alarm. At first, all I see is the outline of a very wide, very tall woman. She takes up the entire door and has to turn her body sideways to walk through. Her jowls rest on her breasts and I stare in awe of her magnitude.

"Why have we not eaten all the foods?" Her voice booms.

It's then that I notice the small blue cake she's holding. My mouth waters.

"Do we not like the chickens and potatoes and salads? Maybe we need cakes?" Each of her S's whistles, and when she holds up the cake, she grins from ear to ear.

I stare in shock and wonder, and she sets the cake right in front of me. She brushes her hands together and nods to the yawning Laticus, motioning to the cake.

"Yours is coming in a jiffys," she says. As she says it, someone else comes in and sets a cake in front of Laticus.

"Pippa." She pats her chest and then looks dismayed that we're not already eating the cake.

"Are you the Pippa from all the—"

"We are," she says proudly. She heaves her bulk into a chair, out of breath. "We own all the Pippas in all the Regions. You mights be wondering why you're here?"

"Yes," I say, slowly. "We are."

I sneak a look at Laticus and his mouth is open. He shuts it quickly and we exchange a look.

"First of alls, let's get one thing established, yes?" Pippa stands up. Grabbing the hem of her dress, she lifts it to her chest, exposing hairy legs. I can't keep the shock off of my face. All of a sudden her dress is entirely up, exposing every inch of her body from the waist down. My eyes are drawn to the cradle of hair between her mighty thighs. I blink once…twice…I'm not seeing things. She has a penis.

"You're trans?" I say.

Pippa shakes her head.

"We were born like this, it has sperms and everything." She looks quite proud to say so.

I shake my head, confused.

"We were born a man, sweethearts. My mother was afraid they'd take us so she made us a girl instead."

Laticus and I look at each other, but Pippa doesn't seem to notice.

She's dropped her skirt by now and holds out her arms. "Surprise!"

"Surprise indeed," I say.

"We're older than your Folsom, by the way. Which makes us," she points between her legs, "the oldest working penises in the Regions."

I don't know whether to be more surprised by her revelation or the fact that she just called him my Folsom.

"So, do people know?" Laticus, who's been silent until now, is leaning forward in his chair.

"Not many," Pippa says more solemnly this time. "But there are more of us. We hide in plain sight."

He shakes his head. "But why? The End Men, they need you—"

"Boy, and that's what you are, make no mistakes, the End Men are the Society's prisoners. We don't need no End Men. Some of us want to live our lives in peaces. Besides, we're attracted to mens and mens are in short supply. No offenses," she says, looking at me.

"None taken."

Pippa pulls her skirt over her knees and pats her hair down.

"So…why are we here exactly?" I ask.

She looks at me in surprise, one of her painted eyebrows lifting in time with her lips. "You called your friend Kaspers for helps, didn't you?"

I look at her doubtfully. "You know Kasper?"

"Know him…oh we know him. Shits was already stirring, Gwen. Before you started mouthing offs like the emotional train wrecks you are."

I frown at her, but she doesn't notice.

"You gave feets to what was already started. But you're in deep shits and now we have to hides you until we can get you out."

"Out where?" I ask.

"Of the Regions."

"Laticus too?"

"And Folsom." She nods.

My heart leaps. "Do you know where—"

"Not yet."

My face drops and she reaches over to pat my knee. "You get some rests. We have to get back to it."

With that, she leaves the room in the same way she arrived. With grandeur.

"Where do you think we are?" Laticus asks.

"I don't know. Lower end somewhere?" We stare at the cakes, unsure of what to do.

Laticus doesn't respond. We wait long enough to get antsy. He looks at the ceiling.

"I'm so sick of being bored all the time." He stands up and paces around the tight room.

The woman with the gun comes in a few minutes later. She looks less hostile now that I know she's not one of the governor's people.

"I'll take you to your room," she says.

Our room is an eight by ten storage closet with bunk beds underneath Pippa's restaurant. To get there, we go down a dark elevator shaft and then we're hit with bright fluorescent lighting. If I think about it too much, I'll go crazy. Once inside the room though, it's similar to the SIMS. In fact, for a moment I wonder if I'm in one. The woman notices me taking it all in.

"Have you done a SIM before? I can show you how to sign in if you'd like…"

I must go all dreamy-eyed by the way the woman does a double take and grins.

"Have at it," she says and leaves.

All I can think about is Folsom's SIM. I don't care about my own, I just want to watch his five or six dozen times. When Laticus goes to take a shower across the hall, I lie down on the bottom bunk and sign in with Folsom's password: Foley97. One day I hope to ask about his connection with the number ninety-seven.

When I see the purple silk it's like a conditioned response…I'm immediately in the moment with the simulation, remembering the way he made me feel the last time I watched too. I stare at us and wish he could feel how desperate I am for him. My heart quickens at the sight of him, the rush almost like he's really here, when the bed we're on fades away. Suddenly, it's just Folsom and he's looking right at me. At least it seems that way.

"Hey. You're here. Or maybe you're not and I'm talking to myself. I just needed to get some things off my chest."

I look around the room, confused for a moment.

"I was hoping that whatever happened, you'd come back in here." He smirks and rubs an eyebrow. "I *hoped* you would be back," he adds. "I had to add this in case I never get a chance to tell you…I never wanted this life, Gwen. I'm sure you know that by now. I've done what was expected of me. I've served the people and my country. I've managed okay because I've been on autopilot, barely even noticing my surroundings. And then I walked into your house that day and you noticed me. Not the fact that I was a man, or had a dick, or that I could give you a baby. You saw me…and my boots." He smiles distantly like he's remembering, and I smile too, covering my mouth with my hand. "Autopilot was comfortable and you've made me uncomfortable. I'd been living without feeling anything and now I feel everything. Even if nothing externally changes in my life, the way you make me feel…I'm changed. Because I got the chance to know you. I can't ever forget you. And I'll always wish things could be different for us." His voice breaks, but he quickly regains it. "I'm in love with you. It's the only piece of me the Society doesn't own." The view changes abruptly; it's the two of us standing on top of a large mountain, overlooking a valley of jagged rocks and trees and a river at the bottom. It's beautiful and I stare at it for a long time before looking at the two of us: him so tall and imposing and me barely eye level with his shoulder, yet we look like we fit. The picture stays there for so long that I imagine Folsom did the same thing, watched longingly for a life that will never be.

I fall asleep crying but happier than I've been since he's been gone. He told me he loved me...

THIRTY-FOUR

GWEN

It's been weeks. Weeks of waiting, weeks of the stuffy basement room underneath Pippa's.

"I don't know how you did it for so long, being locked up at Genome Y," I say to Laticus.

"I wasn't really given a choice." He's on his bed above me, reading a book Pippa brought for him. He hasn't looked up since she dropped it off. "I would have just worked if they let me. It's better than being a prisoner."

"Do you still feel that way?" I ask him.

I hear him set his book down, the paper fluttering. I can picture him frowning up at the ceiling like I've seen him do before.

"Yes."

I bury my face in my hands, glad that he can't see me. If this is what having a teenager is like, I'm not ready.

"You're entitled to your own feelings about things, Laticus. But before you develop a solid opinion on anything, make sure you examine all sides."

I hear him retrieve his book and turn a page. But I know he's thinking.

A few days later, Pippa comes down to bring us cake and to visit. She tells us about the riots in the Green Region, the marches in Blue and Purple.

"And here?" I ask her. "What's happening in Red?"

Pippa looks down, and I see shame on her face.

"Tell me what's happening?" I leave my half-eaten slice of cake on the bed and lean toward her. Laticus is listening. I hear the bed springs creak above me as he turns to face our gregarious host.

"They're arresting anyone who disturbs the peaces," she says. "The governor has issued Region-wide curfews and put restrictions on public gatherings. She's trying to quench the thirsts."

"Well, we can't let that happen," I say. "Not when everyone has worked this hard. She's trying to take eyes off the Red so the President can't blame us for igniting a revolution."

"Rights you are, but the people are scared."

"So let's make them un-scared."

"Maybe if that was a words." Pippa raises her eyebrows.

I want to call her out on that one so bad, Queens of Making the Words, but I resist.

"I want to do something," I tell her. "Let me do something!"

Pippa nods slowly. Her hands are clasped between her knees; she fills my entire room.

"It's a risk. But if you're willings—"

"I'm willing," I say quickly. "Get the people together. I'll stir them up."

Doctor Hunley comes to pick me up from Pippa's two days later.

We drive to the edge of downtown in a run-down neighborhood and there are people lined up outside the building, waiting. For what, I'm not sure. She turns off the car and tells me to wait while she gets my door. I step outside and the cheers are deafening. Women cry and touch my hands and shoulders and hair; they hand me small candies and chocolates, and knitted booties for the baby.

I'm so overwhelmed that I start to cry and am handed pretty hankies with lace trim. They remind me of the ones Phoebe used to make my mother and I get homesick for her. We walk past everyone and before I step up the stairs, the door opens and there she stands. *Phoebe.* I gasp and hug her before being led into the old building. She walks alongside me, tending to my hair and telling me how pretty I look.

"You know I don't look pretty. You just love me," I whisper, leaning my head against hers.

"I have never been prouder of you, sweet girl," she says. "I'm getting the word out. We all are." She motions to the women around her.

"This is where the heart of your message is being received," Doctor Hunley says, leaning into my ear. "These people who don't have the resources to buy their way to a family…they're able to see the reality of the situation and aren't blinded by greed. The data you brought up in your latest post…would you tell us more about that? These women feel like they have finally been understood."

I move to the podium and when the noise gradually dies down, I begin to speak. All of my failures and shortcomings seem to have led me to this very place, today, so I can be the one that finally says what needs to be said.

"Before the age of women, there was the age of men."

You could hear a pin drop in the room, it is so quiet.

"In that age, we were ravished, sold into marriages, denied an education, raped and blamed, and refused equal treatment. I'm beyond grateful to be with you today in this age of women. But I am also grieved. The age of men is over and so is our oppression. And what has oppressed us is near extinction. Unfortunately, we will follow shortly behind them." I swallow hard, my emotions reaching their peak. The faces staring up at me are conflicted. They are listening to me, rapt attention on their faces. I flex my hands where they can't see, hoping I don't look as wrung out as I feel.

"The problem lies not with men, or women, but with humanity. Perhaps we lost it, but there's a good chance we never found it. And what has been done to us for thousands of years must not be done to them now…the men. In the age of women, we must rise for the sake of our humanity. Let us decline rather than once again turn humans into slaves. We must not repeat history; we must rewrite it. To do so, we must unite. Unite in our defense of justice for all women *and* for all men."

I step back to signify that my speech is over, my eyes glued to the floor.

There are thirty seconds where I panic. I've said too much or perhaps too little. I've not made sense. I consider the fact that I have no allies, and I'll be escorted right to jail. And then I look up as I hear the sound of one pair of hands, slapping vigorously together. An older woman with dark skin and a severely curved back. Her hair is the color of snow and she looks too fragile to clap that hard, but there's a look of anger and determination on her face. I smile at her faintly, grateful for her support. And then five more stand up…ten. They're all clapping, a small thunder in the room. I let out a haggard breath as the rest of the women stand up together. How many? Six hundred? Seven? I glance at the doctor whose lips are pursed as she too gazes at the sea of faces. She looks over and catches my eyes, smiling faintly as if she's both happy and terribly moved.

"Well done," she mouths.

Doctor Hunley tells them I need to rest and that our visit today has been against the support of the governor.

"I'll continue posting the messages Gwen gives me and we will meet again…someplace larger next time. Invite everyone you know," Doctor Hunley says. "And for those of you who are in a place where you can…I have this reminder for you." She holds up a laminated page with eye-catching font and reads aloud: "Stop providing what the elite are accustomed to demanding. It starts with us."

Phoebe helps me down the steps and to the car. She hands me a container with my favorite dessert: lemon cake.

"Be encouraged and take care of that baby boy. Be on guard day and night," she says in my ear, trying to keep the worry from her eyes. I know her so well.

"It helps me just to see your face," I tell her.

The cheers are still ringing in my ears when we leave. I'm exhausted but rejuvenated. Everyone in the car is giddy.

"I didn't know there were so many," I say.

"How often do you leave the upper end?" The driver looks at me knowingly from the rearview mirror.

Touché.

The doctor turns around in her seat to look at me. "They've been here, Gwen. They have no voice. Much like the End Men. And if you want to create a movement, you find like-minded people and give them a name for their cause. This isn't just about the End Men. It's about humanity, like you said."

Before I get out of the car, Doctor Hunley reaches for my arm and looks to make sure I'm listening. "Gwen, be careful."

I nod. "I'll do my best."

Pippa's basement room feels especially like a prison cell when I return, but seeing all of those kind faces today…I have a new purpose. What helps the most, though, is holding onto the promise that we will save

Folsom and Laticus from the Society soon. Everything will be okay if they are safe.

Over the next couple of weeks, I write posts and start exposing the facts behind Genome Y, along with a view of my brief time in the compound. Each week, a new tidbit, such as:

> *Treatment of the people continues to decline.*
>
> *The End Men require drugs to perform multiple times daily.*
>
> *Genome Y spent three million dollars last year on the new sperm injection research.*
>
> *The numbers of the impoverished grow exponentially in each Region—why are we killing the people on our planet in our efforts to repopulate it?*

Pippa sweeps down to the basement one night, waving her Silverbook. "We need to cut your hairs," she says, wrinkling her nose. "We can't have you leaving my presences looking like such menaces."

She shows picture after picture of me speaking at what I thought were clandestine meetings.

"I couldn't care less about my dull, split-end hair. This means there's a leak and it could be someone who's watching our every move!" I glance at the article underneath and go cold. I suddenly feel very small and like I'm not equipped to finish what I started.

War is coming, it says.

THIRTY-FIVE

GWEN

The smell of grease and garlic, the clatter of silverware and plates, laughter and the banging of doors as customers come and go—these are the sounds and smells of my day. At night, when things grow quiet and Pippa locks up the restaurant, I can't sleep. I listen to the sound of Laticus breathing, my toes curling and uncurling under the covers, waiting for morning to come. My body is cumbersome, but my mind is not. It races through possibilities: how long can they keep us here before we're found? Where is Folsom? Will I give birth in this dungeon room with nothing to look at besides these brick walls? The baby kicks at my ribs, little feet stretching. Not much longer now. I can't bend over, and my feet have swollen so much I can't fit into shoes. Pippa lends me a pair of hers and I waddle around with pink furry slippers. I wait for the days they tell me there's a rally. I live for the excitement of sneaking out after it's dark, being ushered into buildings where women are crammed together, their faces eager and expectant. After a few times of us leaving, Laticus asks to come.

"We can't trusts that it's safe for yous out there," Pippa explains. "You're who everyones is looking for."

"They're looking for Gwen too," he argues.

"Yeah, to arrest her. They want to sell your manhoods to the highest bidders."

"Why is that so bad?" He jumps back in.

Pippa raises a majestic eyebrow at him.

"Because if they can do it to yous, they can do it to anyones."

He doesn't argue back.

"Yeah, thinking about that ones, right? Maybe your mom's…"

Laticus blinks at her, the muscles in his jaw twitching.

"Uh-huh," she says, looking at me. "They always thinks they know everythings."

"Let me come with," he says. "I'll wear a disguise."

Pippa and I exchange a glance. It's risky, but perhaps we could pull it off.

The first time Laticus comes out in a wig and heels, I think I might go into labor right then from laughing so hard. Laticus is not an attractive woman, but once Pippa tones down the makeup, he's passable for getting into the crowded places without being too noticeable.

At the first rally, he stands quietly in the back watching the women, seemingly fascinated by their passion. He listens to me too, a slight scowl on his face. When we are back in our room at night, he's quiet and I don't press him. I don't know if it's making a difference or not, but I'm glad he's listening.

Pippa comes downstairs one evening when Laticus has already fallen asleep. She holds a finger to her lips and motions for me to follow her. I've not been upstairs into the restaurant very often, just once when Laticus and I snuck up for ice cream. When we reach the dining room, I see that all the lights have been turned off and the parking lot outside is empty. We turn into a kitchen where a

Silverbook is on. I stand quietly as she turns up the volume, my eyes already glued to the governor.

"Good evening, Red Region," she says, looking directly at the screen. "The wind of change is often met with resistance. Sometimes it can be hard to remember what we're striving toward once the dissenters confuse the issues with slander and false truths." She clutches her hands together, the gloves tapping lightly together. "I'd like to remind you exactly how far we've come since the epidemic took the men. We've been rebuilding—not just the technology we lost, but our crops are now all organic, cancer has dropped by ninety-four percent, the crime rate has dropped so drastically—did you know that our former prisons have been condensed by eighty-seven percent? We've found peace. This age of women, the term touted recently, has been an age of progress, and while some have had to sacrifice themselves to help us rebuild, it has been done in a decent and timely order. No one is a slave in this country. We have rebuilt on our terms, and once there are more men in our Regions again, we will keep the progress moving forward. It is not the end of men, but the beginning. We must not decline! To do so would bring an even bigger fall to the age of *humanity* and we'd be back to a time of disease and war. I urge you, do not listen to these rumblings of dissent and confusion. If we give ear to the voices who have no real evidence to back up the so-called facts, we will not just decline, we will disappear."

She pauses, and it's as if she can see me through the screen, her gaze is so venomous.

"I've asked our Chief of Police to close."

Commander Hoffa steps forward and doesn't bother with a greeting. "There is a warrant out for Gwen Allison's arrest. Anyone found harboring her will be found in contempt. Contact the alert at the bottom of the screen if you have any information regarding her."

A picture of me fills the screen and the alert icon flashes.

I look up and Pippa stares back with defiance.

"We won't let them wins," she says.

I'm languidly eating an English muffin with peanut butter and strawberry jelly when Doctor Hunley rushes in. I spot the urgency on her face and my heart lurches into a gallop. Laticus is suddenly next to me, looking between us with concern.

Pippa labors into the room not seconds after, her breathing ragged. "We have to leave. Quickly. Get your shoes on," she says to Laticus.

He nods once and turns to find his shoes. Our questions are stilled by the looks on their faces. Obey now, ask later. Pippa wrings her hands from the corner of the room. There are too many of us in here; it's making me claustrophobic. The doctor looks like she wants to say more, but she grabs my arm instead and helps me to the exit. I walk, an easy directive. It's the only thing I can do. If I need to bend, if I need to crawl, will I be able to? I try to not think about all the things I can't do.

I turn around at the top of the stairs, making sure Laticus is following, and Pippa has him by the arm.

"We have him," she assures me. "No time for your sasses today, young mans," she warns him.

When we reach the last door, Doctor Hunley stops and Pippa moves forward, hugging me.

"Go with the lights, little warrior," she says. She smells like onions and I breathe her in for what I sense is the last time.

I open my mouth to respond, but she turns to Laticus. "Take care of each others, yes?"

He nods and she swallows him up in a hug.

"Thank you," I tell her one last time as we get in the car.

The light is always so bright as we leave the underground, but today it's not much different than below. The sky looks like it's throwing a temper tantrum, dark and brooding with lightning flashing here and there. When we drive a few blocks, the first raindrop hits and hundreds quickly follow.

We speed through, the driver seemingly oblivious to the rain, and Doctor Hunley sits in the front seat, glancing back at us every few minutes. She says something to the driver in low tones and I sit forward, trying to hear her.

"Where are you taking us?" I finally interrupt.

She turns around and I notice how tired she looks. Her nails are bitten down to the quick. I have no idea what she's been doing these last weeks, how the strain of keeping us hidden has affected her. I reach out and rest my hand on top of hers. She's been a true friend, even before this started. She looks back at me in surprise and then nods like she knows what I'm thinking.

"We're getting you out. Somewhere safe."

I look at Laticus who gazes out the car window, eyes glazed over. Teenagers aren't meant to be holed up in tiny basement rooms for weeks at a time. He looks tense…eager—ready to jump from the car and sprint through the rain. I take his hand and squeeze it hard.

"Sounds like we're getting out of here," I tell him. He nods, mute. I don't want to scare him. "Just do everything they tell you to do, okay? They've been working on a plan for a long time."

"Do you think they've found Folsom?" he asks.

"If not today, I think it will be soon," I whisper. I say this as much for myself as I do for him.

"We're close," the doctor says. "When we step out of the car, move quickly…that's all you have to do. Okay? Stay calm, and we will have you airborne before you know it."

I nod and take a deep breath, looking out the window. I'm afraid. I move slowly, my belly large. If we have to move quickly I'll slow everyone down. We drive to an abandoned building. I recognize it—it once was a school back when we needed such large institutions to educate our children. The grounds are dark, and I squint to make out our surroundings. The remains of a playground sit collapsed, a lone swing hanging by a single chain. The car drives slowly. I hold my stomach as we bounce around, flinching when we hit the deep ditches. Finally we stop. There are no lights. Everything is bathed in darkness.

"Gwen? Are you ready?" Doctor Hunley looks at me and lowers her head, eyes always assessing.

Laticus grips my shoulder and gives me a little shake. "Don't get scared on me now," he teases, though I can see in his own eyes that he's terrified.

"Never. Let's do this." I muster up enough enthusiasm in my voice that he looks relieved.

Our car doors are opened for us and we step out. I don't look up at first, too busy seeing who has Laticus. I wish I'd gotten out on his side. The rain has dwindled to a mist, but the wind is picking up. It's going to pour again soon.

When I look up, I see my sister. She smiles weakly at me and I freeze.

"What are you doing here?" I look at her in alarm, backing away. The back of my calves hit the wet steel of the car and I shake my head.

"I'm here to help," she says slowly. "I need you to come with me."

"What do you mean *help*?"

Sophia glances around, irritated. "We don't have time for this," she says.

I stay where I am, fingers pressing into cold metal. I don't trust her. She sighs.

"He's my nephew," she hisses.

My eyebrows draw together, and at first I don't know who she's talking about. Then I lift a hand to my belly and our eyes meet.

"I'm a bitch, but I'm not heartless…you think you're the only one who can be swayed by a cause?"

She holds out her hand and I only hesitate for a minute before I take it. There are so many questions I want to ask her, but she gives me a look that means I'm to be quiet.

We move toward the front of the car, where Laticus is waiting, his shoulders hunched forward. Doctor Hunley embraces us both in turn. It's brief…hurried. There's more to say but no time.

"You've changed the course of history," she says to me. "You woke us up..."

A sound is getting closer: a dull, whopping noise. We all listen, our bodies still.

Where's Folsom? Where's Folsom?

The blade slap gets closer. I look around the parking lot and something catches my eye—a glint in the grass. Without looking away I lay a hand on the doctor's arm.

"There's someone out there," I say quietly.

Before she can respond, the lights from the helicopter appear, glowing eyes in the dark. Our eyes move up to watch as the helicopter hovers over the parking lot. My hair lifts around my face, tendrils snaking across my eyes and mouth. I push it behind my ears, as Laticus presses close to my side. In my peripheral vision, I see movement to our right. While the others stare up at the approaching helicopter, I watch a vehicle appear, driving slowly, headlights off.

"Doctor Hunley," I say. But she doesn't hear me because the chopper is above us now, so loud I can barely hear my own voice. I put my hand on her arm as the car door opens.

I'm about to shout a warning when I see him.

Folsom!

He doesn't notice me at first, stepping out of the car. I watch his head lift to study the helicopter and I'm given a glimpse of his profile. My heart drops at his appearance.

Even in the dark I can tell he's lost weight. I wave off the mosquitoes that hum around my face and will him to look at me.

And then he does, his eyes lowering from the sky. Everything stills when he sees me. We're in a bubble, just the two of us. Not even the rain, or the people, or the beating of the helicopter's blades can reach us. I run toward him, ignoring the doctor's calls. Wanting only to touch him, smell his skin. He catches sight of my huge belly and his eyes light up. We're moving toward each other, only a few yards separating us.

And then everything turns upside down. First I hear the choked sound of Doctor Hunley as my name is torn from her lips. I turn as a popping sound fills my ears, and I see the doctor fall, her body hitting the ground as she collapses onto her side. I glance back at Folsom, and then run toward her, falling on my knees and into a puddle of her blood. She's choking, blood coming from her nose and mouth. She convulses once and then her body stills, eyes empty. Sophia pulls me to my feet. She's yelling something but I can't make it out. *The doctor is dead, the doctor is dead.*

"Come on," she yells in my ear.

The helicopter has landed, its lights illuminating the parking lot. It's then that I see the guards rushing out of one of the buildings, weapons aimed at us. Sophia tugs at my arm, pulling me toward the copter. My eyes search for Folsom and Laticus. Where are they? I can't leave without them. Oh my God, the guards are shooting at us! I struggle to get away from Sophia to make sure Folsom is still standing. The whites of her eyes spread around her irises in panic.

The guards keep shooting, but then I see women in civilian clothes coming from the sides of buildings, shooting at the guards.

We run toward the helicopter, me holding onto my stomach. A blood-curdling scream stops me. I turn my head just as Sophia goes down. I scream her name and drop to my knees beside her. A steady stream of blood flows from her arm. I press down on it to stop the blood but it rushes through my fingers. A tourniquet! I pull off my shirt and tie it above the wound as she winces and gasps beneath me.

"You have to go," she says. "If they catch you—"

"I'm not leaving you," I say firmly. More shots pop around us and I lie over her body until it stops. *Please, God, please let Folsom and Laticus be all right.*

I need to get her to the helicopter, but I can't do it on my own. And how long will it wait for us before the pilot thinks it's too dangerous and leaves?

"You have to stand up," I say to Sophia. "I'll help you get to the helicopter."

She shakes her head. "There's only room for three."

Me. Folsom. Laticus. It doesn't matter. I'm not the one hurt. When they find out my sister was helping us, they'll throw her in jail. I'm helping her to her feet when Folsom stumbles to us. I want to grab him, kiss his face. No time.

"She's been shot. Help her."

He doesn't hesitate before scooping her off the ground. I run beside him as we head for the copter, looking around for Laticus. I see him running toward us, across an open expanse of parking lot. I want to scream at him to keep his head down, move faster, but there's too much noise. Hands are pulling Sophia into the helicopter. Folsom pushes me forward so I can go next, but I pull away, my eyes on Laticus. I see the glint of something shiny behind him and I scream as the shot is fired. I hear Folsom say his name and then he's running toward the boy with me following. Laticus falls to his knees, his eyes wide. Folsom reaches him first, catching him before he hits the ground.

He finds Laticus' bullet wound, his face blanched of all color. Blood is seeping out of the wound, staining his shirt crimson.

The boy's eyes are closed, his mouth open in shock.

"We have to get him to the helicopter," Folsom says calmly. Too calmly. My entire body is shaking as he begins to pick him up.

"Go!" I say. "I'm right behind you!"

He nods, rushing forward.

Sophia's words repeat in my head. "*There's only room for three.*"

"Gwen!" Folsom calls over his shoulder.

From the far end of the field, I see half a dozen figures in black moving toward the helicopter, guns raised. I back up a step.

Folsom reaches the door and hands Laticus to them, then turns back for me. When he doesn't see me, his face crumples in confusion. I take another step back and suddenly realization dawns on his face. He's about to move toward me when hands grab at him, pulling him backward through the open door. He fights them, pulling away, his eyes trained on my face. But it's too late. It begins to lift from the ground.

I see him mouth my name as they hold him, his eyes crazed.

"I love you," I scream at the wind. But they're too far away for him to hear me.

THIRTY-SIX

FOLSOM

Fall interrupts summer early, the leaves moody, eager to drop. I stand in their midst, the air sweet with rot. We've been here for a month. Sophia hates it: the cabin, the woods, the food. Her complaining never stops, but I'm grateful for it. The silence would be too much to bear. I laugh at her and then she laughs too. Immediately after laughing she cries. And then she laughs again.

"It's pregnancy hormones," she says.

Her arm is healing nicely. I change the bandage for her. There will be a scar where the bullet entered and some nerve damage they say, but she's alive. A wind picks up and leaves rattle through the clearing, sending a fresh shower of reds and yellows down on my head.

I think of Laticus, the same as I do every day. Of his lifeless body in the helicopter, the medic unable to revive him. We'd barely been in the air for five minutes when he died in my arms. I'd wanted to die right then. Die instead of him, die so that Gwen could be flying to safety, instead of me. I'd done this to him, brought him into the world only to die right before his sixteenth birthday. And the woman I loved was in danger, her belly swollen with another of my sons. Sophia, who saw the look on my face as I cradled my son on the floor, started to cry. I could tell she was scared out of her mind, but she lowered herself next to me and put an arm around my shoulders as I sobbed. I lost everything in one day.

I hear my name yelled from the cabin and I run, jumping over a fallen tree and skidding down an incline. When I reach the doorway, Sophia is standing in the kitchen holding a pot, a puddle around her feet.

"It's time," she whimpers. She's panicked. I can see it in her eyes.

"Hey," I say.

She looks up at me wide-eyed. Her toes lift off the ground to avoid the mess.

"We know what to do. We're ready."

She nods, but she doesn't look convinced.

"Sophia," I say firmly.

"What?"

"We've got this."

What starts out as a smile ends in a scream. She goes down on one knee, her face contorted. I scoop her up and carry her to the bed. Then I get the towels, the scissors, the water. We're prepared. The doctor told us what to do.

"What if something goes wrong?" She leans up on her elbows, sweat already dampening her hair despite the chill in the air. Sophia is not blond. She has two inches of dark hair on the crown of her head. The same color as Gwen's. I look away quickly.

"The house is a mile away. I'll take the quad and get help if we need it."

She nods and falls back down into the pillows. She opens her legs and I check to see if she's crowning.

"I was making dinner," she says, breathless. "In the oven…"

I nod. Once a week the doctor brings us supplies, boxes of food. Sophia, who is restless and bored, has taken over the task of cooking, though what she makes is barely edible.

I jump up and run to the oven, turning it off. Before I leave, I peek inside. Looks like bread. Black bread.

"Did you save it?" she asks when I come back.

"Yes. It looks delicious. You need to push."

Twenty minutes later and I'm holding my daughter. She screams louder than Sophia, and she has a full head of dark hair.

"Is she okay?" She lifts her head, worry along the edges of her voice.

"Yes." I try to hold back the things I'm feeling, the awe at what I just witnessed. No wonder they outlasted us, their contribution to human race eclipsing ours in its magnitude. A body able to grow another body. I am in awe of the process. And something else…a connection to the child. I didn't just deliver a baby, I delivered my flesh and blood: a nose, and eyes, and coloring handed down from generation to generation. I hand her to Sophia.

"Her name?" I ask.

"What would you like to name her? She's your daughter," Sophia says.

An offering.

If I name this child, she is mine in body and mind. I excuse myself. Stumbling outside, I walk away from the cabin, the wet grass hitting my knees. The sky is luminous as the sun sinks behind the trees, a bright blue with streaks of pink. I think of Gwen, and like always when I pull her to mind, something begins to ache behind my ribcage. I rub absently at my chest as I stare at the sky. I've lived numb for so long that every time I feel something I want to identify it, give it a name. For Gwen it's love. I don't know if she's had the baby, or if she's safe. Once we left the Regions, we were cut off from any news, secluded out here in the woods. Dr. Hein, who lives in the main house, reached out to her contacts, promising me she'd find out what she could. But so far there has been no news of Gwen. The Red Region was unusually quiet after we escaped, Governor Petite only emerging once to make a statement about the rebels and how they'd be reprimanded in due course. Before we crossed over to Canada, Laticus' body was sent back to the Black Region, to his mother. I wrote her a letter to tell her how her son had died, though I doubted it would ever reach her. The Black Region blamed the Red for his death, the Red blamed the rebels, and the Society blamed me. I don't really know who is to blame, perhaps all of us.

I pull a piece of Laticus' shirt from my pocket and hold it in my fist. This has to end. I was unsure before, but now I know. Gwen is alive. She'll find a way, and she'll protect our boy with her life. I will protect the people I love. I will fight for them like they fought for me.

I say their names out loud: Gwen, Jackal, Sophia, Kasper, my daughter, and my son.

THIRTY-SEVEN

GWEN

The pain is gripping. It holds my body tense as it works its way through my lower abdomen and back, a dull knife sawing through tendons and muscle. I roll onto my side and scream, holding onto the bedpost as people rush around me. I've been tucked away in dome six at Genome Y with doctors I don't recognize. They hover, never giving me a moment's peace as I progress through labor.

"Get her legs up," I hear someone say.

And then—"Gwen, we're going to need you to push, darling. Can you do that for me?"

I open my eyes and stare into my mother's face. She nods at me encouragingly. I let them lift my legs, a nurse on each side, and push them back up toward my body.

"Push, Gwen, push," Mother instructs.

I push with all my might, the pain so intense I think I'm going to pass out. I scream as I push and the nurses coo their encouragement. When I think I can't go on for a second longer, I feel a rush of something warm between my legs, and then a piercing wail. The doctor snips his cord, the cord that has connected my body to his for thirty-nine weeks. We are no longer two souls inhabiting one body. I weep for both the separation and the miracle that she lays on my chest. I hold his slimy, purple body to my own, barely able to keep my head up I'm so tired. Everyone's eyes are on my son; they all stare in wonder.

"The Red Boy," I hear someone say. And I hold him tighter because he's not the red boy, he's my boy—mine and Folsom's.

"What's his name, Gwen?" my mother asks. When I open my eyes, I see that hers are glossy with tears. I don't know. I haven't thought about a name. I say the first thing that comes to mind.

"Rebel."

Mother flushes with anger, but one of the nurse's eyes widen.

"I'll let the Regions know that their Rebel is born," she says.

I nod, and they take him from me to be cleaned and weighed and swaddled.

Rebel Donahue's birth is celebrated throughout all twelve Regions, but mostly in the Red Region. The media has run his name and are calling him The Red Rebel, remarking on the fact that his father is still missing. They spend equal time speculating about whether I'm sending Folsom messages through the name of his new son, and where Folsom is.

I am.

I'm sending them all a message.

I spend three days holding my son, touching his velvety skin and staring into his tiny face. It's his feet that get me the most: perfect, and wrinkled, and miniature. Who knew feet could be so beautiful? I feed him and rock him in my arms, barely able to stand being apart from him even if it's a few minutes.

My mother comes to visit us, her eyes drawn and downcast. We are not the same. Something changed between us when I stopped being the "good daughter."

When you question the world your parents set up for you, it changes the relationship, it makes them question themselves, and then no one knows where they stand anymore. She holds Rebel for a few minutes, staring down at him like she's trying to figure out all six pounds of him. How could a baby cause so many problems? She's thinking about my sister, we all are. News of her helping the rebellion and smuggling Folsom and Laticus out of the Region has shaken the entire country. No one knows if they're even alive. It's taken the focus off of me, but I know that won't last.

I can't get them off of my mind. I don't know where they are or if Sophia's given birth to my niece. It tears me up inside knowing that she is without her family. She sacrificed herself for both me and Folsom and all that time I was questioning whether or not she even loved me. *Folsom is with her*, I tell myself. He will take care of all of them.

My heart hurts when I think of Laticus. In the hours of staring at my baby and being so grateful he is healthy, I pray for Laticus to be okay. He's young. *He will survive this*, I console myself.

When I close my eyes, I can still feel Folsom's lips on mine. The scruff on his face grazing my cheeks as he kissed me over and over, the way "I'm in love with you" sounded when he said it. And now he's just gone, and I'm aching inside. I don't know when or if I'll ever see him again; his absence feels like the drag of a match that will never ignite.

One of the nurses I know tells me that they can't arrest me for kidnapping or arson since there was no evidence. Her aunt works in the governor's office.

"They're saying you're a traitor to the Regions. That you're disturbing the peace and inciting riots."

"They can't arrest me for that," I say.

"Freedom of speech isn't what it used to be, Gwen. There are limits to what is tolerated. The governor is trying to get something to stick. She wants you punished."

I've not told them anything about who took us, just that we were kept in a basement and fed three times a day. The story is that the rebels in the Black Region retaliated against the Red by trying to take both of us.

After three days I'm told we're to be released. My mother arrives to pick us up. An emotionless statue, she stands near the door holding Rebel while I pack up the last of our things. She is unusually quiet. When I turn around, the bag slung over my shoulder to tell her I'm ready, she's not there. I blink around the room in shock, and then I run for the door. I fling it open and it hits the wall with a heavy thud as I run down the corridor barefoot. My feet slap at the floor. I can hear the roar of my heart in my ears. *She took him to the car to get him strapped into his seat*, I tell myself. That's all. I'd laugh about this later, think about what an overprotective mother I am. I turn a corner, heading for the front of the building. It's a Saturday. Genome Y is mostly empty. I can see them, oh God, I can see them. Just up ahead on the other side of dome three. I hit the button to open the door. It doesn't move. I hit it again. My mother hasn't seen me yet. Rebel is asleep in her arms. *He's okay, he's okay*, I tell myself over and over. I wave my arms and she catches sight of me, but instead of walking over to open the door, she turns her back. I pound on the door with my fists and then I stop. Three people are walking down the corridor toward her, too far for me to make out who they are at first. When they move closer, I'm frozen. I don't move a limb. The governor, a woman in uniform—police—and Langley. The three of them have an exchange that lasts no more than a few seconds, then they all look over their shoulders at me, and the uniform nods. My mother very gently hands the baby to Langley. I begin to sob, my knees threatening to buckle. I hold myself up. *I will not fall.* I have to get to my son. He's right there, I just need to get to him. Langley looks at my baby, a smile pressed to her lips. Then her gaze lifts and she looks right at me, right into my eyes before turning on her heel and walking toward the door. My mother follows her out, and they disappear into a sharp burst of light as the front entrance opens for them. I'm screaming, I can't feel my fists as they pound on the glass, I can't feel anything but an all-encompassing panic. And then the governor and the officer are on my side of the glass. I try to push past them, but the officer grabs my arms and pulls them behind my back. I don't feel the pain. I struggle against her, kicking and heaving. The governor presses a button on the wall and an alarm sounds. People run into the room, people I used to work with. I look for Corinne, but she's nowhere to be found. They grab my arms. I feel a sharp prick in my neck and suddenly I don't have the energy to fight anymore. My limbs go limp, my head swims, the governor blurs in and out of my vision.

"You're the problem, Gwen," I hear her say. She's right in my face, an inch away. I can smell her breath and see the pores on her nose. "This is exactly why you can't be trusted to take care of that baby. He's our future, Gwen…"

My eyes close, I can't keep them open, but I can still hear her voice.

"Don't worry, Langley will take good care of him. She's his mother now."

And then everything goes black.

Thank you for reading our words. Without you, we're just two best friends making up stories together. For every blog, every reader, every review, every kind word, and even the not so kind…we're grateful you're reading our work and giving it wings. ~ Tarryn Fisher & Willow Aster

The *End of Men* series continues with *Jackal,* coming soon! We can't wait for you to find out what happens with Folsom and Gwen and the new characters we hope you'll love just as much.

Add Jackal to your Goodreads list:
www.goodreads.com/book/show/40144365-untitled

Folsom's Playlist:
https://open.spotify.com/user/1226318453/playlist/0nD2lFQEfKiF1rWkdbNezi

Tarryn Fisher is the New York Times and USA Today Bestselling Author of nine novels. Born a sun hater, she currently makes her home in Seattle, Washington with her children, husband, and psychotic husky. Tarryn writes about villains.

AUTHOR LINKS:

www.tarrynfisher.com

www.facebook.com/authortarrynfisher

https://instagram.com/tarrynfisher/

https://twitter.com/Tarryn__Fisher

The Opportunist

Dirty Red

Thief

Mud Vein

Marrow

*F*ck Love*

Bad Mommy

Atheists Who Kneel and Pray

Never Never series

Willow Aster is the USA Today bestselling author of five novels. Willow loves nothing more than writing the day away—anywhere will do. Her husband and two children graciously put up with her endless daydreaming and make fun of her for reading while cooking.

AUTHOR LINKS:

www.willowaster.com

www.facebook.com/willowasterauthor/

www.instagram.com/willowaster1/

https://twitter.com/WillowAster

True Love Story

Fade to Red

In the Fields

Maybe Maby

Lilith

Made in the USA
Columbia, SC
17 June 2018